普通高校应用型人才培养规划教材

U0095751

视听说英语教程

（教师用书）

主　编　王秀珍

副主编　徐　江　宁克建

编　者　李　琳　孙　言　徐　玮

　　　　唐湘茜　张琼尹　王　燕

　　　　戴　雷　濮　琼

经济科学出版社

图书在版编目（CIP）数据

视听说英语教程（教师用书）／王秀珍主编 . —北京：
经济科学出版社，2009.8
普通高校应用型人才培养规划教材
ISBN 978 - 7 - 5058 - 8574 - 5

Ⅰ . 视… Ⅱ . 王… Ⅲ . 英语—听说教学—高等学校—教
学参考资料Ⅳ. H319.9

中国版本图书馆 CIP 数据核字（2009）第 160083 号

责任编辑：范　莹　肖　萍
责任校对：杨晓莹
技术编辑：董永亭

视听说英语教程（教师用书）
王秀珍　主编
经济科学出版社出版、发行　新华书店经销
社址：北京市海淀区阜成路甲 28 号　邮编：100142
编辑部电话：88191417　发行部电话：88191540
网址：www. esp. com. cn
电子邮箱：esp@ esp. com. cn
北京欣舒印务有限公司印刷
华丰装订厂装订
印数：0001 - 2000 册
787×1092　16 开　15.5 印张　450000 字
2009 年 9 月第 1 版　2009 年 9 月第 1 次印刷
ISBN 978 - 7 - 5058 - 8574 - 5　定价：24.00 元

普通高校应用型人才培养规划教材
编 审 委 员 会

总　序

　　经过几年的快速发展，我国教育已进入高等教育大国的行列，按照党的十七大精神，向建设人力资源强国迈进。数以千万计的学生在各级、各类高等学校学习各种知识和培养能力，为成为社会主义的建设者和新时期的应用型人才而努力。高等教育从"精英化"到"大众化"的转变，除了数量的扩大外，必须在培养目标、教学内容、教学方法、教材等方面进行改革，以适应培养不同类型人才和不同类型高校的教学需要。

　　独立学院自开办以来，在教学各方面，特别是教材基本沿用了普通本科的教学资源，这给特色教育和定向教学带来了诸多不便，难以达到教委设定的教学目的。有鉴于此，我们在"服务于地方，培养应用型人才"这一总的目标指导下，组织了一批教学经验丰富、致力于教学改革研究、在相关课程方面有较深造诣的教师，按教育部的教育培养规划，编写了这套适合独立学院本科教学的系列教材，旨在有针对性地培养应用型高等学历人才，因此我们称这套教材为"普通高校应用型人才培养规划教材"。

　　我们编写这套教材的基本思想是：对基本原理、基本理论，重在结论和应用。理论部分遵循教学大纲，不求深入全面，但求适用，对相关理论做必要的引介。书中编列了较多的例子和习题，增加了学生自我训练、独立解题的素材，期望帮助学生加深对理论知识的理解和应用。我们力求这套丛书在内容结构上既区别于传统本科教材，又不同于高职高专教材。在理论知识方面既有一定的系统性，也兼顾了现代性；既注重知识间的逻辑性，也突出了知识的应用性；在够用、实用、适用的前提下，还编入一些有深度知识的链接，供要求进一步提高的学生自学之用。本套教材在文字上力求准确易懂，适当增加例图，有较好的可读性，便于学生自学。

　　由于我们的水平有限，书中难免出现一些问题，敬请各位教师和广大学生给予细心的指正和热情的帮助。在此，对于大力支持这套教材出版发行的经济科学出版社也一并表示真诚的感谢。

教材编审委员会

甘德安

2008 年 1 月

前言

　　《英语视听说教程》是一本根据新的教学理念，集视、听、说于一体的适合于独立学院英语专业学生入学阶段强化训练的教材。旨在让学生接受与中学阶段完全不同的英语学习方式，为后期的英语教学作一个过渡和铺垫。本教材分为学生用书和教师用书各一册。

　　《英语视听说教程》（教师用书）对照学生用书分为相应的12个单元，每单元按Background knowledge, Reference Key, Listening Scripts及Translation的顺序进行编写。本教材内容可安排96学时，为期8周时间完成。具体做法是，每周12学时，其中视听6学时，视说4学时，语音2学时。该学时安排的框架在使用过程中可根据各校具体情况自行调整。在使用本教师用书时，授课教师应注意以下几点：

　　（1）在授课过程中，教师应引导学生听懂书中的视听材料，指导学生口头表达材料的主旨大意、相关细节，做到复述基本正确。

　　（2）在句子跟读环节，教师不仅要注重句子的准确性，还应该鼓励学生认真模仿语音、语调以及感情色彩。

　　（3）在视听、视说每个单元中，我们编写了Additional Listening Material和Additional Video-audio Material，老师在授课时可以选择使用，时间充裕时，可以作为正常教学材料，也可以作为家庭作业让学生课后练习使用。

（4）听力技巧的掌握是学生今后英语学习的基础，教师应该首先吃透书中的讲解，结合自己的经验，在课堂上精讲多练，还可以课后推荐英语学习网站，经典练习书籍供学生课后进行巩固练习。

（5）充分利用语音训练2学时，帮助学生了解学习语音的重要性，打好语音、语调基础，注意纠正学生常见的孤僻发音，课程结束时可进行班级语音比赛。

参编者均为视听、视说、语音课的任课教师，通过实践，他们积累了较丰富的经验。而本教材正是各位教师教学理念、教学方法、教学研究的集体结晶。本书的听力和视频部分的文字材料由Phillipa, Peter, Jennifer, Tim和Sean校对，对此，我们表示衷心地感谢。

由于编者水平和经验有限，教材中难免还有不足之处，希望各位读者不吝赐教。

编　者

2009年8月

Contents

Contents

Contents

Contents

I   Background Knowledge

1. Language Points

Preview Exercises

(1) **finance**   n.   the commercial activity of providing funds and capital/ 财政，财务

e. g. He is an well-known expert in finance.

(2) **senior students**   students in the third or fourth year of the college/ 大三、大四学生

Listening Material

(1) **journalist**   n.   a writer for newspapers and magazines /记者，新闻 工作者

e. g. This journalist's works are popular among young people.

Reference words: reporter, press conference

(2) **interview**   v. /n.   the questioning of a person (or a conversation in which information is elicited); often conducted by journalists/面谈，访问，接见

e. g. The two rival politicians came/were brought face to face in a TV interview.

(3) **occupation**   n.   the principal activity in your life that you do to earn money /职业

e. g. Riding is her favorite occupation.

Reference words: job, career, profession, work

Listening Skills

(1) The ways of "direct choice and indirect choice" are the means to get the correct answer while doing the short conversation. While teaching the students, the definition of these two ways should be explained in detail. And then, do the sample exercises.

(2) **in charge of**   assign a duty, responsibility or obligation to/负责

1

e. g. You're responsible to whoever is in charge of sales.

（3）**vacancy**　　n.　being unoccupied /空缺，空白

e. g. We still have vacancies for secretaries but other positions have been filled.

（4）**count on**　　depend on/依靠，指望

e. g. You can count on me.

（5）**optional course**　courses possible but not necessary; left to personal choice /选修课

e. g. Music is one of the optional courses in our college.

2. Cultural Background

（1）The related elements involved in greetings and introductions

If you want to get a suitable, polite greetings and introductions, the following elements students should be familiar with: How to call a name, country, and different ways of greetings and introductions.

①　Name formation（Omitted）

②　Important capital, name of a country（Omitted）

（2）Introduction to the ways of greetings

The useful ways of greetings:

How's everything?

What's up?

What's new?

What's happening?

How are you?

Nice to meet you.

How have you been?

Long time no see.

（3）Different ways of introduction

Introduction is the beginning of the conversation with a stranger. A good introduction can help you more in the communicative society.

The main content of self-introduction:

Greeting, Your name, Your age, Your nationality, Your work, Your education, Your hobby, Your wishes, Ending.

e. g. Hello, I'm very glad to have a chance to introduce myself. My name is River Xu.

I am 44 years old. I am from Wuhan. I am a college teacher. I was graduated from Air force Radar College. I like singing and dancing. I hope we can make friends with each other. Thank you!

Introduction to each other:

Sample 1: A: Hello, I am... I am from... How do you do?

　　　　　B: Hello, I am... I am from... How do you do?

Sample 2: A: Hello! This is...

　　　　　B: How do you do?

　　　　　A: ..., this is...

　　　　　C: How do you do?

II Reference Key

Part One

1. Preview Exercises

(1) Dictation

Would you introduce yourself briefly to each other, please? My name is Wen Yue. My major is international finance. I'm a senior student now. My name is Shi Wenwen. My major is computer. I'm now a junior. My name is Zhu King. My major is also international finance.

(2) Questions

①They are attending CET4 oral test. They are making self introduction...

②OK. My name is..., I'm... you may call me... I major in...

2. Listening Material

Task 1

C　D

C, engineer, police officer, businessman, lawyer, teacher, student, D

Task 3

(1) Personal   (2) spells   (3) 5552340   (4) 5557894   (5) occupation

3. Additional Listening Material

Task 1

D   D

Task 2

C   B   C

Task 3

(1) dinner   (2) read   (3) watch   (4) talk   (5) same   (6) different   (7) work

4. Video-aural Material

Task 1

C   C

Task 2

D   A   C

Task 3

(1) meet   (2) chair   (3) letter   (4) young   (5) last   (6) Miss or Mrs.

5. Listening Skills

plug   n.   an electrical device with two or three pins that is inserted in a socket to make an electrical connection/电插头

indicator   n.   a device for showing the operating condition of some system /指示器

pocketbook   n.   a pocket – size case for holding papers and paper money/皮夹子

limp   v.   walk impeded by some physical limitation or injury /跛行

e. g. He was born with a slight deformity of the feet which made him limp.

turned down refuse to accept/拒绝

e. g The board turn down all approach on the subject of merger.

· **semester** n. one of two divisions of an academic year/学期

e.g. I have completed 12 semester credits now and shall have completed8 more
by the end of June.

Part Two

1. Preview Exercises

(1) When we meet a stranger, we often say "How are you?"; and when we meet a stranger,
we often say "How do you do?". About introduction, I think we should greet to somebody first and introduce my name, age, and other things.

(2)(omitted)

2. Warming up Exercises

(Please see background knowledge)

3. Listening Material Review

Task 1

They are good friends. This is because the boy is invited to her home and watches her family
photos.

Task 2

(1) Yes. It is. Because there are nine people in her family. They are…

(2) In my opinion, personal information should include name, age, gender, degree, contact
way, etc.

(3) She has no job at present. She just wants to take part in an interview.

Task 3

(1) According to the clip, I think the woman is very kind, beautiful and ready to work.

(2) Ana and her boy friend are watching her family photos. She is patiently introducing his
family members. And then, a telephone comes in. It says Ana will have an interview
tomorrow. And she just gives her personal information to the caller.

Task 4

(1) Your father is from Ireland and your mother is from Mexico.

(2) I was from Mexico, but I am American. And you?

(3) Joe is a lawyer. Jack is a teacher. And Bill is a student.

(4) My information for the interview tomorrow with Nancy Marquette.

4. Video-aural Material Review

Task 1

This is because they are strange to each other. This is the first time for them to meet.

Task 2

(1) Maybe he is practicing saying hello to audience.

(2) Everyone there can be a host. I think if you work hard, you will be a host very soon.

(3) The name of the TV station is called "Hello America". I just find it on the screen.

Task 3

(1) They work very hard. They will be good hosts in the future.

(2) This clip tells a story happening in a newly made TV station called "Hello America". The young hosts are greeting each other. Some of them are practicing very hard.

Task 4

(1) I'm Susan Webster. It's nice to meet you, Carol.

(2) This letter says I am the host.

(3) Susan, it's nice to meet you. What's your last name?

(4) Miss or Mrs. Susan Webster?

5. Additional Video-aural Material

Task 1

They are going to attend a party given by his teacher. The address is 410 Pine Street, apartment 203.

Task 2

(1) No. They just go to a wrong place. They mix 203 with 302.

(2) According to the announcement board, we find it is "end of exam party".

(3) No. They fail in finding his teacher. But they know some other new friends.

Task 3

(1) They just find a wrong address. So they just go to a wrong place and find a wrong person.

(2) Bob and Jennifer are classmates. They decide to attend a party given by his teacher. However, they forget the exact address. So they just go to a wrong place.

Task 4

(1) What is the apartment number?

(2) Well. It's nice to meet you. Are you Terry's friends?

(3) I think he is over there. My name is Bob. Bob Freeman.

(4) This is my husband, John.

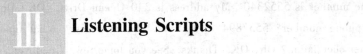

III Listening Scripts

Part One

1. Preview Exercises

Thank you. Now, would you introduce yourself briefly to each other, please? My name is Wen Yue. My major is international finance. I'm a senior student now. My name is Shi Wenwen. My major is computer. I'm now a junior. My name is Zhu King. My major is also international finance.

2. Listening Material

A: That's my father. Pastrick Baino Webster.

B: Is he Irish?

A: Yes. He's from Dublin Ireland.

B: Your father is from Ireland and your mother is from Mexico.

A: Yes. I'm Mexican and Irish. I'm from Mexico, but I am American. And you? Where are your parents from?

B: My parents are English.

A: What does your father do?

B: My father is a journalist.

A: Oh, And what does your mother do?

B: She is a singer.

A: A singer?

B: Yes. My mother is a singer. Who are they?

A: They are my brothers.

B: Six brothers?

A: It's hot.

B: Mm. Good. Denis is an engineer. Dan is a police officer. Peter is a businessman.

A: How old is he?

B: He is 35. Joe is a lawyer. Jack is a teacher. And Bill is a student.
Excuse me. Hello! Hi, Carol, how are you? I'm fine, thanks. It's Carol. Personal information? OK. I'm 25 years old. My middle name is Ana, Susan Ana Webster. It spells Ana, a-n-a. My phone number is 5552340. My address is 340 Ocean Drive. OK? Oh, Carrol, what's your phone number? 5557894. OK. Yes. An interview? What time? Who's that? What's her occupation? Oh, OK. Thanks. See you tomorrow. Goodbye.

A: What's that?

B: My information for the interview tomorrow. With Nancy Marquet.

A: Nancy Marquet. Is she from France?

B: No, she is from England.

A: Marquet. Is Marquet an English name? How do you spell it?

A: Marquet.

B: What time is it?

A: 12 o'clock.

B: Well. See you tomorrow.

A: OK. John?

B: Yes.

A: See you tomorrow.

B: Goodbye, Susan.

3. Additional Listening Material

Hi. My name is Andy. I'm 23. This is my house. I live here with my mum, and my dad, and my sister Susan. Susan is 17. She is a high school student. It's OK here, really. This is my room. Nice. Huh, weekdays I get up about 6. Then I have breakfast with my family.

Then I go to work. I drive to work. I am a police officer. This is the police station. I start at 9 o'clock. It's a great job. I work outside. I work with people. At noon I usually go to lunch. At one o'clock, I work again. At five I go home. Weekday nights I stay at home. I eat dinner, I read, I watch TV. I talk with Susan. Every night is the same. But weekends are different. Friday, Saturday and Sunday I work at Ivories. I start at 9 o'clock. I am a singer. But on Monday, I am a police officer.

4. Video-aural Material

Carol: Good morning, Steven.

Steven: Good morning Carol.

Carol: Hi. Mike.

Mike: Good morning, Carol.

Hello, Linda. Good morning Carol.

(Good morning. My name is Jake Celsir...)

Carol: Hi. I'm Carol Green.

Jake: Hi, Carol. Good morning. My name is Jake Celsir.

Carol: I like, my name is Jake Celsir.

Jake: My name is Jake Celsir.

Carol: Hello, my name is Carol Green.

Susan: I'm Susan Webster. It's nice to meet you, Carol.

Carol: It's nice to meet you, too.

Coffee?

Susan: Yes, please.

Carol: This is the chair for the host.

Susan: I'm the host.

Carol: Maybe.

Susan: Maybe?

Carol: Maybe. Maybe Jake is the host. Maybe John is the host. Maybe you are the host.

Susan: This letter says I am the host. Linda Marino, please.

Carol: She is Linda Marino.

Susan: She is Linda Marino? Really? She is very young.

Carol: Linda, Linda.

Linda: Hi. I'm Linda Marino.

Susan: I'm Susan Webster.

9

Linda: Excuse me, Susan.

Susan: He is John P. Banks.

Carol: Susan, this is John Banks. John, this is Susan.

Susan: Hello, John, it's nice to meet you.

John: Susan, nice to meet you. What's your last name?

Susan: Webster.

John: What?

Susan: Webster. W-e-b-s-t-e-r.

John: Oh. Welcome to WEFL, Susan Webster.

Susan: Thank you.

Jake: Well. Hello. My name is Jake Celsir. What's your name?

Susan: Jake... really. This is Susan Webster.

Jake: Miss or Mrs. Susan Webster?

Susan: Ms Susan Webster.

Linda: Susan, Steven.

Susan: Nice to see you again, Steven.

Steven: Call me Steve.

Susan: John P. Banks.

John: Susan Webster.

Jake: Ms Susan Webster.

Carol: Jake...

5. Listening Skills

Sample practice

(1) W: Do you want dollars or pounds?

    M: I want pounds. Two tens and a five, please.

    Q: How much money does the man want?

(2) W: Can you come to my birthday party tomorrow afternoon, Uncle Smith?

    M: I'd like to, Mary. But I can't. I'll in surgery at three o'clack. I'll be operating on a patient then.

    Q: What is the profession of the man?

(3) W: What kind of gas do you want?

    M: I don't know really. This is a rented car. And it's the first time I am getting gas. What kind of gas does it take?

Q: Who is the woman?

(4) M: How time flies! Last month I was in Pairs and now I'm in Seoul.

W: Is it the first time for you to be here?

Q: Where was he last month?

(5) M: Do you check the power plug and press the play button?

W: Yes. The power indicator wasn't on and it was running. But somehow the sound didn't come through.

Q: What was the woman probably trying to do?

(6) W: Did Hellen tell you about the fight she and her husband had last night?

M: Yes. That really got her nervous when he found that photograph in her pocketbook.

Q: How did Helen's husband react for the photograph?

(7) W: Marlin, what has happened? How come you are limping?

M: It's not too bad. I was a big lucky. The seat belt saved me.

Q: What has happened to the man.

(8) M: Would you get me through to Mr. Lemon, please?

W: I'm sorry. He is with a patient.

Q: What does the woman mean?

(9) W: If I were you, I would have accepted the job.

M: I turned down the offer of it would mean frequent business trips away from my family.

Q: Why didn't the man accept the job?

(10) M: You were seen hanging about the store on the night when it was robbed, weren't you?

W: Me? You must have made a mistake. I was at home that night.

Q: What are they talking about?

(11) M: Prof. Kennedy has been very busy this semester. As far as I know, he works until midnight every day.

W: I wouldn't have troubled him so much if I had known be was so busy.

Q: What do we learn from the conversation?

(12) W: Excuse me, sir. You are not supposed to be here. This area is for airport staff only.

M: I'm sorry, I didn't note the sign.

Q: What do we learn from the conversation?

Additional training

(1) W: I heard you got a full mark in math exam. Congratulations!

M: Thanks! I'm sure you also did a good job.

Q: What's the probable relationship between the two speakers?

(2) W: Hi, Tony. How did your experiment go yesterday?

M: Well, it wasn't as easy as I had thought . I have to continue doing it tonight.

Q: What do we learn from the conversation?

(3) M: I hear you are moving into a new apartment soon?

W: Yes, but it is more expensive. My present neighbor plays piano all night long.

Q: Why is the woman moving?

(4) W: Mr. Jones, your student, Bill, shows great enthusiasm for music instruments.

M: I only wish he showed half as much for his English lessons.

Q: What do we learn from the conversation about Bill?

(5) W: Oh, dear! I'm starving, I can't walk any farther.

M: Let's go to the restaurant across the street and get something to eat.

Q: Where are the two people?

(6) W: Why didn't you make an appointment to see the doctor last week when you first twist your ankle?

M: The injury didn't seem serious then . I decided to go today, because my foot still hurt when I put my weigh on it.

Q: Why didn't the man see the doctor earlier?

(7) M: I wonder if Suzy will be here by 5 o'clock.

W: Her husband said she left home at 4 : 30. She should be here at 5 : 10, and 5 : 15 at the latest.

Q: What time did Suzy leave home?

(8) W: When will you be through with your work, John?

M: Who knows? My boss usually finds something for me to do at the last minute.

Q: What do we learn from the conversation?

(9) W: I don't know what I'm going to wear to the party . All of my clothes look so old and I can't afford something new.

M: Why don't you wear your black silk dress?

Q: What is the woman going to do?

(10) M: How did you like yesterday's play?

W: Generally speaking, it was quite good. The part of secretary was played wonderfully, but I think the man who played the boss was too dramatic to be realistic.

Q: How does the woman feel about the man's acting in the play?

Part Two

Additional Video-aural Material

Girl: Is that it?

Boy: Yes. 410 Pine street.

Girl: OK.

What is the apartment number?

Oh, quick. Bob.

I think it's 302.

Really.

Yes. 302.

Hello.

Hi. It's Bob and Jennifer. Oh. There it is. 302.

Hi. Come in . I'm Eduardo.

Hi, Eduardo... nice to...

It's... Eduardo.

Eduardo. Sorry. It's nice to meet you. I'm Jennifer.

And I'm Bob.

Well. It's nice to meet you. Are you, um, Terry's friends?

Terry? (Eduardo)

Oh, excuse me.

Who is Terry?

I don't know. I think she's Doctor Robert's wife.

And where is Doctor Robert?

I don't know.

Hi, I'm Ken.

Are you John's friend?

No, Ken, I'm his student. My name's Jennifer.

Student?

Excuse me Jennifer.

Excuse me. Are you Eduardo?

No. I'm not. I think he is over there. My name is Bob, Bob Freeman.

Nice to meet you. I'm...

Nice to meet you.

Are you in my math class?

Math class? No. I'm a friend of Terry's.

Is Doctor Robert here?

Doctor Robert? No. I don't think so.

Time for tea, everyone.

Yes. Help yourselves.

That's not Doctor Robert.

No, it's not.

Hi. Are you, um, Naomi's friends?

No, I am Bob and this is Jennifer.

Hi. Nice to meet you.

Nice to meet you, too. My name is Terry and this is my husband, John.

Hi, nice to meet you.

Is this your apartment?

Yes, it is. And you are...

Bob, and I'm Jennifer. We are in Doctor Robert's class.

Oh, John Robert.

He is in apartment 203 I think.

This is the department 302.

Oh, oh, oh.

That's OK. Please. Oh no, it's no problem, please.

Oh, OK. Thank you. Yes. Thanks.

So you're students then.

Translation of the Listening Materials

Part One

1. Preview Exercises

请简单互相介绍一下。我叫文越，我的专业是国际金融，我是大学三年级学生。我叫施文文，计算机专业，我是大二的学生。我叫朱庆，也是国际金融专业的。

2. Listening Material

A：那是我的父亲 Pastrick Baino Webster。

B：他是爱尔兰人吗？

A：是的。他来自爱尔兰的都柏林。

B：你父亲来自爱尔兰你母亲来自墨西哥。

A：一个爱尔兰人和一个墨西哥人。我出生在墨西哥，但是我是一个美国人。你呢？你的父母是哪里人？

B：我父母是英国人。

A：你父亲是干什么的？

B：我父亲是一名记者。

A：哦，那你母亲呢？

B：她是一个歌唱家。

A：一个歌唱家？

B：是的。我母亲是一个歌唱家。他们是谁？

A：他们是我的兄弟。

B：6 个兄弟？

A：茶很烫。

B：嗯，是的。Denis 是一个工程师。Dan 是一个警官。Peter 是一个商人。

A：他多大了？

B：他 35 岁了。Joe 是个律师。Jack 是个老师。还有 Bill 是个学生。

我接一个电话。你好！你好，Carol，最近过得怎么样？我很好，谢谢。Carol 打来的。个人信息？好的。我 25 岁。我的中间名是 Ana，Susan Ana Webster。它是这样拼写的 A-n-a，Ana。我的电话号码是 5552340。我的住址是 340 Ocean Drive。好了？哦，Carol，你的电话号码是？5557894。好的，是的。面试？时间是？是谁面试？什么职业？哦，好的。谢谢。明天见。再见。

A：那是什么？

B：我明天面试的资料。和 Nancy Marquet 一起。

A：Nancy Marquet。她来自法国吗？

B：不，她来自英国。

A：Marquet。Marquet 是一个英文名字吗？怎么拼写它？

A：M-a-r-q-u-e-t。

B：现在几点了？

A：12 点。

B：明天见。

A：好的。John？

B：是的。

A：明天见！

B：再见，Susan。

3. Additional Listening Material

你们好，我叫 Andy，我 23 岁。这是我的家。我与我的妈妈、爸爸和我的妹妹 Susan 住在这里。这是我妹妹 Susan，17 岁。她是高中学生。好的，就这里了，这是我的房间，看起来挺漂亮，是吧。平时我大约 6 点起床，和家人吃早餐，然后就上班。我开车上班。我是警察。这是警察局。我 9 点开始工作。工作不错。我在外面执勤。我的工作是与人打交道。中午，我去吃中餐，1 点又开始工作。5 点下班。平时晚上就待在家里。吃晚餐，读书，看电视，与 Susan 聊天。每天晚上都是如此。但是周末不同。周五、周六、周日我在 Ivories 工作，9 点开始上班，我是一名歌手。但是周一，我又成为警察了。

4. Video-aural Material

Carol：早上好，Steven。

Steven：早上好，Carol。

Carol：你好，Mike。

Mike：早上好，Carol。

你好，Linda。你好 Carol。

（早上好，我是 Jake Celsir……）

Carol：你好，我是 Carol Green。

Jake：你好，Carol。早上好，我是 Jake Celsir。

Carol：我喜欢这样说，我叫 Jake Celsir。

Jake：我叫 Jake Celsir。

Carol：你好，我是 Carol Green。

Susan：我是 Susan Webster。很高兴见到你，Carol。

Carol：我也很高兴见到你。

　　　　喝咖啡吗？

Susan：好的，谢谢你。

Carol：这是主持人的位置。

Susan：我是主持人。

Carol：可能吧。

Susan：可能？

Carol：也许。可能 Jake 是主持人，也许 John 是主持人，也许你是。

Susan：这封信说我是主持人。请问，Linda Marino。

Carol：她是 Linda Marino。

Susan：她是 Linda Marino 吗？真的吗？她很年轻啊。

Carol：Linda，Linda。

Linda：你们好，我是 Linda Marino。

Susan：我是 Susan Webster。

Linda：Susan，请多关照。

Susan：他是 John P. Banks。

Carol：Susan，这是 John Banks。John，这是 Susan。

Susan：你好，John，很高兴认识你。

John：Susan，很高兴认识你。你姓什么？

Susan：Webster。

John：什么？

Susan：Webster。W-e-b-s-t-e-r。

John：哦，欢迎来到 WEFL，Susan Webster。

Susan：谢谢你。

Jake：嗯，你好，我是 Jake Celsir，你叫什么？

Susan：Jake…… 真的，这是 Susan Webster。

Jake：称你为女士还是夫人？

Susan：叫 Susan Webster 女士。

Linda：Susan，Steven。

Susan：再次见到你很高兴，Steven。

Steven：叫我 Steve。

Susan：John P. Banks。

John：Susan Webster。

Jake：Susan Webster 女士。

Carol：Jake……

5. Listening Skills

（Omitted）

Part Two

Additional Video-aural Material

Girl：是这里吗？

Boy：是的，Pine 大街 410 号。

Girl：好的。

房间号是多少？哦，快点，Bob.

我想是 302 吧。

是吗？

是的，302。

你好。

你好，我们是 Bob 和 Jenifer。到了，这是 302。

你好，请进，我是 Eduardo。

你好，很高兴见到你。

我是 Eduardo。

Eduardo，对不起，很高兴见到你，我是 Jennifer。

我是 Bob。很高兴见到你，你是 Terry 的 朋友？

Terry？（Eduardo）

哦，我离开一下。

谁是 Terry？

我也不知道啊，我想是 Robert 博士的妻子。

Robert 博士在哪里啊？

我不知道啊。

你好，我是 Ken。
你是 John 的朋友？
不是，Ken，我是他的学生，我叫 Jennifer。
学生？对不起，我要离开一下。

对不起，你是 Eduardo？
不是，我想他在那边。我是 Bob，Bob Freeman。
很高兴见到你，我是……
很高兴见到你。
你是我们数学班的么？
数学班？不是的，我是 Terry 的朋友。
Robert 博士在吗？
Robert 博士？没有啊。

现在是吃茶点的时间，来宾们。
是啊，大家随意啊。
那不是 Robert 博士。
是的，他不是。
你好，你是 Naomi 的朋友么？
不，我是 Bob，她是 Janifer。
你们好！见到你们很高兴。
见到你们也很高兴。我叫 Terry，这是我的丈夫 John。
你好，见到你们很高兴。
这是你的房间？
是啊，你是……？
Bob，我是 Jennifer。我们是 Robert 博士班上的。
我想他住在 203 房间。
这是 302 房间。
哦，哦，哦。
那好吧。哦不，这没问题。
哦，好的。谢谢，是的，谢谢。
所以你们是他的学生啊。

I Background Knowledge

1. Language Points

Preview Exercises

(1) **institute** n. an association organized to promote art or science or education /学院，协会

e. g. A database is supplied by American Geological Institute and dealing with earth sciences.

(2) **approximately** adv. (of quantities) imprecise but fairly close to correct/近似地，大约

e. g. The plane will be taking off in approximately five minutes.

Listening Material

(1) **take the lead** be the first to do something, hoping that others will copy you/带头

e. g. She always takes the lead when we plan to do anything.

(2) **cutlery set** tableware implements for cutting and eating food/刀具

e. g. A cutlery set includes knives, forks, spoons, etc.

Additional Listening Material

(1) **give a hand** help somebody/帮助某人

e. g. It's too heavy. Please give me a hand.

(2) **be disciplined in** obeying the rules/对……循规蹈矩

e. g. That old man is always disciplined in everything he does.

(3) **get offended with/at** cause to feel resentment or indignation/生气

e. g. He is offended at being ignored.

e. g. He was offended that we didn't agree with him.

Video-aural Material

(1) **on behalf of** representing; for the sake of/代表;为了

e. g. The agent spoke on behalf of his principal.

The legal guardian must act on behalf of the child.

(2) **etiquette** n. rules governing socially acceptable behavior /礼仪,礼节,成规

e. g. The forms of ceremony and etiquette should be observed by diplomats and heads of state.

Listening Skills

(1) The ways of "direct choice and indirect choice" are the means to get the correct answer while doing the short conversation. While teaching the students, the definition of these two ways should be explained in detail. "Direct choice" here means a question designed for learners to choose among the four choices directly from the conversation they have just heard. In other words, just judging from synonyms or similar word or from the words matching. While "indirect choice" means a question designed for learner to choose from some clues between the lines or the tone of voice.

(2) **in charge of** assign a duty, responsibility or obligation to /负责

e. g. You're responsible to whoever is in charge of sales.

(3) **vacancy** n. being unoccupied /空缺, 空白

e. g. We still have vacancies for secretaries but other positions have been filled.

(4) **count on** depend on/依靠,指望

e. g. You can count on me.

(5) **optional course** courses possible but not necessary; left to personal choice /选修课

e. g. Music is one of the optional courses in our college.

2. Cultural Background

(1) Bad manners in college

① Ride bikes at a speed beyond the limit.

② Cross the road without watching the traffic and lights.

③ Spit everywhere.

④ Take a rude attitude at teachers and classmates.

⑤ Keep silent when being asked to answer questions.

⑥ Litter everywhere.

⑦ Ruin the belongings of others and school.

⑧ Make noise when others are sleeping.

⑨ Disobey teachers when breaking the rule.

⑩ Insult teachers and classmates.

（2）Different good manners between China and other countries

In China	In other countries
① Ask someone to have more again and again.	① Spit four times as a kind of blessing in some East African countries.
② Show guests around their new houses.	② Walk behind the tents when people are having their meals in Arabia countries.
③ Ask "Where are you going?" when meeting on the way.	③ Hug when meeting each other in many countries.
④ Pat one's shoulder when showing happiness or encouragement.	④ Talk about the weather when meeting for the first time in English-speaking countries.
⑤ Serve guests at a restaurant.	⑤ Express directly whether they like or dislike the food offered.
⑥ Eat together with all the family members.	⑥ Walk on the side closer to the traffic with ladies on the street.
⑦ Give your seats to the old or women with babies in their arms.	

II Reference Key

Part One

1. Preview Exercises

（1）Dictation

kids; tobacco; one-third; die;

（2）Questions

• I think it is a bad manner. First, it is against the rule of the college. Second, it is not healthy.

- In my opinion, good manners in colleges should be as follows:
① be in class on time;
② respect teachers;
③ regard classmates as brothers and sisters;
④ be honest in the examinations and so on.

2. Listening Material

Task 1

D   C

Task 2

A   A   D

Task 3

(1) suggests   (2) hostess   (3) listed   (4) rules   (5) considered   (6) elbows

3. Additional Listening Material

Task 1

C   A

Task 2

A   C   C

Task 3

(1) words   (2) constructions   (3) extremely   (4) pressure   (5) communication
(6) offended

4. Video-aural Material

Task 1

D   B

A B B

Task 3

(1) definitely (2) specials (3) passed (4) completed (5) excused (6) comment

(7) delicious

5. Listening Skills

Sample practice

(1) – (5) CBACD   (6) – (10) DADBA

Additional training

(1) – (5) AAADB   (6) – (10) BADDA

Part Two

1. Preview Exercises

(1) teacher; children; play; poor

(2) It is a bad manner using mobile phones in the classroom. First, it can interrupt the teaching. Second, it belongs to impolite behavior to teachers.

2. Warming up Exercises

(1) According to the clip, I think the first impression she gives me is that she is impolite, rude and poorly-cultured.

(2) What I get impressed is chiefly from her language, her appearance, her dressing and posture.

(3) The woman gives me a bad impression.

3. Listening Material Review

Task 1

It tells us the basic rules for the table manners.

Task 2

(1) Don't eat with your mouth open; don't put your elbows on the table; start with the cutlery set on the outer most of the plate and work your way in; never speak with your mouth full.

(2) Say "excuse me" or "I want to wash my hands" before you leave the table.

(3) When you use the cutlery set in a wrong way, it's no need to be panic.

Task 3

(1) Pay attention to the table seat order; don't finish eating all the food; talk with the host or hostess while eating with some praising words, and so on.

(2) This is a program of introduction to table manners. It tells us what we should do and what we should not do while eating.

Task 4

(1) Hello. Welcome to another BBC Learning English programme.

(2) And that's considered very rude.

(3) And remember never speak with your mouth full.

(4) But remember if you used the wrong knife for a dish, don't panic.

4. Video-aural Material Review

Task 1

It is most probably for children.

Task 2

(1) We should say "May I please have this" or you can ask "Could you please tell me some of your specials".

(2) They have to give their comment on the meal and show their appreciation.

(3) Give your order; say "thank you" when the meal has been passed; give your comment on the meal.

Task 3

(1) According to "expertvillage. com" and the content, we can guess it is a program given to common people, given by host and helped by experts invited.

（2）（*Omitted*）

Task 4

（1）…"May I please have this" or you can ask "Could you please tell me some of your specials".

（2）And also how to order when you are at the restaurant.

（3）…saying please and thank you when it has been passed something or ask for something.

（4）…and they might comment the meal is delicious.

5. Additional Video-aural Material

Task 1

How to make a successful interview.

Task 2

（1）Be punctual; shake hands firmly; look the interviewer in the eye; speak in positive terms; sit alert in your interview and show your humor, smile a little; write a "thank you" note.

（2）It means "acting or arriving or performed exactly at the time appointed".

（3）To express your interest in the job and why you think you are qualified.

Task 3

（1）No. I don't. But I will do it when I am in summer holidays.

Yes, I do. It is a challenge.

（2）This clip gives us some suggestions about how to make a successful interview. In his suggestion, he mentions good manners in the interview.

Task 4

（1）Be punctual for interviews, but no earlier for five minutes.

（2）A firm handshake is important, and looks the interviewer in the eye.

（3）Speak in positive terms about your school and your previous employers.

（4）sit alertly during your interview and show you're humor, smile a little.

Part One

1. Preview Exercises

An estimated 22 percent of American high school <u>kids</u> smoke, and according to Cathy Backinger, chief of the <u>tobacco</u> Control Research Branch at the National Cancer Institute in the
United States, approximately <u>one-third</u> of young smokers will eventually <u>die</u> from a smoking-
related illness.

2. Listening Material

Hello. Welcome to another BBC Learning English programme. I'm Helen. This week we're
going to answer a question from Jenny. Yes, Jenny is going to have a formal dinner with her
friend's parents. And she would like some help with formal English table manners. Alright,
Jonathan suggests taking the lead from your host or hostess. And Liz listed a few basic table
manner rules. First, don't eat with your mouth open. Like this (making noise). And that's
considered very rude. Second rule, don't put your elbows on the table. Personally, I think
this rule applies in formal dinner situations, not when you're having a casual meal with
friends. Liz also mentioned the cutlery set, the knives, forks and spoons. So just remember
to eat from outside in. Yes, start with the cutlery set on the outer most of the plate and work
your way in. And remember never speak with your mouth full. Well, I hope we've covered
the basics for table manners. But remember if you used the wrong knife for a dish, don't panic.

3. Additional Listening Material

Hi Lee. Hello everyone. Welcome to BBC Learning English. Today we've got a question on
good British manners.

I am interested in English culture very much, for example, so I want to know English manners. My Chinese name is Chen Manzhu.

Well, this is a big question to talk about, but I think what we are concentrating on today is good manners in public places. The first person we spoke to is Marie:

Well, I think my idea of politeness really is just general consideration for other people. For example, if you see a mum struggling with a couple of kids with a pram or pushchair trying to get upstairs at a railway station, I just think it common courtesy really to try and give a hand. Marie thinks that to be polite you need to have a general consideration for other people. So it's common courtesy to give a hand. The word courtesy is spelt c-o-u-r-t-e-s-y.

Well generally I find British people extremely polite, very disciplined in things. For example, when I travel on the tube I always see that there is always somebody who gives up their seat for a pregnant woman or elderly people or women with children. I have great admiration for British way of life because there is a lot things people can learn from this in other parts of the world.

This is a very typical example. On the tube people will give up their seat for pregnant women, elderly people or women with children. Bharti said that she is full of admiration for the British way of life.

Well another example is how and when you can use your mobile phone. Listen to Dermit:

I think one example of British good manners compared to perhaps certain other nationalities is in the use of mobile phones. I have noticed when I am abroad in meetings if people's mobile phone rings, people immediately pick it up and answer and I think here in the UK, certainly people with good manners don't use their mobile phones in meetings. If you are having a meal in a restaurant, it's better not to use it. Of course during a show or cinema you would obviously turn it off.

So the message from Dermit is people with good manners don't use their mobile phones in meetings, restaurants or the cinema. Another thing is the polite way British people talk to each other. Here's Martina:

British people are very polite in the way they talk. They are just so lovely. They use a lot of words like please and thank you and excuse me and constructions of sentences are extremely polite. Even in the situation when there is a lot of pressure in the air they would be talking to you in a very very polite manner and they would make sure that the communication is on a very very polite level and nobody gets offended with the way they speak to them.

Yes, I quite agree with Martina there. We do use please and thank you a lot. She said that we make sure that communication is very polite so that nobody gets offended. And last but not least, is the habit of queuing. Here is Lorraine:

British people like to queue I think mainly because it's a tradition. And they are very polite and basically don't like to upset other people. So we will all queue at the bus stop while increasingly now others do not and they form their own queue at the other side of the bus stop, but we are so polite we won't say anything.

Here Lorraine said that queuing is a British tradition and basically we don't want to upset other people. She said British people are so polite they even don't complain when others don't queue.

4. Video-aural Material

Hi, I'm Marine. And on behalf of expertvillage.com, I will be discussing proper dining etiquette, and this session is on teaching your children how to properly excuse themselves when they have finished eating and also how to order when you are at the restaurant. When you're at the restaurant and the waiter comes to your order, you should definitely say "May I please have this" or you can ask "Could you please tell me some of your specials" and with your children too teaching them proper manners of the table, saying please and thank you when they've been passed something or ask for something. Also when they have completed their meal, they should ask to be excused that they finished, and they might comment that the meal was delicious. And certainly you have to…let them know if it's alright to be excused but that's proper for children to thank for the meal, and to make a comment how they like it and then ask that if they can be excused.

5. Listening Skills

<u>Sample practice</u>

(1) M: Hello, Lucy, do you have some change? I have to take a bus to my office.

W: Why not use my car? Let's go.

Q: What will the man most probably do?

(2) M: Can you show me the book you bought yesterday?

W: Sorry, I left it at home, but after class you can go together with me to my home.

Q: Where does this conversation most probably take place?

(3) M: I am worried about those classes I missed when I was sick.

W: I will try to bring you up today on what we've done.

Q: What can we learn from this conversation?

(4) W: Hey Dan. Is it the first time for you to meet Susan's parents?

M: Yeah, next weekend. Fortunately, her father loves to drink, so we will have much more to talk about.

Q: What can be infered about Dan?

(5) W: Professor White's presentation seemed to make me sleep.

M: How could you sleep through it? It is one of the best that I have ever heard on this topic.

Q: What does the man think of Professor White's presentation?

(6) W: I am looking for good quality paper to type my term paper. I don't see any on the shelf.

M: I saw some in the storeroom this morning. I will go and check for you.

Q: What does the woman want to buy?

(7) M: It seems that we'll have another fine day tomorrow. Let's go to the seaside.

W: OK. But we'll have to leave very early, otherwise we'll get caught in the traffic.

Q: What does the woman suggest?

(8) M: Do you know James? He is in your class.

W: Certainly. He is in charge of our class and he is a good-looking guy.

Q: Why did the woman remember James so well?

(9) W: The man at the garage thinks that I don't take good care of my car.

M: Nor do I. I can see some scratches on the outside, and the inside is in a mess, too.

Q: What does the man think of the woman's car?

(10) M: Beautiful day, isn't it? Do you want to go shopping with me?

　　　W: If you don't mind waiting while I get prepared.

　　　Q: What does the woman mean?

Additional training

(1) W: I'm told you've bought some gifts for your family?

　　　M: Well, I've bought a mobile phone for my father and two shirts for my sister, but I haven't decided what to buy for my mother, probably some jewels.

　　　Q: Who did the man buy the mobile phone for?

(2) W: Look! It says they have a vacancy of a junior sales manager, and it seems like it's a big company. That'll be good, for you might have to travel a lot.

　　　M: Do they say anything about education degree or working experience?

　　　Q: What are they talking about?

(3) W: I think we've covered everything. What about tea break before we move on to the next item?

　　　M: Good idea. I really can't wait another minute.

　　　Q: What does the woman suggest doing?

(4) W: Tom, what happens if it rains? What are we going to do then?

　　　M: We'll have to count on good weather, but if it does rain, the whole thing will have to be put off.

　　　Q: What do we learn from the conversation?

(5) W: You took an optional course this semester, didn't you? How is it going?

　　　M: It's awful. It seems like the more the professor talks, the less I understand.

　　　Q: How does the man feel about the course?

(6) W: Mark is playing computer games.

　　　M: He should have prepared for his lessons.

　　　Q: What does the man think Mark should do?

(7) M: This year's basketball season will be disappointing.

　　　W: But most others think differently.

　　　Q: What does the woman mean?

(8) M: Is this the gate for flight 914 to Hong Kong?

　　　W: Yes, but I'm sorry the flight has delayed because of the weather. Please wait for further notice.

Q: What do we learn from this conversation?

(9) M: Excuse me. I'd like to place an advertisement for a used car in China Daily.

W: OK, but you have to run your advertisement for a month.

Q: Where is the conversation most probably taking place?

(10) M: I spent so much time designing my letter of application.

W: It's worth making the effort. You know how important it is to give a good impression.

Q: What do we know about the man?

Part Two

Additional Video-aural Material

Hi, I'm Gordon, I'm here about the job opening, PANG! Hi, I'm here about the job ... PANG! Hi, PANG!

The word you hear most often during a job hunt? "NO, NO ..." One expert says you can expect 20 rejections before you get your first "MAYBE", so don't be down on yourself.

Be sure your resume is flawless, or you'll never see the inside of an interviewer suite?

Be punctual for interviews, but no earlier than five minutes.

A firm handshake is important, and look the interviewer in the eye.

Don't be a dudda dude.

Speak in positive terms about the school and your previous employers.

Sit alertly during your interview and show you're humor, smile a little.

And follow up every interview with a "Thank You" letter, expressing your interest in the job and why you think you are qualified.

Translation of the Listening Materials

Part One

1. Preview Exercises

据估计 22% 的美国高中生吸烟，而且根据美国国家癌症学会烟草控制研究中心主任 Cathy Backinger 说，大约 1/3 的年轻吸烟者最终会死于与吸烟相关的疾病。

2. Listening Material

大家好。欢迎收听另一个 BBC 学英语节目。我是海伦。这周我们将会回答来自珍妮的问题。是的，珍妮将要参加她朋友的父母举行的一个正式聚餐。她需要我们帮助她了解一下英国正式聚餐时的餐桌礼仪。好的，Jonathan 建议要效仿男主人和女主人。这里利兹列出了几条基本的餐桌习惯规矩。第一，不要在吃东西的时候张着嘴，就像这样（发出声音），这会被认为是很粗鲁的。第二，不要把你的手肘放在桌子上。就我个人观点来看，这条规矩只是在非常正式的聚餐时候应该遵守，在和朋友们一起比较随意的情况下就不必要了。利兹还提到了餐具的摆放，刀、叉、勺。好吧你只要记住应该从最外面开始往里面拿。是的，首先拿起盘子最外面的餐具然后开始往里面进行吧。还要切记千万不要在你满口食物的时候说话。好了，希望我们对餐桌礼仪所介绍的已经够全面了。但是也请记住如果你用餐时用错了刀叉，也没必要惊慌失措。

3. Additional Listening Material

李，你好。大家好。欢迎收听 BBC 英语学习节目。今天我们来谈论一下关于英国礼节的话题。

我对英国的文化很感兴趣，因此我很想了解一下英国礼节。我的中文名字叫陈嫚姝。

当然，这是个很大话题，但是我们现在来浓缩一下，只谈论公共场所的礼节。第一个和我们一起谈话的人是 Marie：

好的，我认为礼貌行为应该是这样的，就是应该为别人考虑一下。例如，当你在地铁站看到一位母亲推着一辆坐有两个小孩子的婴儿车艰难地爬楼梯的时候，我认为大家都会认为应该上前去帮忙。礼貌（courtesy）这个词的拼写是这样的 c-o-u-r-t-e-s-y。帮助别人是很普遍的礼貌行为。

我发现英国人普遍都非常有礼貌，非常遵守秩序。比如我在地铁里经常看到有人会主动把座位让给孕妇或者老年人以及带着孩子的女士。我非常赞赏英国的生活方式，因为他们让世界上其他国家的人都能从中学习很多东西。

这是个很典型的例子。在地铁里人们会让座给孕妇、老人以及带孩子的女士。Bharti 说她完全赞赏英国人的生活方式。

好了，另一个例子是什么时候以及怎样使用你的移动电话。听听看 Dermit 是怎么说的：

我想到一个例子，与其他某几个国家比较起来英国的好习惯还体现在他们用手机上。我出国开会的时候如果我的电话响了我会马上接听，但是我注意到在英国大部分人不会在开会的时候用电话。还有当你在酒店吃饭的时候最好不要用手机。当然在戏院看表演或在电影院的时候你绝对应该关机。

这就是来自 Dermit 的信息，关于人们在会议厅、酒店、电影院不用手机的好习惯。接着我们来看看另外的英国人与别人交谈时候的好习惯。这是来自 Martina 的信息：

英国人在与人交谈的时候习惯非常好。他们就是如此的可爱。他们会用到许多礼貌的词汇比如"请"、"谢谢"、"对不起打扰了"，他们还会把句子组织得非常得体。即使在气氛非常压抑紧张的情况下，他们也会非常非常礼貌地与你交谈而且会确保谈话发生在一个和谐水平而不会有任何人因为他们的说话方式而生气。

是的我非常同意 Martina 的观点。我们确实用到很多请和谢谢之类的词汇。她说的很对，我们会保证交流的礼貌进行不让任何人生气。最后而且也很重要的一点，就是排队的习惯。这是 Lorraine 提到的：

我想，英国人喜欢排队的主要原因是这是一个传统。而且他们非常懂礼貌，基本上不愿意给人添麻烦。因此我们在车站排队的时候，尽管逐渐增多的人不会站队或者他们自己在一边又排起一对，我们也会保持礼貌而不说任何什么。

Lorraine 在这里说到了，排队是英国的一个传统，而且我们大多数人不愿意麻烦别人。她说到英国人非常礼貌以至于都不会和不排队的人争吵。

4. Video-aural Material

嗨，我是 Marine。代表 expertvillage.com 网站，我将会继续讨论合适的就餐礼节，这次是为了让你的孩子们知道在吃晚饭后如保礼貌地离开，以及怎样在餐厅点菜。当你在餐厅服务员来点菜时，你可以明确地说："可以帮我点一份这个吗？"或者你可以问："可以告诉我你们有什么特色菜吗？"为了教育你的孩子有个良好的餐桌习惯，当菜传过来或你要求什么东西的时候你应该说请和谢谢。还有当他们用餐结束时，孩子们应该说他们吃完了，准备离开了。他们可以评论一下食物是多么的可口，你必须让孩子们明白要求离开是否合适,但他要对饭菜进行感谢是合适的,要表达他们是如何喜欢,然后再问问是可以离开。

5. Listening Skills

（Omitted）

Part Two

Additional Video-aural Material

嗨,我是 Gordon,我来这里找工作,呼! 你好! 我来找工作! 呼!

这是你在找工作期间听到的最多的词吗:"不,不……"一位专家说到,在你得到第一个"可能可以"之前你会受到 20 个拒绝,因此,不要对自己失望。

一定做到的是简历是完美的,不然,你是不会见到面试组成员的。一定要准时参加面试,但也不要早于五分钟。稳健的握手也很重要而且要与面试官目光相对。不要表现出一个花花公子。可以说说你学校的积极生活以及说些前雇主的好话。面试时,要正襟危坐,但也要表现得人性化一点,笑一笑,并且每次面试之后要写一封感谢信,在信中表达你对这份工作的兴趣,并且告诉他们你为什么能够胜任这份工作。

I Background Knowledge

1. Language Points

Preview Exercises

(omitted)

Warming up Exercises

(omitted)

Listening Material

steer clear (of someone or something) to avoid someone or something /绕过，避开

e. g. Steer clear of the rocks ahead.

Kid shall steer clear of that park, it does not seem safe.

Additional Listening Material

(1) **permanent** adj. continuing or enduring without marked change in status or condition or place /永久的,持久的

e. g. They established their permanent abode here.

Nothing can assure permanent happiness.

(2) **resume** n. a summary of your academic and work history /简历,履历

e. g. Please send a detailed resume to our company.

Video-aural Material

(1) **wander** v. move about aimlessly or without any destination, often in search of food or employment/徘徊

e. g. The boy was wandering around.

Please don't wander off the point.

(2) **entrench** v. put something or thoughts firmly in one's mind /坚持, 固定（本意为: 挖战壕）

e. g. Arguments that only entrench you more firmly in error.

The enemies were strongly entrenched on the other side of the river.

(3) **drag down**　exert a force with a heavy weight/拖垮

　　　　　　　　Reference words: bear down, bear down on, press down on, weigh down

　　　　　　　　e.g. President, dragged down by corruption scandals, will resign Monday or Tuesday, Prime Minister said.

　　　　　　　　I'm afraid the children will all be dragged down to his level.

(4) **negative**　adj.　characterized by or displaying negation or denial or opposition or resistance; having no positive features/否定的, 负的, 消极的

　　　　　　　　e.g. I have a negative opinion on the value of this idea.

(5) **clutter**　n.　a confused multitude of things /混乱

　　　　　　　　Reference words: jumble, muddle, fuddle

　　　　　　　　e.g. His room is in a clutter so I have to tidy it up.

Additional Video-aural Material

(1) **opponent**　n.　a contestant that you are matched against/对手, 敌人

　　　　　　　　e.g. Never underestimate your opponent.

　　　　　　　　She is one of the strongest opponents of tax reform.

(2) **profoundly**　adv.　to a great depth psychologically/深深地

　　　　　　　　e.g. I am profoundly touched.

　　　　　　　　His feeling has been harmed profoundly.

(3) **incredible**　adj.　beyond belief or understanding/难以置信的

　　　　　　　　e.g. That's the most incredible coincidence I've ever heard of!

　　　　　　　　He has an incredible house!

Listening Skills

(omitted)

2. Cultural Background

Some famous sayings and proverbs about confidence:

No cross, no crown.

没有苦难，就没有快乐。或译为"不经历风雨，怎么见彩虹"。

Self-confidence and self-reliance are the mainstays of a strong character.

自信和自力更生是坚强品格的柱石。

Confidence in oneself is the first step on the way to success.

自信是迈向成功的第一步。

Anyhow, spring will return to us.

春，无论如何也会回到人间。——陶行知

Skill and confidence are an unconquered army.

技能和信心是无敌的军队。

Nothing seek, nothing find.

无所求则无所获。

Preview Exercises

The man in the video is called Paul Potts. He is 36 years old, once working as a cell phone salesman. He went to Italy to learn Opera when he was 28. Today, Paul Potts is the winner of the program Britain's Got Talent in 2008 and released his first album *One Chance*. (listening)

Zhang Juanjuan won the archery gold medal on August 14th in Beijing Olympic Games and this is China's first archery gold medal. (speaking)

Li Xiaopeng won parallel bars gold medal in Beijing Olympic Games and this is his fourth Olympic gold medals. (speaking)
(More information about Olympic can be found in Unit Nine Olympics.)

Warming up Exercises

Phelps won 8 swimming gold medals in Beijing Olympic Games and became the very person who has won the most gold medals in one Olympic Games. (speaking)

Liu Xiang is the first Asian people who won the 110 meters hurdle gold medal in 2004, but he quitted the 2008 Beijing Olympic Games because of his heel wound. (speaking)

Additional Listening Material

This material is taken from an American radio program called *This I Believe*. It invited people from every walk of life to share their special stories with audiences. This black girl told us the life of being a black in today's America.

Video-aural Material

This video is a clip taken from the video "25 tips for develop super self-confidence and self-esteem" and this video in our textbook tells the first 6 tips. You can watch it in www. you-tube. com . And if you want to find more information to help your students to build self-confidence you can google the website www. toastmaster. com which is introduced in this video.

Additional Video-aural Material

This speech is delivered by Hillary Clinton when she won the New York senator in 2000.

The State of New York is a state in the Mid-Atlantic and Notrheastern regions of the United States and is the nation's third most populous state. The state is bordered by New Jersey and Pennsylvania to the south, and Connecticut, Massachusetts and Vermont to the east. The state has a maritime border with Rhode Island east of Long Island, as well as an international border with the Canadian provinces of Quebec and Ontario to the north. New York is often referred to as New York State to distinguish it from New York City.

The United States Senate is the upper housee of the bicameral United States Congress, the lower house being the House of Representatives. Each U. S. state is represented by two senators, regardless of population. This ensures equal representation of each state in the Senate. U. S. Senators serve staggered six-year terms. The chamber of the United States Senate is located in the north wing of the Capitol building, in Washington D. C. , the national capital. The House of Representatives convenes in the south wing of the same building.

The Senate is a more deliberative body than the House of Representatives because the Senate is smaller and its members serve longer terms, allowing for a more collegial and less partisan atmosphere that is somewhat more insulated from public opinion than the House. The Senate is considered a more prestigious body than the House of Representatives, due to its longer terms, smaller membership and larger constituencies.

Hillary Diane Rodham Clinton (born on October 26 , 1947) is the 67th United States Secretary of State, serving in the administration of President Barach Obama. She was a United States Senator from New York from 2001 to 2009. As the wife of Bill Clinton, the 42nd President of the United States, she was the First Lady of the United States from 1993 to 2001. She was a leading candidate for the Democratic presidential nomination in the 2008 election.

After moving to New York, Clinton was elected as senator for New York State in 2000. That election marked the first time an American First Lady had run for public office; Clinton was also the first female senator to represent New York. In the Senate, she initially supported the George W. Bush administration on some foreign policy issues, which included voting for the lrap War Resolution. She subsequently opposed the administration on its conduct of the war in lrap, and opposed it on most domestic issues. She was re-elected by a wide margin in 2006. In the 2008 presidential nomination race, Clinton won more primaries and delegates than any other female candidate in American history, but she narrowly lost to Senator Barack Obama. As Obama's Secretary of State, Clinton is the first former First Lady to serve in a president's cabinet. More information will be from the website: www. hillaryclinton. com.

Listening Skills

(1) *The Readers' Guide to Periodical Literature* is a reference guide to recently published articles in periodical magazines and scholarly journals, organized by article subject. The Readers' Guide has been published regularly since 1901 by The H. W. Wilson Company, and is a staple of public and academic reference libraries throughout the United States; a retrospective index of general periodicals published from 1890 to 1900 is also available.

Originally, The Readers' Guide was published on a biweekly basis, with later issues incorporating the previous content in larger copies until the index for the entire year was published. This format has since been complemented with an online version which is marketed to libraries.

(2) The term Golden Age comes from Greek mythology and legend, but can also be found in other ancient cultures. It refers either to the earliest, and most ideal age in the Greek range of Golden, Silver, Bronze, and Iron Ages, or to a time in the beginnings of humanity which was perceived as an ideal state, or utopia, when mankind was pure and immortal. A "Golden Age" is known as a period of peace, harmony, stability, and prosperity. In literary works, the Golden Age usually ends with a devastating event, which brings about the Fall of Man.

3. Listening Skills

(1) To grasp the first and the last sentence.

The first sentence which usually gives the topic and indicates the coming contents is always the topic sentence of long conversation. The last sentence always gives the conclusion or results of their talking. Both of them are crucial to the understanding of the whole conversations.

(2) To focus the repeated words and phrases.

The repeated words and phrases usually supply the keys.

(3) To underline the key words of the choices.

To grasp the key words of the choices before the listening will save you much effort when you are doing the exercise and offer some reference for you to anticipate what the conversation will be talking about.

(4) To take note of the numbers, names, address, times, etc.

Pay special attention to the numbers, names, address and times, which are illogical and hard to remember, therefore, you'd better to write them down.

II Reference Key

Part One

1. Preview Exercises

Dictation:

(1) mobile phones (2) Opera (3) career (4) confident

Questions:

(1) When I have the first sight of this man, I think he is a little bit fat and without good appearance. I can not trace anything special or excellent from his appearance.

(2) I think his singing is fantastic! From him, I can see even the most ordinary man has his shining point, and never underestimate ones ability.

2. Warming up Exercises

I think I am special, because I am the unique individual in the world. I am good at singing and dancing. I am outgoing and easy to get along with. Although I am a lump of coal now and I believe I will be a diamond someday.

3. Listening Material

4. Additional Listening Material

5. Video-aural Material

(3) flash your biggest and your best smile at yourself

(4) do things that make you feel good

(5) listen to you

(6) talk to you

(7) remove negatives

6. Listening Skills

Sample Practice: (1) D (2) B (3) B (4) C

Additional training: (1) A (2) A (3) D

Part Two

1. Preview Exercises

(1) They are champions/Olympic gold winners and they are famous for/ gain great fame in/ enjoy good reputation in archery/ parallel bars.

(2) I can find/see/trace confidence/determination in their face/gestures.

2. Warming up Exercises

(1) In the first picture, Phelps was swimming during 2008 Olympic Games and he won 8 gold medals in Beijing. The exciting moment recorded in the second picture was in the year 2004 after Liu Xiang won the gold medal of 110 meters man's hurdle race. The third picture recorded the sorrow moment that Liu Xiang quitted from the 2008 Beijing Olympic Games because of his heel wound.

(2) It is hard to have confidence when you fail. / You can still own confidence when you fail.

(3) You can forget the failure and tell yourself everything will be fine. /You should find out your weakness and try to overcome it. / You can tell yourself you are excellent. It is only a chance to test your determination.

3. Listening Material Review

Task 1

The material tells us several ways to build our confidence and these methods are every suitable to girls.

Task 2

(1) It means to dress properly and suitably.

(2) Gossip means wagging one's tongue; speaking about others and revealing secrets or intimacies.

(3) When you can express yourself clearly, you'll gain confidence and you'll become a better public speaker.

Task 3

(1) I think it is very useful, having confidence is good for our study and work. I can list more ways to build confidence, for example:

❖ Talk about it with friends and loved ones.

❖ Remember that no one is perfect.

❖ Be thankful for what you have.

❖ Be positive, even if you don't feel positive.

❖ Stick to your principles.

❖ Help others.

❖ Stop worrying.

(2) It tells us 6 ways to build our self-confidence. The methods are to dress well, walk faster, stand up straight, compliment others, speak up and work out.

Task 4

(1) Walking 25% faster will make you look and feel more important.

(2) And taller people are naturally more confident than shorter people.

(3) The fact is, by looking for the best in others, you can also find the best in yourself.

(4) Improving your ability to speak in front of others is important in feeling more confident.

4. Video-aural Material Review

Task 1

It tells us 6 ways to build our confidence, especially when you are in tough situations.

Task 2

(1) How you expect others to love you is the way you love yourself. So how can you expect others to love you if you don't love yourself?

(2) Tell yourself how lucky you are; tell yourself how lucky you are to be you! And praise yourself for every good and positive thing that you can attribute to yourself.

(3) Anything that gives you a positive feeling about yourself will increase your self-confidence and your self-esteem. It can be anything from listening to some music, taking hikes, doing volunteer work or even just taking a bath.

Task 3

(1) I think this clip is very useful. It tells us 6 methods to build our self-esteem. But it is hard to take them into practice. Take the sixth method "to remove from a negative environment" for example, it says when your friends complain to you, just tell them we do not want to listen to these negative things, but in fact it is very hard to say these words to your friends. Maybe it will ruin your friendship. Anyhow, I will try my best to follow most of those tips, for I think these will do me much good.

(2) The video tells us 6 tips to build our self-esteem. They are to love yourself, look in the mirror, do things that make you feel good, listen to you, talk to you and remove negatives.

Task 4

(1) And tell yourself: looking good; or, wow, I love me. Or any other similar phrase that expresses your own self-esteem in a positive light.

(2) The more positive energy you have, that you bring to your life, the more that'll come on the outside.

(3) And once you begin to do that, you'll take confidence in the feelings of what your body's trying to tell you.

(4) Wander in your mind and have a conversation with yourself about anything.

5. Additional Video-aural Material

Task 1

She is Hillary Clinton and she won the election of New York in 2000. This was her speech at that moment. She expresses her thanks to those who supported her and she also promised what she would do in her mission.

Task 2

(1) 16 months and 3 debates.

(2) They discussed jobs matter, downstate and upstate, health care matters, education matters, the environment matters, social security matters, a woman's right to choose matters.

(3) She thanked them for opening up their minds and hearts to accept her as a member of them, and giving her the chance to serve them as the senator of New York State.

Task 3

(1) Hillary's speech is very encouraging. Her voice is very determined and she is an excellent public speaker.

(2) At the beginning, Hillary recalled her time-consuming and pain-taking election journey. And she expressed her thanks to her supporters and the former New York senator. And she also talked about the issues the people concerned. At last, she promised all the citizens she would do her best to serve the New York people.

Task 4

(1) It all matters and I just want to say from the bottom of my heart, thank you, New York!

(2) Thank you for opening up your minds and your hearts, for seeing the possibility of what we could do together for our children and for our future here in this state and in our nation.

(3) I am profoundly grateful to all of you for giving me the chance to serve you.

(4) I would like all of you and the countless New Yorkers and Americans watching to join me in honoring him for his incredible half century of service to New York and our nation.

 Listening Scripts

Part One

1. Preview Exercises

"By day I've sold mobile phones. My dream is to spend my life doing what I feel I was born to do…"

"Paul, what are you here for today, Paul?"

"To sing Opera. "

"I've always wanted to sing as a career. Confidence's always been sort of like a difficult thing for me. I always find a little bit difficult to be completely confident in myself. "

"Okay, ready when you are. "

2. Listening Material

When you dress well, you feel better, and increase your self – confidence.

This may sound silly, but you should walk faster. People with confidence walk quickly. They have important work to do and they don't have all day to do it. Walking 25% faster will make you look and feel more important.

Stand up straight. By practicing good posture, you'll notice how much more confident you feel. With better posture, you'll be slightly taller. And taller people are naturally more confident than shorter people.

Compliment others. Help break this cycle of negativity and get in the habit of praising other people. Steer clear of gossip and make an effort to compliment other people. The fact is, by looking for the best in others, you can also find the best in yourself.

Speak up and don't be afraid to say what you think. Make an effort to speak up at least once in every group discussion. When you can express yourself clearly, you'll gain confidence and you'll become a better public speaker. Improving your ability to speak in front of others is important in feeling more confident.

Make time to work out. Improving your physical appearance will have a huge effect on how you feel about yourself. Working out also gives you more energy to improve your attitude at home and at work. Plus, the discipline to work out consistently is just another way to reassure yourself that you're capable of a lot when you set your mind to it.

3. Additional Listening Material

I've been searching for a job for months with no success. I was just about ready to settle into permanent unemployment and a deep depression when my sibling suggested that I try something I never before considered. Why don't you put a different name on your resume, they propose, something less ethnic-sounding and easier to pronounce, something that doesn't set off alarm bells as my name apparently does.

Out of the question, I said, if they don't want Sufiya Abdur-Rahman then they don't want me.

I'm the daughter of two 1970s African-American converse to a slum. I am black, I am proud and I don't shy from showing it.

I learned along with every other American school kid that at one point in this country, being black meant being less than human. But that never made me wish I wasn't black. I love that my African people were among the most individual in the world and I'm constantly amazed that my ancestors survived a period of unimaginable hardship and forever grateful to my grandparents fight for equal rights and equally admire my brothers for creating a music and culture with impact worldwide.

So I can never mask who I really am, not even to get a job.

For me, I haven't turned to lies that black is beautiful, not a condition to rise above. For as long as it takes, I'll keep being Sufiya Abdur-Rahman on my resume and everywhere else I go.

4. Video-aural Material

The first one you can do is to love yourself. Now this takes a bit of practice and looks kind of funny, but try, it'll work for you. When you wake up, give yourself a big hug. And do the same thing when it is time for you to go to bed at night. Now some of you may have heard this before, but how you expect others to love you is the way you love yourself. So how can you expect others to love you if you don't love yourself? So practice the morning and evening hugs for about 2 weeks, or maybe 3 weeks if you're kind of like me old-fashioned, stubborn and it's hard to get. And you'll see that it works really well in your lives.

Now the second technique: look in the mirror. So every time you pass a mirror, look into it and flash your biggest and your best smile at yourself. It might feel kind of strange first but eventually it'll make you feel brilliant about yourself. And tell yourself: looking good; or, wow, I love me. Or any other similar phrase that expresses your own self-esteem in a positive light. Do this often enough to entrench it inside your sub-conscious mind. Do that and it will become reflected on the outside of your outer life. So now you have two techniques: love yourself and look in the mirror.

But the third thing: do things that make you feel good and that can be anything from listening to some music, taking hikes, doing volunteer work or even just taking a bath. Anything that gives you a positive feeling about yourself will increase your self-confidence and your self-esteem because you are taking yourself into a positive energy. The more positive energy you have, that you bring to your life, the more that'll come on the outside.

Now the fourth thing: listen to you. Nobody knows you better than you know yourself, no matter how many times or how many people try to tell you differently. Nobody knows you better than you know yourself. So, if your body, if your mind, or your gut is telling you something, I want you to take notice of it. And don't worry about what other people may possibly have to say about it, listen to you, learn to develop that inner intuition that comes from inside. And once you begin to do that, you'll take confidence in the feelings of what your body's trying to tell you.

The fifth thing: talk to you. Yeah, not like you're crazy or something like that, but in times of stress, take a timeout break . Wander in your mind and have a conversation with yourself about anything. Tell yourself how lucky you are, tell yourself how lucky you are to be you! And praise yourself for every good and positive thing that you can attribute to yourself. Remember the way it is on the inside is the way it is on the outside. Your outer world is merely a microcosm of what's going on inside. Too often we dump a lot of garbage and false beliefs into our sub-conscious mind. Thereby it causes our outer world to shift focus and change to become like those beliefs.

So the sixth thing is to remove negatives. If anything feels like it's dragging you down, get rid of it. If it's clutter, tidy up. If it's a friend full of negativity, explain nicely that you don't really feel up to talking to them right now. If you have people in your lives constantly dumping negative thoughts and words at you, explain to them that you don't have time to listen right now and remove yourself from that negative environment. Always seek to be in positive and motivating environments.

5. Listening Skills

<u>Sample practice</u>

W: Hello, Gary. How're you?

M: Fine! And yourself?

W: Can't complain. Did you have time to look at my proposal?

M: No, not really. Can we go over it now?

W: Sure. I've been trying to come up with some new production and advertising strategies. First of all, if we want to stay competitive, we need to modernize our factory. New equipment should've been installed long ago.

M: How much will that cost?

W: We have several options ranging from one hundred thousand dollars all the way up to half a million.

M: OK. We'll have to discuss these costs with finance.

W: We should also consider human resources. I've been talking to personnel as well as our staff at the factory.

M: And what's the picture?

W: We'll probably have to hire a couple of engineers to help us modernize the factory.

M: What about advertising?

W: Marketing has some interesting ideas for television commercials.

M: TV? Isn't that a bit too expensive for us? What's wrong with advertising in the papers, as usual?

W: Quite frankly, it's just not enough anymore. We need to be more aggressive in order to keep ahead of our competitors.

M: Will we be able to afford all this?

W: I'll look into it, but I think higher costs will be justified. These investments will result in higher profits for our company.

M: We'll have to look at the figures more closely. Have finance drawn up a budget for these investments?

W: All right. I'll see to it.

Additional training

W: Sir, you've been using the online catalogue for quite a while, Is there anything I can do to help you?

M: Well, I've got to write a paper about Hollywood in the 30s and 40s, and I'm really struggling. There are hundreds of books, and I just don't know where to begin.

W: Your topic sounds pretty big. Why don't you narrow it down to something like …uh … the history of the studios during that time?

M: You know, I was thinking about doing that, but more that 30 books came up when I typed in "movie studios".

W: You could cut that down even further by listing the specific years you want. Try adding "1930s" or "1940s" or maybe "Golden Age".

M: "Golden Age" is a good idea. Let me type that in …Hey, look, just 6 books this time. That's a lot better.

W: Oh… another thin you might consider …have you tried looking for any magazine or newspaper articles?

M: No, I've only been searching for books.

W: Well, you can look up magazine articles in the Reader's Guide to Periodical Literature. And we do have the *Los Angeles and Times* available over there. You might go through their indexes to see if there's anything you want.

M: Okay, I think I'll get started with these books and then I'll go over the magazines.

W: If you need any help, I'll be over at the Reference Desk.

M: Great, thanks a lot.

Part Two

Additional Video-aural Material

You know, you know, we started this great effort on a sunny July morning in Pinders Corner on Pat and Liz Moynihan's beautiful farm and 62 counties, 16 months, 3 debates, 2 opponents, and 6 black pantsuits later, because of you, here we are.

You came out and said that issues and ideals matter, jobs matter, downstate and upstate, health care matters, education matters, the environment matters, social security matters, a woman's right to choose matters. It all matters and I just want to say from the bottom of my heart, thank you, New York!

Thank you for opening up your minds and your hearts, for seeing the possibility of what we could do together for our children and for our future here in this state and in our nation. I am profoundly grateful to all of you for giving me the chance to serve you.

I will—I will do everything I can to be worthy of your faith and trust and to honor the powerful example of Senator Daniel Patrick Moynihan. I would like all of you and the countless New Yorkers and Americans watching to join me in honoring him for his incredible half century of service to New York and our nation. Senator Moynihan, on behalf of New York and America, thank you.

 # Translation of the Listening Materials

Part One

1. Preview Exercises

"白天我卖手机。我的梦想是用我的生命去做那些我天生就适合的事情。"
"坡,你今天唱什么?"
"唱歌剧。"
"我一直都想将歌唱作为我的事业。自信对我来说一直都是比较困难的事情。我一直觉得让自己完全自信很困难。"
"好,准备好了就开始吧。"

2. Listening Material

当你着装得体的时候,你会感觉更良好并增强自信。

也许这听起来有点傻,但是你得走快一点。自信的人都走的比较快。他们有很多重要的事情要做而他们没有整天的时间去做这些事。比平常走快 1/4 会让你看起来并且也感觉自己更重要。

挺直腰板。练习良好的身姿，你会感觉到你更自信。拥有良好的姿势，你会比平常稍微高一点。而身高较高的人比那些个子矮的人更自信。

赞美他人。打破这个消极循环，学会赞美他人。澄清那些谣言而且努力的去赞美他人吧。而事实就是：在发现他人的优点的同时也会发现自己的优点。

大声地表达，不要害怕说出自己的想法。尽可能在每次小组讨论的时候发一次言。你能在清楚地表达自己当中获得自信，并且成为一个优秀的公众演讲者。提高在公众面前演讲的能力对提高自信心很重要。

找时间锻炼身体。提升你的外形对提升你的自我感觉有很大的作用。锻炼身体同样也能给你更多的能量来改善你对家庭和对工作的态度。而且，坚持锻炼身体也能通过另外一个方式告诉你只要你打定了主意，你就能做成任何事。

3. Additional Listening Material

几个月来我一直在找工作却没有成功。当我兄弟姐妹们建议我尝试下那个我从未考虑过的方法的时候我刚做好了长期失业的准备，并陷入了消沉中。"为什么不在你的简历上换一个名字呢，换一个不是那么带种族特色的，拼写容易一点的，不像你名字那样明显的让人觉得不同的名字呢?"他们建议说。

绝不可能。我说道："如果他们不录取 Sufiya Abdur-Rahman，那么他们就不是要录取我。"

我是两个出生于 20 世纪 70 年代的非洲籍美国人的女儿，住在贫民窟。我是黑人，我为此感到骄傲，并从不羞于承认这点。

我从在美国其他学校上学的孩子处了解到至少一点，在这个国家成为黑人就意味着低人一等。但这并不会让我希望自己不是黑人。我热爱非洲人民，他们是世界上最独特的人种之一。而且我一直都惊讶于我的祖辈能够经受住那段让人无法想象的艰难时期，并且对我的父辈们努力争取平等权利表达无尽的感激。我也同样敬佩我的兄弟姐妹们，他们创造的音乐和文化影响着全世界。

因此我绝不会掩饰自己的本来身份，即使因此找不到工作。

我并不想是要谎称黑色是美丽的，但是我的肤色不应该是我的困扰。无论何时我都会在简历上写上我的名字 Sufiya Abdur-Rahman，无论我走到哪里我依然是 Sufiya Abdur-Rahman。

4. Video-aural Material

你要做的第一件事就是爱自己。这一点需要很多的练习而且听起来有点搞笑，但是一定要尝试，它有用。当你醒来的时候给自己一个大大的拥抱，晚上睡觉的之前再做一遍。也许你们有人之前曾经听过你想要别人如何爱你，就要以同样方式爱自己。所以你不爱自己怎么能期望别人爱你呢？那么就这样早晚练习2周吧，如果你像我那么守旧或者固执，恐怕需要3周。不过随后在你的生活中你会发现它真的很有用。

第二件事是照镜子。每次经过镜子前，站定，给自己一个最大最灿烂的笑容。开始的时候你会觉得有点奇怪，但是最后你会感到很愉快。告诉自己我看起来不错，或者我爱我自己或者其他任何相似的能够增强你的自信心的语言。经常练习这个动作以让这个观点牢牢的留在你的潜意识里，而且它的作用会反映在你的外在生活中。现在你有2个技巧了：爱自己和照镜子。

第三件事就是做让你感觉愉快的事。这些可以是听音乐，远足，做义工，甚至是泡个澡。任何给你积极感觉的事都可以增强你的自信心，因为它们会带给你积极的能量。当你为你的生活中注入越多积极的能量，你的外在生活表现就会越好。

第四件事就是听自己的。无论多少次或者多少人试图告诉你，你是怎么样的人，但是没有任何人比你更了解你自己。如果你的身体、心灵或者勇气告诉你什么，我希望你能够重视它。不要担心别人会为此有所微词，倾听自己的内心，学会培养来自你的内心的内部信息。一旦你开始这样做，你就会从自己的身心传递的信息中获取信心。

第五件事就是和自己对话。不是在你濒临疯狂或者类似的情况下，只是在面对压力的时候，让自己松口气。松懈下你的大脑或者和自己来场可以是任何话题的谈话。告诉自己是多么的幸运，成为我自己是多么的幸运。赞美自己，为你做的那些一切所有积极美好的事情。记住内心的行为方式就是你的外在行事方式。你的外部世界表现仅仅是你的内心世界的一个微观反映。很多时候我们向我们的潜意识灌输了太多的垃圾信息和错误的观念。因此也让我们的外部世界转换了重心，转移到了这些错误的观念上。

第六件事就是远离消极。如果任何事可能会拖垮你，甩掉它。如果事情很混乱，那么整理清楚。如果你有朋友充满了消极的观点，那么耐心的向他解释你现在不想与之交谈。如果你的生活中有人持续不断的向你灌输消极的想法和语言，那么告诉他们你现在没有时间听他们诉说并且从那样消极的环境中脱离出来。要让自己呆在积极的充满希望的环境里。

5. Listening Skills

Sample practice

女：你好，盖瑞，最近好吗？

男：很好，你呢？

女：一般吧。你有时间看下我的计划吗？

男：没有，时间不多。我们能现在看下吗？

女：当然。我一直想要开发一些新的产品和广告策略。首先，如果我们想要保持竞争力，我们需要让我们的工厂更加现代化。很早以前就该安装新设备了。

男：那要花多少钱？

女：我们有几个选择，从10万到50万都有。

男：好，我们得和财务讨论这个事情。

女：我们也应当考虑下人力资源，我一直在和人事部门和员工谈话。

男：情况怎样？

女：我们可能需要雇佣一些工程师帮助我们的工厂现代化。

男：广告做的怎么样了？

女：市场部有一些关于电视广告的有趣的点子。

男：电视？这对我们来说是不是贵了点？像往常那样在报纸上做广告有什么不好吗？

女：说实话，那个已经不能满足要求了。为了继续保持领先优势，我们需要更激进。

男：那我们有能力承受吗？

女：我会跟进的。但是我认为高投入会有相应的回报的。这些投入最终会为公司带来更多的利润。

男：我们应该更具体的的了解这些数据。财务部门有没有这些投资的预算？

女：好的，我会跟进的。

Additional training

女：先生，你用这个网上目录已经很长一段时间了，有什么我可以帮你的吗？

男：哦，我准备写篇关于好莱坞三、四十年代的论文。我正难以抉择呢，这里有上百本书，我不知道从哪一本开始看起。

女：你的题目听起来有些大，你为什么不缩小一点呢，比如说那段时间的工作室的历史之类的？

男：我正准备这么做，但是我输入电影工作室，就会有30多本书。

女：你可以通过添加具体的时间来进一步缩小范围。试一下20世纪30或40年代，黄金年代。

男：黄金年代是个好主意。让我试一下，啊！看，这次只有6本书了。好多了。

女：你也可以考虑另外一个方法，你有没有试过找杂志和报纸上的文章？

男：没有，我一直在搜索书。

女：那你可以在读者指南或者期刊文学上找文章。我们这里有《洛杉矶》和《时代》杂志。你可以看看它们的索引有没有你要的东西。

男：好。我想我要开始查阅这些书和那些杂志了。

女：如果你需要任何帮助，请到咨询台找我。

男：太好了，谢谢。

Part Two

Additional Video-aural Material

我们是在七月的一个阳光灿烂的早上，从帕特和丽兹·莫伊尼汉夫妇位于频德角的美丽农场开始迈出了这艰难的一步，然后辗转六十二个县，历经过十六个月、三场辩论，打败了两个竞争对手，穿破六套黑色便服。如今，在你们的支持下，我们终于胜利了。

你们说，各项议题和观念非常重要——全州的就业问题是重要的，医疗保健是重要的，教育是重要的，环境是重要的，社会保险是重要的，还有妇女选择权是重要的。这些全都重要，而我只想衷心道一声：谢谢你，纽约！

感谢你们开放思想，不存成见，感谢你们相信我们携手为子孙后代、为我州，以至全国的未来而共同努力的美好前景。我对你们每个人都深怀谢意，感谢你们给了我一个为大家服务的机会。

我将以参议员丹尼尔·帕特里克·莫伊尼汉为榜样，尽自己最大的努力不负众望。我恳请你们所有人、诸位正在收看直播的纽约市民和美国人民，同我一起向他致敬，感谢他这半个世纪以来为纽约和美国做出的巨大贡献。莫伊尼汉议员：我代表纽约和美国人民，感谢你。

Unit Four Gratitude

I Background Knowledge

1. Language Points

Preview Exercises

(1) …has brought many challenges/碰到很多挑战, 遇到很多问题

e. g. This year has brought many challenges to this state.

(2) lifting our economy from a recession/重振经济

e. g. The policy from the government lifted our economy from a recession.

(3) an outpouring of compassion and relief/激情与信念的流露

e. g. Her speech is an outpouring of compassion and relief.

Listening Material

(1) **dime**　n.　a coin worth 10 cents/一角硬币

e. g. Jobs like his are a dime a dozen.

(2) **critically**　adv.　in a critical manner/相当地

e. g. Years later the young woman became critically ill.

(3) owe　v.　to pay someone money because you have borrowed from them/欠, 亏欠

e. g. How much do you owe?

(4) baffle　v.　be a mystery or bewildering to/为难, 困惑

e. g. These questions baffled me a lot.

(5) feel stronger physically/感觉浑身是劲

e. g. He felt stronger physically.

(6) to increase his faith in something/更加相信……

e. g. He increased his faith in God and the human race after reading the Bible.

(7) for the consultation/咨询

e. g. The expert in this field was called in for the consultation.

(8) …take it to his heart so much/把某事、某物放在心上

e. g. They take their exam to their heart so much.

(9) gown　n.　a long dress/女士礼服, 医生白大褂

e. g. Doctor White dressed in a white gown.

Additional Listening Material

（1）buoyant　adj.　characterized by liveliness and lightheartedness/心情愉快的

　　　　　e. g. She sings a long in a buoyant mood.

（2）manifold　adj.　various/多种多样的

　　　　　e. g. The uses of this machine are manifold.

（3）blessing　n.　making the sign of the cross over someone in order to call on God for protection; consecrate/祝福

　　　　　e. g. The rain will be a blessing for the farmers.

Video-aural Material

（1）agony　n.　intense feelings of suffering; acute mental or physical pain/痛苦, 创痛（极度的）

　　　　　e. g. I've suffered agonies with toothache.

（2）W. W. Uncle Walt

　　惠特曼，美国著名诗人。从小热爱民主和自由，他只读过五六年书，十几岁就外出谋生。他当过排字工人、木工、泥水匠、农村教师和编辑等。惠特曼勤奋好学，利用业余时间阅读了大量世界文学名著。他从 19 世纪 40 年代起开始写诗，于 1855 年出版了《草叶集》的第一版。他在一封给朋友的信中说："记着，这本书是我从 1838 年至 1853 年间在布鲁克林的生活中涌现出来的，其中吸进了千百万个人和十五年的生活；那种亲密，那种热烈，那种陶醉，简直是无与伦比的。"

（3）**barbarian**　n.　a member of an uncivilized people/野蛮人

　　　　　e. g. The barbarians conquered Rome.

（4）**gibberish**　n.　unintelligible talking /急促而不清楚的说话

　　　　　e. g. Don't talk gibberish.

（5）wail　n.　a cry of sorrow and grief/悲叹　v.　悲叹

　　　　　e. g. The wind wailed in the forest all night.

（6）mumbling　v.　ineffectual chewing（as if without teeth）/喃喃

　　　　　e. g. What are you mumbling about? I can't understand a word!

Listening Skills

（1）**temporally**　adj.　with regard to temporal order/时间的，当时的，暂时的，现世的，世俗的

　　　　　e. g. The Pope has no temporal power in modern society.

（2）**readiness**　n.　the state of having been made ready or prepared for use or action

(especially military action) /预备，准备，敏捷

e. g. She shows great readiness to learn.

(3) hypothesis   n.   a message expressing an opinion based on incomplete evidence/假设

e. g. Several conclusions flow from this hypothesis.

2. Cultural Background

(1) It is essential for the children to learn gratitude now and then because they are the cores of the family . They have themselves rather than others in their mind due to birth control policy or one kid for a couple policy. So it is very important to educate our kids to express their gratitude to parents, teachers and friends. Learning gratitude is actually to learn how to respect people. During the process of growing up, children have received so much love and concerns from the adults. It reminds them to love and help others. What first comes to them is to comprehend what their parents have done to them, what their teachers have done and what their friends have done, which will surely help them to own the feeling of gratitude in their life-long time.

(2) Listening prediction strategy

Listening prediction strategy influences listening comprehension greatly. Accordingly, it becomes an essential part when practising listening. In order to maximize the application of prediction strategy, teachers must elaborate the prediction awearness and techniques both.

Ⅱ   Reference Key

Part One

1. Preview Exercises

(1) Dictation

The past year has brought many challenges to our nation, and Chinese have met every one with energy, optimism and faith. After lifting our economy from a recession, manufacturers and entrepreneurs are creating jobs again. Volunteers from across the country came together to help hurricane victims rebuild. And when the people of Wenchuan, Sichuan suffered a brutal earthquake attack, the world saw Chinese's generous heart in an outpouring of compassion and relief.

(2) Questions

① Our Chinese people have uncommon experiences this year. We have met many difficulties, like earthquake, economic crisis and poisoning baby milk powder.

② Chinese people never give up facing the sufferings.

2. Listening Material

Task 1

A   D

Task 2

A   C   B

Task 3

(1) nerve   (2) owe   (3) replied   (4) bottom   (5) stronger physically

(6) critically   (7) specialists   (8) consultation   (9) determined

(10) Dr. Kelly requested the business office to pass the final bill to him for approval

3. Additional Listening Material

Task 1

C   D

Task 2

C   A   B

Task 3

(1) granted   (2) buoyant   (3) seldom   (4) stretch   (5) characterizes

(6) suffered   (7) faculties   (8) concentration   (9) stricken

(10) Darkness would make him more appreciative of sight; silence would teach him the joys of sound

4. Video-aural Material

B   A

D   D   C

(1) sitting   (2) agony   (3) out of   (4) misery   (5) poem   (6) inside

(7) embarrassing   (8) Isn't   (9) worst

(10) I think you have something inside of you that is worth a great deal

5. Listening Skills

Sample practice: (1) B   (2) C   (3) A

Additional training: (1) B   (2) C   (3) D

Part Two

1. Preview Exercises

(1) —People in Wenchuan, Sichuan suffered a brutal earthquake attack.

   —Volunteers from across the country came together to help hurricane victims rebuild.

   —After lifting our economy from a recession, manufacturers and enterpreneurs are crea-

   ting jobs again.

(2) The past year has brought many challenges to our nation, and Chinese have met every

   one with energy, optimism and faith.

2. Warming up Exercises

(1) Family members are important to us. When we were young, we loved to play with them.

   When we were grown up, we left them and only came to them when we need something

   or when we are in trouble. No matter what, family members will always be there and

   give everything they could to make us happy.

(2) Family is the warmest place in this world. Our family provides us encouragement, sup-

port and cares for us no matter where we are and what we do.

(3) "Teacher" is a special image in students' minds. It represents love, capability, and knowledge for them. Teacher's day is designed to thank what teachers have done daily and annualy.

Once there was a song sing that "You've got a friend. Winter, spring, summer or fall – all you've got to do is call – and I'll be there." Many people expect that their friends will always there. They expect friendship to last forever.

> To be kind.
> To be considerate.
> To be supportive.
> To go out with my friends.
> To talk to my friends about most things.

3. Listening Material Review

Task 1

A young boy was once helped by a girl when the boy was in difficulty. Years later, the boy became a well-skilled doctor who rescured the girl from a fatel illness.

Task 2

(1) Yes, the young girl helped the little boy. She provided a glass of milk to the boy.

(2) Howard Kelly was actually the young boy whom the young girl once helped. The boy became a doctor years later.

(3) Yes, the young girl recovered from the illness at the end. Doctor Howard Kelly gave her successful therapy.

Task 3

(1) No, the girl had no enough money to pay. When she worried a lot, the doctor cancelled her bill for return to the offer which the young girl once gave him.

(2) The boy was once helped by the girl.

Task 4

(1) "You don't owe me anything," she replied. "Mother has taught me never to accept pay for a kindness."

(2) When he heard the name of the town she came from, a strange light filled his eyes.

(3) He went back to the consultation room and determined to do his best to save her life.

(4) Dr. Kelly requested the business office to pass the final bill to him for approval.

4. Video-aural Material Review

Task 1

The students praised Mr. Keating's courses a lot.

Task 2

(1) Some of them finished the class but some of them didn't.

(2) Mr. Anderson thinks that everything inside of him is worthless and embarrassing. Isn't that right, Todd? Isn't that your worst fear? Well, I think you're wrong. I think you have something inside of you that is worth a great deal.

(3) The truth is like a blanket.

Task 3

(1) You push it, stretch it, it'll never be enough. You kick at it, beat it, it'll never any of us. From the moment we enter crying to the moment we leave dying, it will just cover your face as you wail and cry and scream.

(2) The students received a lot from Mr. Keating's class. Their appreciation is possibly expressed by their words, rewards and behaviors.

Task 4

(1) Mr. Anderson thinks that everything inside of him is worthless and embarrasssing.

(2) You can do better than that. Free up your mind. Use your imagination.

(3) Give him action. Make him do something.

(4) From the moment we enter crying to the moment we leave dying, it will just cover your face as you wail and cry and scream.

5. Additional Video-aural Material

Task 1

Martial wants more.

（1）Ray is done. And Martial is done. And Elise is done.

（2）The family lives in Long Land.

（3）The family is full of happiness and warm. A kid willl be contented and joyful if she/he lives in such a family.

（1）There are 5 people in the family, parents, twins and a girl.

（2）The grand-parents live on the other street.

（1）We want presents.

（2）Martial wants more.

（3）Kay is done. And Martial is done. And Elise is done.

（4）OK. Cookie, coodie, and cookie.

III Listening Scripts

Part One

1. Preview Exercises

The past year has brought many challenges to our nation, and Chinese have met every one with energy, optimism and faith. After lifting our economy from a recession, manufacturers and entrepreneurs are creating jobs again. Volunteers from across the country came together to help hurricane victims rebuild. And when the people of Wenchuan, Sichuan suffered a brutal earthquake attack, the world saw Chinese's generous heart in an outpouring of compassion and relief.

2. Listening Material

One day, a poor boy who was trying to pay his way through school by selling goods door to door found that he only had one dime left. He was hungry so he decided to beg for a meal at the next house.

However, he lost his nerve when a lovely young woman opened the door. Instead of a meal he asked for a drink of water. She thought he looked hungry so she brought him a large glass of milk. He drank it slowly, and then asked, "How much do I owe you?"
"You don't owe me anything, " she replied. "Mother has taught me never to accept pay for a kindness. " He said, "Then I thank you from the bottom of my heart. " As Howard Kelly left that house, he not only felt stronger physically, but it also increased his faith in God and the human race. He was about to give up and quit before this point.

Years later the young woman became critically ill. The local doctors were baffled. They finally sent her to the big city, where specialists can be called in to study her rare disease. Dr. Howard Kelly, now famous was called in for the consultation. When he heard the name of the town she came from, a strange light filled his eyes. Immediately, he rose and went down through the hospital hall into her room.

Dressed in his doctor's gown he went in to see her. He recognized her at once. He went back to the consultation room and determined to do his best to save her life. From that day on, he gave special attention to her case.

After a long struggle, the battle was won. Dr. Kelly requested the business office to pass the final bill to him for approval. He looked at it and then wrote something on the side. The bill was sent to her room. She was afraid to open it because she was positive that it would take the rest of her life to pay it off. Finally she looked, and the note on the side of the bill caught her attention. She read these words...

"Paid in full with a glass of milk. "

Tears of joy flooded her eyes as she prayed silently: "Thank You, God. Your love has spread through human hearts and hands. "

3. Additional Listening Material

Most of us take life for granted. We know that one day we must die, but usually we picture that day as far in the future, when we are in buoyant health, death is all but unimaginable. We seldom think of it. The days stretch out in an endless vista. So we go about our petty task, hardly aware of our listless attitude towards life. The same lethargy, I am afraid, characterizes the use of our faculties and senses. Only the deaf appreciate hearing, only the blind realize the manifold blessings that lie in sight. Particularly does this observation apply to those who have lost sight and hearing in adult life? But those who have never suffered impairment of sight or hearing seldom make the fullest use of these blessed faculties. Their eyes and ears take in all sights and sound hazily, without concentration, and with little appreciation. It is the same old story of not being grateful for what we conscious of health until we are ill.

I have often thought it would be a blessing if each human being were stricken blind and deaf for a few days at some time during his early adult life. Darkness would make him more appreciative of sight; silence would teach him the joys of sound. Now and then I have tested my seeing friends to discover what they see. Recently I was visited by a very good friend who had just returned from a long walk in the woods, and I asked her what she had observed. "Nothing in particular, " she replied. I might have been incredulous had I not been accustomed to such responses, for long ago I became convinced that the seeing see little.

4. Video-aural Material

Keating: Mr. Anderson, I see you sitting there in agony. Come on, Todd, step up. Let's put you out of your misery.

Todd: I, I didn't do it. I didn't write a poem.

Keating: Mr. Anderson thinks that everything inside of him is worthless and embarrassing. Isn't that right, Todd? Isn't that your worst fear? Well, I think you're wrong. I think you have something inside of you that is worth a great deal.

Keating: I sound my barbaric yawp over the rooftops of the world. W. W. Uncle Walt again. Now, for those of you who don't know, a yawp is a loud cry or yell. Now, Todd, I would like you to give us a demonstration of a barbaric yawp. Come on. You can't yawp sitting down. Let's go. Come on. Up.

Keating: You gotta get in yawping; stance.

Todd: A yawp.

Keating: No, not just a yawp. A barbaric yawp.

Todd: Yawp.

Keating: Come on, louder.

Todd: Yawp.

Keating: No, that's a mouse. Come on. Louder.

Todd: Yawp.

Keating: Oh, good god, boy. Yell like a man!

Keating: There it is. You see, you have a barbarian in you, after all. Now, you don't get away that easy.

Keating: The picture of Uncle Walt up there. What does he remind you of? Don't think. Answer. Go on.

Todd: A m-m-madman.

Keating: What kind of madman? Don't think about it. Just answer again.

Todd: A c-crazy madman.

Keating: No, you can do better than that. Free up your mind. Use your imagination. Say the first thing that pops into your head, even if it's total gibberish. Go on, go on.

Todd: And, and all the time he's mumbling.

Keating: What's he mumbling?

Todd: M-mumbling, truth. Truth is like, like a blanket that always leaves your feet cold.

Keating: Forget them, forget them. Stay with the blanket. Tell me about that blanket.

Keating: Good god, boy, there's a poet in you, after all. There, close your eyes. Close your eyes. Close them. Now, describe what you see.

Todd: Uh, I-I close my eyes.

Keating: Yes?

Todd: Uh, and this image floats beside me.

Keating: A sweaty-toothed madman?

Todd: A sweaty-toothed madman with a stare that pounds my brain.

Keating: Oh, that's excellent. Now give him action. Make him do something.

Todd: H-his hands reach out and choke me.

Todd: Y-Y-Y-you push it, stretch it, it'll never be enough. You kick at it, beat it, it'll never any of us. From the moment we enter crying to the moment we leave dying, it will just cover your face as you wail and cry and scream.

Keating: Don't forget this.

Part Two

1. Listening Skills

Sample practice

When US spacewoman Joan Higginbotham is not flying and working in space, she might be found somewhere on earth giving a speech. Higginbotham, who grew up in Chicago and became an engineer before joining NASA, that is the National Air and Space Administration, gives about a dozen speeches a year. Each speech is different because she tailors her remarks to each audience. Through interviews and E-mails, she finds out in advance her listeners' educational level and what information they want to know. On the subject of space walks, for example, audiences vary in their interests and how much complexity they can comprehend. To elementary school children, Higginbotham may discuss a problem that many kids want to know about. "How do spacemen in a spacesuit eat, drink, and go to the bathroom?" Her answer is "The spacesuit is really a small spacecraft with room for food and water-containers, and a waste-collection system." To a high school audience, she might satisfy a curiosity that often arises in her pre-speech interviews with students who obviously have seen many science fiction movies. "Do spacemen carry weapons in case they encounter enemies in space?" Her answer is "No". To scientists, she might provide technical details on such topics as the design of spacesuits that protects spacemen from the deadly temperature extremes of space. Just as elaborate preparation is required for success in space, Higginbotham says that it's important for speakers to learn as much as possible about their listeners before a speech because every audience is different.

Additional training

There are between 3000 and 6000 public languages in the world, and we must add approximately 6 billion private languages since each one of us necessarily has one. Considering these facts, the possibilities for breakdowns in communication seem infinite in number. However, we do communicate successfully from time to time. And we do learn to speak languages. But learning to speak languages seems to be a very mysterious process. For a long time, people thought that we learned a language only by imitation and association. For example, a baby touches a hot pot and starts to cry. The mother says, "Hot, hot!" And the baby, when it stops crying, imitates the mother and says, "Hot, hot!" However, Noam Chomsky, a famous expert in language, pointed out that although children do learn some words by imitation and association, they also combine words to make meaningful sentences in ways that are unique, unlearned and creative. Because young children can make sentences they have never heard before, Chomsky suggested that human infants are born with the ability to learn language. Chomsky meant that underneath all the differences between public and private languages, there is a universal language mechanism that makes it possible for us, as infants, to learn any language in the world. This theory explains the potential that human infants have for learning language. But it does not really explain how children come to use language in particular ways.

2. Additional Video-aural Material

Mother: Yes, I know. He has gone 4 days and 16 minutes late.

Father: Hey!

Daughter: Daddy!

Twins: A ...

Daughter: We want presents.

Twins: Mom ...

Father: Martial wants more.

(Telephone is ringing.)

Father: Ray is done. And Martial is done. And Elise is done.

(Elise is screaming.)

Father: OK. Cookie, cookie, and cookie.

Father: Hi! Honey!

Mother: Hi!

Ⅳ Translation of the Listening Materials

Part One

1. Preview Exercises

　　过去的一年中国人遇到了很多困难，但是在每个挑战面前，中国人都乐观无比，满怀信心，精神百倍。为了重振经济，制造商与企业家都在不断地创造工作机会。来自全国各地的志愿者集合在一起，帮助灾区人民重建。当汶川大地震发生，整个世界都目睹了中国人团结一心的激情与信念。

2. Listening Material

一天，一个贫穷的小男孩为了攒够学费正挨家挨户地推销商品。饥寒交迫的他摸遍全身，却只有一角钱。于是他决定向下一户人家讨口饭吃。

然而，当一位美丽的年轻女子打开房门的时候，这个小男孩却有点不知所措了。他没有要饭，只乞求给他一口水喝。这位女子看到他饥饿的样子，就倒了一大杯牛奶给他。男孩慢慢地喝完牛奶，问道："我应该付多少钱？"

年轻女子微笑着回答："一分钱也不用付。我妈妈教导我，施以爱心，不图回报。"男孩说："那么，就请接受我由衷的感谢吧！"说完，霍华德-凯利就离开了这户人家。此时的他不仅自己浑身是劲儿，而且更加相信上帝和整个人类。本来，他都打算放弃了。

数年之后，那位女子得了一种罕见的重病，当地医生对此束手无策。最后，她被转到大城市医治，由专家会诊治疗。大名鼎鼎的霍华德-凯利医生也参加了医疗方案的制定。当他听到病人来自的那个城镇的名字时，一个奇怪的念头霎时间闪过他的脑际。他马上起身直奔她的病房。

身穿手术服的凯利医生来到病房，一眼就认出了恩人。回到会诊室后，他决心一定要竭尽所能来治好她的病。从那天起，他就特别关照这个对自己有恩的病人。

经过艰苦的努力，手术成功了。凯利医生要求把医药费通知单送到他那里，他看了一下，便在通知单的旁边签了字。当医药费通知单送到她的病房时，她不敢看。因为她确信，治病的费用将会花费她整个余生来偿还。最后，她还是鼓起勇气，翻开了医药费通知单，旁边的那行小字引起了她的注意，她不禁轻声读了出来：

"医药费已付：一杯牛奶。"

喜悦的泪水溢出了她的眼睛，她默默地祈祷着："谢谢你，上帝，你的爱已通过人类的心灵和双手传播了。"

3. Additional Listening Material

我们大多数人认为生命理所当然，我们明白总有一天我们会死去，但是我们常常把这一天看得非常遥远。当我们身体强壮时，死亡便成了难以想象的事情了。我们很少会考虑它，日子一天天过去，好像没有尽头。所以我们为琐事奔波，并没有意识到我们对待生活的态度是冷漠的。我想我们在运用我们所有五官时恐怕也同样是冷漠的。只有聋子才珍惜听力，只有盲人才能认识到能见光明的幸运。对于那些成年致盲或失聪的人来说尤其如此。但是那些听力或视力从未遭受损失的人却很少充分利用这些幸运的能力，他们对所见所闻不关注、不欣赏。这与常说的不失去不懂得珍贵，不生病不知道健康可贵的道理是一样的。

我常想如果每一个人在他成年的早些时候，有几天成为了聋子或瞎子也不失为一件幸事。黑暗将使他更珍惜光明;沉寂将教他知道声音的乐趣。有时我会试探我的非盲的朋友们，想知道他们看见了什么。最近我的一位非常要好的朋友来看我，她刚刚在树林里走了很长时间，我问她看见了什么。"没什么特别的，"她回答说。如不是我早已习惯了这样的回答，我也许不会轻易相信，因为很久以前我就相信了有眼人看不见什么。

4. Video-aural Material

基廷：安德森先生，我看你坐在那里，局促不安，来吧，让我们把你从痛苦中解脱出来。

托德：我，我，没写，我没有写诗。

基廷：安德森先生认为他的想象毫无价值，羞愧难当，是这样吗，托德？这是你的恐惧吗？那么，我认为你错了，我认为你的想象是宝贵的。

基廷：惠特曼在诗中写道："我站在世界之巅，发出野性的呼唤!"你们可能不知道，yawp 是指大声喊叫，托德，来，来演示下什么是野性的呼唤。来吧，你是不可能坐着喊叫的。来吧。

基廷：你要大声喊出来,站直。

托德：A yawp。

基廷：大点声，野性的呼唤。

托德：A yawp。

基廷：来吧，大点声。你像老鼠叫，来，大声点。

托德：A yawp。

基廷：很好，非常好，像个男人。

基廷：惠特曼的画像在那里，看到你想到什么？别思考，就这么回答，来。

托德：一个……一个疯子。

基廷：什么样的疯子？别思考，就这么回答，快!

托德：一个疯狂的疯子。

基廷：你可以做的更好。放开你的思想，展开你的想象。把第一个跳入脑海的东西说出来，甚至可以是胡言乱语，来吧，快。

托德：他一直在喃喃自语……

基廷：他在喃喃自语什么？

托德：他在喃喃……他在说……真理……真理就像，就像一床毯子，像一床总也盖不住脚的毯子。

基廷：别管他们，别管他们，继续说，继续说那床毯子。

基廷：真不错，你心中有诗，闭上眼睛，闭上眼睛，描述下你现在看到了什么。

托德：我……我眼睛被蒙住了。

基廷：是的，你看到什么？

托德：嗯……我看到有东西在我周围飘荡。

基廷：那个令人齿冷的疯子吗？

托德：那个令人齿冷的疯子正冷眼盯着我。

基廷：很不错，现在让他做点什么，他对你怎样了？

托德：他的手伸出来卡住我的脖子。

托德：真理就像一床总让你双脚冰凉的毯子。你怎么扯，怎么拽，总也不够。踢也好，打也好，它总也盖不住我们。从我们哭着降生。到我们奄奄一息。它只会盖住你的脸。不管你如何痛苦。不管你如何痛苦。如何叫喊。

基廷：别忘了这个，记住！

Part Two

1. Listening Skills

Sample practice

　　美国女宇航员琼·希金博特姆现在不在太空中遨游，她可能正在某个地方演讲。琼·希金博特姆成长于芝加哥，在加入美国宇航局之前，是一名工程师。每年都有十几场演讲。每一次演讲的内容都不一样，她都是根据观众量体裁衣设计的。每次演讲前，她都要通过采访或者是电子邮件，提前了解听众的教育水平和相关的信息。举例来说，就太空行走而言，观众对其难度的理解是不同的。对小学生，她可能会讲述一些小孩们知道的东西。"请问宇航员们是怎么在太空服中吃饭、喝东西和睡觉的啊？"她回答道，"太空服是一个小型的太空飞船，会提供足够的空间储存食物和水，当然还有垃圾回收系统。"对于中学生，她可能会在演讲前调查学生在看科幻电影中看到那些感到好奇的东西，并在演讲中满足他们好奇欲。"在太空中，一旦遇到了敌人，宇航员们有武器吗？"她回答道："没有。"对科学家，她会根据主题提供技术细节，因为飞船的设计可以防止外太空对宇航员的致命的高温危害。就像进入太空中需要精心准备一样，对于希金博特姆来说演讲者要对听众有足够的了解，因为每一次的听众是不同的。

Additonal training

　　世界上约有3000到6000种通用语言，由于我们每个人都必须知晓一门个体语言，那么还要加上大概60亿种个体语言。从这个事实出发，交流沟通中似乎会出现无数次障碍。但是，每次交流沟通我们都成功的做到了，并且我们也确实学到了如何"说话"。然而学习使用某种语言似乎是个非常神秘的过程。很久以来，人们认为我们是通过模仿和联系来习得某种语言的。比如，一个婴儿碰到一个热锅，放声大哭，他母亲便说："烫！烫！"于是婴儿在停止哭泣后，也接着说："烫！烫！"然而，一位著名的语言专家诺姆·柯盖指出，尽管儿童通过模仿和联系来习得某种语言，他们也会通过某种独特的、天生的、富有创造性的方式来将词汇连成具有意义的句子。由于儿童会造出他们从来没有听到过的句子，柯盖提出人类婴儿天生具有学习语言的能力，他还指出尽管在通用语言和个体语言中存在各种不同，但是确实存在某种适用所有的语言机制，使得我们，比如婴儿，能够学习世界上任何一门语言。这个理论解释了人类婴儿学习语言的潜力，但是却没有很好地解释儿童是如何通过某些特定方式来使用语言的。

2. Additional Video-aural Material

母亲：是的，我明白。他已经出去四天，并且迟到了十六分钟。

父亲：我回来拉！你们好！

女儿：爸爸！

双胞胎兄弟：爸爸……

女儿：有礼物给我们吗？

双胞胎兄弟：妈……

父亲：马修还要吃。

（电话铃声）

父亲：雷吃完啦，马修也吃完啦，啊，爱力丝也吃完啦。

（女儿的尖叫声）

父亲：好吧，来点饼干，来吧，饼干。

父亲：你好！亲爱的！

母亲：你好！

I Background Knowledge

1. Language Points

Preview Exercises

(1) **to have many things in common** to share the same interests or experiences/彼此有很多共同点

e. g. His latest two novels have something in common.

(2) **to earn a living** to earn money that one needs to support oneself / one's family/谋生，挣钱，自食其力

e. g. College education will equip you to earn a good living.

Listening Material

(1) master of business administration (MBA)/工商管理学硕士

(2) **survive** vt. to continue to live after an accident, a war or illness/在事故，战争，疾病之后仍然生存，从……中逃生

vi. to continue to exist after a long time/活下来，幸存；残留

e. g. Only a few houses survived the earthquake.

e. g. The ability of animals to survive decreases.

Additional Listening Material

(1) **constitution** n. a set of basic laws and principles that a country or organization is governed by/一个国家的宪法或组织的法规，章规

e. g. The right to speak freely is written into the Constitution of the United States.

(2) **go into effect** (a law or policy) officially begins to apply or be valid from that particular time/法律，法规生效

(3) **Commonwealth** n. a group of countries that are related politically or economically/联合体，联邦

the official legal title of some U. S. states, such as Massachusetts, Pennsylvania, and Kentucky/美国某些州的官方称呼，例如马萨诸塞，宾西法尼亚，肯塔基

Video-aural Material

(1) **to look forward to sth. / doing sth.** to be excited and pleased about something that is going to happen/期待，盼望

e. g. I'm looking forward to Halloween this year.

(2) **should have done** a subjunctive mood expressing an unfulfilled obligation/此短语表示过去应该做但没有完成的任务

e. g. I'm sorry I missed the speech. You should have told me about it.

Listening Skills

(1) **immigration** n. the process of entering another country in order to live there permanently/移民，外来的移民

(2) **tenure** n. the right to stay permanently in a teaching job/教师的终身任职权

(3) **dismiss** v. to remove someone from their job or position/解雇，开除

e. g. Employees may be dismissed for using illegal drugs.

2. Cultural Background

(1) Residence hall /宿舍

Most colleges and universities in U. S. provide single or multiple occupancy rooms for their students, usually at a cost. These buildings are called dormitory. And the facilities provide not just a place to sleep, but also opportunities for personal and educational growth. However many colleges and universities no longer recognize the word "dormitory" and staff are now using the term "residence hall" or simply "hall" instead.

College cafeteria /大学自选餐厅

A college cafeteria is a type of food service location. In the UK the word "refectory" is often used. Many of these colleges employ their own students to work in the cafeteria. The amount of meals served to students varies from school to school, but is normally around 20 meals per week. Like normal cafeterias, a person will have a tray to select the food that they want, but instead of paying money, they pay beforehand by purchasing a meal plan (meal plan 餐费。例如，14 meals a week 指一个星期可以吃 14 顿饭）．

A school dining location is also referred to as a canteen or dining room.

College library /大学图书馆

A college library is a collection of information, sources, resources, books, and sevices which are organized for use and maintained by a college. In the more traditional sense, a library is a collection of books. Students can get access to the library by using their library cards. Besides borrowing books, students can also do evening study in the library.

(2) Phrases about university activities/大学的活动

independent study 自主学习	student union 学生会
university societies/ clubs 大学社团，协会	part-time job 兼职
postgraduate examination 研究生考试	job interview 面试
evening self-study; morning reading 晚自习，早自习	minor courses 辅修课程
	optional courses 选修课程

(3) Dissertation/毕业论文

For college students, a dissertation is a document that presents their research and findings and is submitted in support of candidature for a degree. A dissertation is also called a thesis. And a typical thesis has a title page, an abstract, a table of contents, a body, and a bibliography. An English major student who is expected to get a B. A. , for example, is required to finish a 5000 words dissertation in English.

(4) Going abroad for further study/出国留学

To go abroad for further study, either master or doctor's degree, students should first study the web sites of schools that interest them. They can find information about how and when to apply, how much it will cost and whether any financial aid is available. And they can probably e-mail the admissions office with any questions.

Wherever students apply, they should start the application process at least two years before they want to begin their studies. Completing the applications and any required admissions tests will take time. Non-native English speakers will most likely have to take the TOEFL, the Test of English as a Foreign Language(托福); IELTS, International English Language Testing System(雅思); GRE, Graduate Record Examination(美国研究生入学考试); or GMAT, Graduate Management Admission Test(管理学研究生

入学资格考试）.

(5) Successful language learner /成功的语言学习者

Successful language learners are independent learners. They do not depend on the book or the teacher; they discover their own way to learn the language. Instead of waiting for the teacher to explain, they try to find the patterns and the rules for themselves.

Successful language learning is active learning. Therefore, successful learners do not wait for a chance to use the language; they look for such a chance. They find people who speak the language and they ask these people to correct them when they make a mistake.

They will try anything to communicate; they are not afraid to repeat what they hear or to say strange things; they are willing to make mistakes and try again.

Finally, successful language learners are learners with a purpose. They want to learn the language because they are interested in the language and the people who speak it. It is necessary for them to learn the language in order to communicate with these people and to learn from them. They find it easy to practice using the language regularly because they want to learn with it.

II Reference Key

Part One

1. Preview Exercises

Dictation

Americans use the term "college students" to mean students either in colleges or universities. Not only that, Americans almost never say "going off to university" or "when I was in university." That sounds British. Instead, they say "going off to college" and "when I was in college."

Questions

(1) Many colleges do not offer graduate studies. Another difference is that universities are generally bigger. They offer more programs and do more research.

(2) Another place of higher education, especially in technical areas, is an institute, like the Massachusetts Institute of Technology.

2. Listening Material

Task 1

A B

Task 2

D C B

Task 3

(1) engineering   (2) differ from   (3) full-time

(4) candidates   (5) experts   (6) federal

(7) temporary

(8) The largest numbers came from China, South Korea, India, Taiwan and Canada. Most of them studied engineering, physical science or life science.

3. Additional Listening Material

Task 1

D C

Task 2

B B A

Task 3

(1) include   (2) division   (3) women   (4) Constitution

(5) note   (6) complex   (7) anniversary   (8) presented

4. Video-aural Material

Task 1

A D

Task 2

B C B

Task 3

(1) sitting down (2) perfectly fine (3) pre-med (4) residency

(5) hospital (6) thrilled (7) exciting (8) possibilities

(9) funny (10) decisions (11) pretty (12) forever

(13) watched (14) wondered (15) quiet (16) drawing

(17) know (18) admire (19) crazy (20) keep in touch

5. Listening Skills

Sample practice

(1) competing (2) spokesman (3) executive (4) recognize

(5) admission (6) unavailable (7) separate (8) version

(9) The TOEFL IBT and the IELTS both measure all four language skills-listening, reading, writing and speaking.

(10) You speak with an examiner who is certified in ESOL-English for Speakers of Other Languages.

(11) IELTS International says the test measures true-to-life ability to communicate in English for education, immigration and employment.

Additional training

(1) completed (2) researchers (3) hired (4) path

(5) seven (6) gain (7) faculty (8) denied

(9) Candidates for tenure may feel great pressure to get research published.

(10) They teach classes. They advise students. And they carry out research. They also serve on committees and take part in other activities.

(11) A visiting professor has a job at one school but works at another for a period of time.

Part Two

1. Preview Exercises

(1) Could you tell me where the library / cafeteria / canteen / residence hall / teaching building / office building / laboratory building / news-stand / automatic vending machine / ATM (Automatic Teller Machine) / multi-media classroom / audio classroom etc. is?

(2) Excuse me. I wonder if you'd mind answering a few questions.

Do you think you could tell me what you think of/about Wuhan?

2. Warming up Exercises

(1) A: Excuse me, could you tell me where the dining room is?

B: Certainly. Go along this road and turn right. You can see the dining hall in front of you.

A: Thanks. I am Helen, a new foreign teacher here. Would you like to show me a-round the campus?

B: It is my pleasure. Let's go to the dining hall first.

A: That's great!

(2) Some words related to the grade, majors, courses and degree.

Grade	freshman, sophomore, junior, senior
Majors	English, Economics, Finance, International Trade, Law, Sociology, Education, Psychology, Chinese Literature, Journalism, Mathematics, Information and Communication Engineering, Computer Science and Technology, Civil Engineering
Courses	Comprehensive English, English Video, Audio and Speaking, Extensive English Reading, Oral English, English Writing, British and American Literature, Society and Culture of English Country , Cultivation of Ethic Thought and Fundamentals of Law, Interpretation, Advanced English Grammar, Selected Readings of English Newspapers.
Degree	Bachelor's degree, Master's degree, Doctor's degree

(3) A: Hello, Jack. How are you doing these days?

     B: Not so bad. I am busy preparing my presentation.

     A: Presentation? For which course?

     B: English Video-aural course. Our teacher asks us to make a class report and it will be my turn next week.

3. Listening Material Review

Task 1

The material is about the difference between college and university.

Task 2

(1) PhD refers to doctor of philosophy degree, or a professional degree in an area like medicine, law or education.

(2) M. D. refers to medical students who receive an degree as "Doctor of Medicine".

(3) The largest numbers came from China, South Korea, India, Taiwan and Canada. Most of them studied engineering, physical science or life science.

Task 3

(1) The requirement of getting a B. A. and PhD.

(2) I like English very much. I believe that interest is the best teacher. / English plays such a crucial role in contemporary world, as long as we desire to join the world, we have to have a good command of English. / Learning English will make job candidates more competitive in the job market.

Task 4

(1) To earn a bachelor's degree, students usually take general subjects during their first 2 years.

(2) After students have a bachelor's degree, they may go on to earn a graduate degree-either a master's degree or a doctorate.

(3) Students can receive a PhD in engineering, social work, education, music, history and a lot of other areas.

(4) A PhD usually requires at least 3 years of full-time study after a bachelor's degree.

4. Video-aural Material Review

Task 1

The clip is about a high school graduate named Fecility who decides to go to New York city for college study.

Task 2

(1) The sentence "I was just wondering... " means " I'd like to know...". The auxiliary "was" indicates politeness.

(2) The phrase "here it goes" is used when people are starting to do something or when something is starting to happen.

e. g. I'll tell you a story. Well, here it goes.

(3) The phrase "would have done" expresses an unfulfilled wish.

Task 3

(1) The girl fell in love with one of her classmate and finally
got the chance to talk to him and made up her mind to
go to the same university with him.

(2) Having a new life in college. / Enjoying university life and having fun. / Studying hard and making progress in English studying.

Task 4

(1) High school was going exactly as it was supposed to.

(2) I urge you to savor the possibilities, embrace life because these...days will not come a-gain.

(3) Sometimes it's the smallest decisions that can pretty much change your life forever.

(4) Yes. I would have said "keep in touch", but unfortunately we never were in touch.

5. Additional Video-aural Material

Task 1

It's about the reasons for choosing a college for the narrator's little girl.

Task 2

(1) It means the time when high-school graduates and their parents visit different colleges in order to make the decision that which college or university they should enter, and it also

means the time when students apply for the admission to a college.

(2) The word "academics" refers to the subjects that students study in school.

(3) "never start a plan too early" here means "It's never too early to start a plan".

    e. g. It's never too old to learn.

    e. g. It's never too late to mend.

Task 3

(1) The father loved his daughter very much.

(2) The father tried to develop five criterions of selecting a college for his daughter, but he actually held just one criterion-distance from home. He wanted his daughter not to go far away from home.

Task 4

(1) I developed five reasons for choosing the perfect one for my little girl.

(2) And last but not least, distance from home which led us to the best choice.

(3) Northeastern. Forty miles from my house. Safe, great education. I can get there in 28 minutes, clocked.

(4) When Melanie finished high school, she'd be going to Northwestern.

III   Listening Scripts

Part One

1. Preview Exercises

Americans use the term "college students" to mean students either in colleges or universities. Not only that, Americans almost never say "going off to university" or "when I was in university." That sounds British. Instead, they say "going off to college" and "when I was in college."

College, university: what's the difference? Colleges and universities have many things in common. Both offer undergraduate degrees in the arts and sciences, for example. And both can help prepare young people to earn a living.

But many colleges do not offer graduate studies. Another difference is that universities are generally bigger. They offer more programs and do more research.

Another place of higher education, especially in technical areas, is an institute, like the Massachusetts Institute of Technology. Yet even an institute of technology can offer a wide choice of programs and activities.

2. Listening Material

To earn a bachelor's degree, students usually take general subjects during their first 2 years. After that they take classes in their major area of study. Students who major in a scientific area receive a bachelor of science degree, known as a B.S. Students in the arts and humanities get a B.A. – a bachelor of arts. Schools may also offer specialized degrees, like a bachelor of music.

After students have a bachelor's degree, they may go on to earn a graduate degree-either a master's degree or a doctorate. A master's degree generally takes 2 to 3 years of full-time study. A master of business administration, for example, takes about 2 years to complete. A doctorate can take much longer. It is the highest degree offered in graduate school. Some programs require 6 years of study or even longer after college. A student may earn a doctor of philosophy degree, known as a PhD, or a professional degree in an area like medicine, law or education.

Medical students, for example, receive an M.D., from the Latin term for "doctor of medicine". Future lawyers receive a J.D., for "juris" or "jurum" doctor, meaning a doctor of law or laws. Someone with a PhD is a "doctor of philosophy". Many people earn a PhD, yet not many are philosophers. The name has survived since the Middle Ages when many areas of study were called philosophy.

Students can receive a PhD in engineering, social work, education, music, history and a lot of other areas. Requirements can differ from one university to another, and from one area of study to another. But the National Science Foundation says American doctoral education is organized around a research experience.

A PhD usually requires at least 3 years of full-time study after a bachelor's degree. Some people first get a master's degree, others do not. PhD candidates must also pass special examinations and carry out original research. Students present their findings by writing a dissertation, a long paper that they have to defend before a group of experts.

Every year, the federal government collects information on research doctorates awarded in the United States. More than 43000 students received a research doctorate in 2005, the most recent year reported. Close to one-third of those doctorates went to foreign students in the United States on a temporary visa.

The largest numbers came from China, South Korea, India, Tai Wan of China and Canada. Most of them studied engineering, physical science or life science.

The University of Illinois awarded the largest number of doctorates to foreign students. The other universities in the top five were Purdue, Ohio State, Texas A&M and Pennsylvania State.

3. Additional Listening Material

The National Center for Education Statistics says more than 4 200 colleges and universities award degrees. These include 2-year schools as well as 4-year schools.

The oldest institution of higher learning in the country is Harvard in Cambridge, Massachusetts. It was established in 1636 as Harvard College. Massachusetts was an English colony at the time. The school was named for a Puritan religious leader. John Harvard gave the college all his books and half his property when he died. At first, Harvard had 1 teacher and 9 students. Today it has almost 20000 students. Nearly 4000 of them this past year were from outside the United States.

There are 14 schools at Harvard. They include Harvard College and the Radcliffe Institute for Advanced Study. Harvard College is the undergraduate division of the university and Radcliffe is a former college for women. So Harvard came first. Later, in 1780, the Massachusetts Constitution went into effect and officially recognized Harvard as a university. Some

Harvard materials call it America's oldest university.

But the University of Pennsylvania calls itself America's oldest university. Penn officials note that the Commonwealth of Pennsylvania recognized their school as a university in 1779. That was one year before Harvard.

Yet the history gets a little complex. Penn considers its anniversary date to be 1740. That was when the Charity School of Philadelphia was established, though it never opened. Benjamin Franklin later presented his ideas for a learning institution that included the Charity School. It opened in 1751 and became the university.

Today, more than 23000 students attend the University of Pennsylvania. 4000 of them come from other countries.

4. Video-aural Material

Felicity: Dear Sally, you should probably be sitting down for this. First of all, everything was perfectly fine. I mean, you know, on paper. High school was going exactly as it was supposed to. I mean, in three months, I'd be at Stanford pre-med; then I'd start my four year residency at one of the Stanford hospital. My dad was thrilled. You know, because he's basically had my life planned out for me since I was pretty much a zygote. I was surrounded by people actually looking forward to their lives.

Headmaster: Benjamin Steven Covington, Felicity Elizabeth, Porter, graduates with honors.

Felicity: My parents' reaction was typically understated.

Headmaster: So on this day, undoubtedly the most exciting of your lives. I urge you to savor the possibilities, embrace life because these...days will not come again.

Felicity: They say crash victims. People who lose a limb-that they can still feel their missing arm or leg, even after it's gone. It's called phantom pain, right? Well, suddenly, I had this horrible thought: "What if high school went away but the feeling of it didn't? I-I mean I didn't feel joy... or sorrow...or anticipation. Things were going so well but all I could feel was...was dread." Three years ago, I held a pint of Ben Covington's blood. I was volunteering at the 10th grade blood drive. That's about as close as we ever got. It's funny. Sometimes it's the smallest decisions that can pretty much change your life forever. I never said that.

Ben's mum: I'm so proud of you.

Ben: Mom, y-you know, you know what? I can not deal with this today! Not today! All right?

Ben's mum: Fine.

Ben: Not today.

Ben's mum: Fine.

Felicity: Excuse me?

Ben: Yeah?

Felicity: I'm Felicity Porter.

Ben: Yeah, I know. I'm Ben.

Felicity: Yeah, I know. I-I was just wondering if, um, you would mind signing my yearbook.

Ben: I don't have mind with me.

Felicity: Oh, that's ok. I-here's a pen for you.

Ben: Thanks.

Felicity: I just got it today, that's why, you know, there aren't any signatures… Except for, um, Mr. Johnson… who's here today somewhere, which I was surprised about. Anywhere would be…great.

Ben: Can you give me just a minute…to do this?

Felicity: Oh, yeah. Yeah, sure…I'll…

Ben: Thanks for asking.

Felicity: Oh, ha, ha…good.

Ben: Luck on you know…

Felicity: Yeah, yeah, yeah. You, too. I'll see ya.

Ben: OK.

Felicity: So this is what Ben Covington wrote: "Dear Felicity, here it goes. I've watched you for four years, always wondered what you were like, what was going in on your mind, all the time that you were so quiet, just thinking, drawing in your notebook. I should've just asked you, but I never asked you. So, now, four years later, I don't even know you, but I admire you. Well, this makes me sound crazy, but I'm okay with that. So take care of yourself. Love, Ben. P. S. I would've said ' keep in touch' , but unfortunately we never were in touch. "

Felicity: Hey, where are you going to college?

Ben: New York. What about you?

Felicity: Suddenly, I know what everyone else was feeling.

5. Listening Skills

Sample practice

Most American colleges and universities accept one or both of the two major tests. One is the Test of English as a Foreign Language , known as the TOEFL. The other is the International English Language Testing System , or IELTS. The TOEFL is given in 180 countries. The competing IELTS is given in 121 countries. 1000000 people each year take the TOEFL , says Tom Ewing , a spokesman for the Educational Testing Service. Same with the IELTS , says Beryl Meiron , the executive director of IELTS International. She says 2000 colleges and universities in the United States now recognize the IELTS. Schools might accept it only for undergraduate or graduate admission , or both. The IELTS is a paper test , while the TOEFL is given on paper only in places where a computer test is unavailable.

The TOEFL paper test costs \$ 150. It tests reading , listening and writing. A separate Test of Spoken English costs \$ 125. The computer version is called the TOEFL IBT , or Internet-based test. The price is different in each country , but generally falls between \$ 150 and \$ 200. The TOEFL IBT and the IELTS both measure all four language skills-listening , reading , writing and speaking. But with the IELTS , the speaking test is done separately as a live interview. You speak with an examiner who is certified in ESOL-English for Speakers of Other Languages. Everyone takes the same speaking and listening tests. But there is a choice of two kinds of reading and writing tests-either academic or general training. IELTS International says the test measures true-to-life ability to communicate in English for education , immigration and employment. Institutions in Britain and Australia jointly developed it.

Additional training

Professors usually need a doctorate degree. But , sometimes a school may offer positions to people who have not yet received their doctorate. Such a person would be called an instructor until the degree has been completed. After that , the instructor could become an assistant professor. Assistant professors do not have tenure.

A person with tenure cannot be easily dismissed. Such appointments are permanent. Teachers and researchers who are hired with the understanding that they will seek tenure are said to be "on the tenure track". Assistant professor is the first job on this path.

Assistant professors generally have five to seven years to gain tenure. During this time, other faculty members study the person's work. If tenure is denied, then the assistant professor usually has a year to find another job.

Candidates for tenure may feel great pressure to get research published. "Publish or perish" is the traditional saying.

An assistant professor who receives tenure becomes an associate professor. An associate professor may later be appointed as a full professor. Assistant, associate and full professors perform many duties. They teach classes. They advise students. And they carry out research. They also serve on committees and take part in other activities.

Other faculty members are not expected to do all these jobs. They are not on a tenure track. Instead, they might be in adjunct or visiting positions. A visiting professor has a job at one school but works at another for a period of time. An adjunct professor is also a limited or part-time position, to do research or teach classes. Adjunct professors have a doctorate.

Another position is that of lecturer. Lecturers teach classes, but they may or may not have a doctorate.

Part Two

Additional Video-aural Material

James Porter: Truth is, he said goodbye years ago, the day she left home. The trouble starts here-college application season. With over 4000 colleges in the US, I developed five reasons for choosing the perfect one for my little girl. Academics, distance from home, campus safety, distance from home, and last but not least, distance from home which led us to the best choice-Northeastern. Forty miles from house; safe; great education. I can get there in 28 minutes, clocked. Now, you can never start a plan too early. I'm James Porter, police chief, husband, dad and the best part of my plan? When Melanie finished high school, she'd be going to Northwestern. You're in! You in!

Translation of the Listening Materials

Part One

1. Preview Exercises

美国人用"college students"一词来指在综合性大学读书或者在高等专科学校读书的学生。不仅如此，美国人在表达大学的概念时从不说"going off to university"或者"when I was in university"。因为"university"一词听起来像英式英语。取而代之，美国人说"going off to college"或者"when I was in college"。

college 和 university 在表达大学这个概念时有什么区别呢？首先它们有很多相似之处，比如，它们都可以授予文学和理学学士学位。而且它们所设的课程都能为年轻人就业谋生做准备。

不同之处在于，许多称作 college 的大学不提供研究生课程。另一个不同在于，被称作 university 的大学总体来说更大，他们提供更多课程和更多领域的研究。

另一个提供高等教育，特别是在技术领域的场所是被称作 institute 的学院，例如麻省理工学院。不过理工学院也有除理工课外大量可供选择的课程和活动。

2. Listening Material

为了取得学士学位，学生通常在大学的前两年学习通识课程，然后再进行他们专业领域的学习。科学领域专业的学生获得理学学士学位，即 B. S.。艺术和人文领域专业的学生获得文学学士学位，即 R. A.。学校也可能颁发专业性的学位，如音乐学士学位。

在取得学士学位后，学生可以进一步攻读研究生课程取得硕士或者博士学位。取得硕士学位一般要经过两到三年的全日制学习。例如，取得工商管理硕士学位要经过两年的学习。而取得博士学位需要更长时间。博士学位是研究生院颁发的最高学位。一些课程需要大学毕业生用六年甚至更长的时间来学习。学生可以获得哲学博士学位，即 PhD，或者在医学、法律、教育等领域方面的专业性博士学位。

例如，医科学生取得 MD，即"mediane doctor"，这是拉丁术语中医学博士的意思。未来的律师取得 JD，即"juris' or' jurum' doctor"，是指法学博士。取得"PLD"的人是理学博士。很多取得哲学博士学位的人并不是哲学家。哲学一词的这个用法沿袭至今是因为在中世纪很多领域的研究都称为哲学。

学生可以获得工程、社会工作、教育、音乐、历史等许多领域的博士学位。取得学位的要求因不同的学校以及不同的学科而不同。美国国家科学基金会认为美国的博士教育是围绕研究能力展开的。

在取得学士学位后，学生至少需要三年的全日制学习来取得博士学位。一些人在这之前取得过硕士学位，另一些人则不然。博士学位的候选人必须通过专门的考试并开展原创的研究，然后撰写很长篇幅的论文来发表研究成果，并通过专家组的答辩。

每年，联邦政府都收集有关在美国授予的研究型博士学位的信息。最新一年的报告显示，在 2005 年有 4 300 多名学生获得博士学位。其中接近 1/3 的人是取得了美国临时签证的外国学生。

这些外国学生中，最多的是来自中国，韩国，印度，台湾和加拿大。而他们中的大部分人研究工程，物理科学和生命科学。

伊利诺伊大学是授予外国学生博士学位最多的大学。其他授予外国学生博士学位排名前五位的大学分别是普渡大学，俄亥俄州立大学，德州农工大学和宾夕法尼亚州立大学。

3. Additional Listening Material

国家教育统计中心表示超过 4200 所大学高校可颁发学位。其中包括两年制和四年制学校。马萨诸塞州剑桥市的哈佛大学是美国的一所资历最老的高级研究院。哈佛大学于 1636 年成立，当时马萨诸塞州还是英国的殖民地。学校以一位清教徒领袖——约翰·哈佛的名字命名。他临死前把自己所有的书籍和一部分他的诗集捐赠给了学校。最初，学校只有 1 名老师和 9 名学生。今天，学校学生几乎达到 20 000 人。去年，学校将近有 4 000 名留学生。

哈佛有 14 所学院。它们包括哈佛学院和拉德克里夫高等研究院，哈佛学院是大学本科分系，拉德克里夫前身是女子学院。因此哈佛先诞生，然后在 1780 年，马萨诸塞州宪法生效官方承认哈佛为大学高校。一部分哈佛文献称哈佛为美国最古老的大学。

但是宾夕法尼亚大学称自己为美国最古老的大学。宾夕法尼亚官员指出宾夕法尼亚州已于 1779 年承认其大学地位。这比哈佛的诞生时间早一年。

然而，历史变得有些复杂。宾夕法尼亚大学认为其纪念日应该追溯到 1740 年，当时费城慈善学校尽管一直没有开放但已经建立。本·杰明后来就大学，包括慈善学校发表了自己的构想。费城慈善学校于 1751 年开放，后来成为大学。

现在，宾夕法尼亚大学有多达 23 000 名学生，其中有 4 000 名留学生。

4. Video-aural Material

Felicity：亲爱的 Sally，你最好还是坐下来听我说。一开始一切都非常顺利。我是说，你知道的表面上的高中完完全全是它该是的样子。我是说 3 个月内我就要去斯坦福读医学预科,然后在斯坦福其中一个附属医院实习 4 年。我爸爸开心死了。你知道在我还是受精卵的时候他已经把我的人生计划好了。我被人群包围着，每个人都很期待自己的未来。

Headmaster：Benjamin Steven Covington，Felicity Elizabeth，Porter 荣誉毕业。

Felicity：我父母的表现还是很保守的。

Headmaster：从今天开始，毫无疑问你们的精彩生活即将起航。我热切的希望你们享受未知，拥抱生活，因为这些日子……不会再来。

Felicity：据说因为撞击事故而失去某部分肢体的幸存者，他们还是能感觉到失去的胳膊或腿即使它们已经不见了。这被称为幻痛 对吗？突然之间我有了这种可怕的想法，如果高中过完了但高中的感觉还在该怎么办？我是说我并没有感觉到开心，或悲伤，或期待。一切都很好，但我唯一的感觉却是不安。3 年前我拿着一品脱 Ben Covington 的血。我为 10 年级的献血活动志愿服务。那是我们距离最近的时候。有趣的是有时最细微的决定却可以永远改变你的生活。我从没那么说过。

Ben's mum：我为你骄傲。

Ben：妈，你知道吗？你知道吗？我不想今天和你纠缠这事，好吗？

Ben's mum：好吧。

Ben：今天不行。

Ben's mum：好吧。

Felicity：打扰一下？

Ben：什么？

Felicity：我是 Felicity Porter。

Ben：我知道，我是 Ben。

Felicity：我知道，我……我想请你在我的年鉴上签名不知道你愿不愿意？

Ben：我没带我的。

Felicity：哦，没关系，我……给你笔。

Ben：谢谢。

Felicity：我今天才拿到，所以这上面还没有签名，除了 Johnson 老师。他今天在这儿出现过，我很惊讶。签哪里都可以。

Ben：可以给我点时间写吗？

Felicity：哦，好的，当然……我就……

Ben：感谢你让我签。

Felicity：好运……你知道……

Ben：是的，是的，你也好运，回见。

Felicity：好的。Ben Covington 写了这些："亲爱的 Felicity，是这样，我远观了你 4 年，总在想你是什么样子。你脑子里在想什么。一直以来你都很安静思考，在笔记本里画画。我应该问你的，但我从没问过。所以，现在 4 年过去了我甚至不认识你。但我欣赏你。听我这么说你会不会觉得我有点毛病？但我不介意你这么想。好好照顾自己，爱你的 Ben。另外我本想说'保持联系'，可很不幸我们从来也没联系过。"

Felicity：嘿！你去哪儿上大学？

Ben：纽约，你呢？

Felicity：还不清楚。突然之间，我明白其他人的感受了。

5. Listening Skills

Sample practice

大多数美国大学和综合性大学都承认这两种主要测试中的一种或两种。一种是 Test of English as a Foreign Language，被称作托福。另一种是 International English Language Testing System，或者叫雅思。托福在 180 个国家设置考点，其竞争者雅思在 121 国家设有考点。教育考试服务中心的一位发言人 Tom Ewing 称每年有 1 000 000 人参加托福考试。雅思国际的行政执行官 Beryl Meiron 称雅思的参考情况也和托福相同。她谈到现在在美国有 2 000 多所大学和综合性大学都承认雅思考试成绩。学校可能只接受大学生的雅思成绩或只接受研究生的或两种都接受。雅思考试采用笔试。而托福只在不能通过电脑进行考试的地方才采用笔试。

托福笔试费为 150 美元。考阅读、听力和写作。口语一门测试的费用为 125 美元。计算机上考试被称为托福 IBT，即因特网为基础的考试。考试费各个国家不尽相同。但一般在 150 美元至 200 美元之间。托福网考和雅思都考察听，说，读，写这四种语言技能。但是在雅思考试中，口语考试是一个单独的现场面试。考生与 ESOL（海外考试处）认证考官进行对话。每个应试者都参加相同的口语和听力考试。但阅读和写作部分的考试有学术类和通用培训类这两种选择。雅思国际称，雅思考试考察学生在教育，移民和就业方面的沟通能力。此考试由英国和澳大利亚的教育机构联合开发。

Additional training

大学教授通常是获得博士学位的人。但是学校有时也提供教师职位给尚未获得博士学位的人。这样的人将被任名为讲师，直到取得博士学位。之后，讲师可能成为助理教授。助理教授没有终身教职权。

授予了终身教职的人是不能被轻易解聘的。这种终身任命是永久性的。教师和研究人员在初聘时就考虑到了终身教职。他们被称为处于终身教职序列中。成为助理教授是迈向终身教职的第一步。

助理教授一般要经过五至七年的时间才能取得终身教职。在此期间，其他教员对其工作评审。如果终身教职的审核未通过，助理教授通常有一年时间找另一份工作。

申请终身教职的的候选人可能会因为要发表研究成果而感到巨大的压力。"出版或者消亡"是人们经常说的话。

获得终身教职的助理教授将成为副教授。之后副教授可能被任命为正教授。助理教授，副教授和正教授有许多工作任务。他们教书，指导学生并进行研究。他们还在委员会任职并参加其他活动。

其他教员则不需要做以上这些工作。他们不属于终身任职序列中的一员。他们可能是兼职或客座教授。客座教授可以在一所学校任专职但同时在另一所学校工作一段时间。兼职教授是用业余时间有限度的兼职做研究或者教书。

兼职教授有博士学位。大学里的另一个职位是授课员。授课员教书，但他们不一定取得了博士学位。

Part Two

Additional Video-aural Material

James Porter：事实上，多年前孩子离开家时，就和父母道别了。问题出现在，申请大学的时候。在全美 4 000 所学校里，我根据五条标准为我的女儿选择了一所完美的学校。学术水平，离家的距离，校园的安全度，离家的距离，最后也是最重要的就是——离家的距离。这让我们做出了最优的选择——西北大学。离我们家 40 英里，安全，教育水平也很好。我在 28 分钟内就可以到达那里，再说早点计划没有坏处。我是 James Porter 警察局长，一位丈夫，父亲，我计划中最好的部分是什么？就是 Melanie 高中毕业后，她去西北大学。

James Porter：你被录取了，你被录取了。

Unit Six Networks

I

Background Knowledge

1. Language Points

Preview Exercises

(1) **disruptive**　adj.　characterized by unrest or disorder /捣乱的，破坏性的，制造混乱的

e. g. He has a disruptive influence on the other children.

(2) **laptop**　n.　a portable computer small enough to use in your lap /便携式电脑，膝上型电脑

e. g. Nowadays students like take laptops to the classroom.

(3) **retake class**　choose to take the course again/重修

e. g. She has to retake English because she failed last term.

(4) **tutor**　v.　be a tutor to someone; give individual instruction /做家教，辅导

e. g. For extra money, she tutors on weekends.

He tutored the child in physics.

Listening Material

(1) **virtual**　adj.　existing in essence or effect though not in actual fact/虚拟的，实质的

e. g. For example, in a virtual space, students can "dissect" a human body, "visit" ancient battlefields, or "talk" with Shakespeare.

(2) **cranky**　adj.　easily irritated or annoyed/怪癖的，不稳的

e. g. A cranky, complaining person can't be getting along with.

(3) **counseling**　n.　something that provides direction or advice as to a decision or course of action/顾问服务

e. g. Credit counseling helped us get out from under.

(4) **addiction**　n.　being abnormally tolerant to and dependent on something that is psychologically or physically habit-forming (especially alcohol or narcotic

drugs)/上瘾

    e. g. His addiction to drugs propelled him towards a life of crime.

(5) **access to**   approaching or having a chance to use/接近或使用的机会

    e. g. Citizens may have free access to the library.

(6) **be attached to**   create social or emotional ties ; cause to be attached/使依恋

    e. g. We are much attached to each other.

(7) **abstain**   v.   choose not to consume; give up/自制，放弃

    e. g. He swore to abstain from smoking.

Additional Listening Material

demonstration   n.   a show or display; the act of presenting something to sight or view/示范，实证

    e. g. She gave us a demonstration of the machine to show us how it worked.

Video-aural Material

conference   n.   a prearranged meeting for consultation or exchange of information or discussion (especially one with a formal agenda)/会议

    e. g. An international conference will be held in Beijing next month.

Listening Skills

(1) SARS, severe acute respiratory syndrome/急性呼吸综合症

(2) **infect**   v.   communicate a disease to/传染，感染

    e. g. The open wound soon became infected.

2. Cultural Background

(1) What is network?

    一般地说，将分散的多台计算机、终端和外部设备用通信线路互联起来，彼此间实现互相通信，并且计算机的硬件、软件和数据资源人家都可以共同使用，实现资源共享的整个系统就叫做计算机网络。

(2) What is the development of network?

    最早的 network，是由美国国防部高级研究计划局（ARPA）建立的。1977～1979年，推出了目前形式的 TCP/IP 体系结构和协议。1980 年所有计算机开始了 TCP/IP 协议的转换工作，建立了初期的 Internet。1983 年全部计算机完成了向 TCP/IP 的转

换，1985 年，美国国家科学基金组织 NSF 采用 TCP/IP 协议将分布在美国各地的 6 个为科研教育服务的超级计算机中心互联，并支持地区网络。1988 年 Internet 开始对外开放。1991 年 6 月，在连通 Internet 的计算机中，商业用户首次超过了学术界用户，这是 Internet 发展史上的一个里程碑，从此 Internet 成长速度一发不可收拾。

（3）Advantages and disadvantages of network

Advantages：

① Information release

② Electronic Mail(E-mail)

③ Online communication

④ Electronic business

⑤ Net phone

⑥ Online office

⑦ Remote education

Disadvantages：

① Addiction

② Human flesh search

③ Cheating

④ Obscene

（4）How to dictate broadcasting news.

① The significance of dictating news of the radio station

A. Have the ability of listening to the foreign radio station.

B. Help you increase the ability of dictation.

② Something about VOA

A. VOA stands for Voice of America.

B. Special English is broadcasted in a slow speed, which is designed especially for learners from non-speaking countries.

C. It has three features：a. the vocabulary is limited in 1500 words widely used in the US. b. It has simple patterns. Its broadcasting speed is 90 words/min.

D. Special English has many programs, such as News, Science Report, Agriculture Report, Words and Their Stories, and Education Report.

E. The timetable for VOA.

VOA Special English	
Beijing Time	Short Wave Frequency(MHz)
6:30 – 7:00 a.m	7.230 9.780 15.445
7:30 – 8:00 a.m	6.180 7.205 11.655 13.640 15.150
8:30 – 9:00 a.m	1.575 1.593 7.200 7.405 9.620 11.695 11.705 11.805 12.005 15.185 15.205
23:30 – 00:00 p.m	1.575 6.105 7.175 9.760 15.460

II Reference Key

Part One

1. Preview Exercises

(1) Dictation

Computers have been used in teaching for more than twenty years. But a new book says that only now are they changing education. And it predicts that a lot more is about to happen.

The new book says the needed disruptive force in education is computer-based learning. Michael Horn, another author of "Disrupting Class", told us about a Boston public school that he visited. Every student at Lilla G. Frederick Middle School in Dorchester, Massachusetts, has a laptop computer.

Computer-based learning offers a way for students to take advanced courses not offered at their school, or to retake classes they failed. It also serves those who can not physically attend school, and students who receive home schooling or need tutoring.

(2) Questions

The advantages and disadvantages of the network are as follows:

Advantages：

① Information release

② Electronic Mail(E-mail)

③ Online communication

④ Electronic business

⑤ Net phone

⑥ Online office

⑦ Remote education

Disadvantages：

① Addiction

② Human flesh search

③ Cheating

④ Obscene

2. Listening Material

Task 1

A　A

Task 2

D　C　D

Task 3

(1) 10th　(2) trial　(3) alone　(4) cool

(5) existed　(6) upset　(7) sought　(8) experts

(9) it is important that children have the opportunity to learn about the Internet.

(10) Some may become so attached that they will spend more than 8 hours a day on the computer playing games or chatting.

3. Additional Listening Material

Task 1

B　A

Task 2

B   D   C

Task 3

(1) offers   (2) undergraduate   (3) range   (4) receive

(5) available   (6) contact   (7) site

4. Video-aural Material

Task 1

A   B

Task 2

B   B   D

Task 3

(1) convenient   (2) conferences   (3) drawing   (4) transport

(5) operated   (6) legs   (7) reduced

5. Listening Skills

Sample practic

American secretary of state Hillary Clinton, has expressed concern about north Korea and possible crisis, Kim Jong-I I is no longer in power. Mrs. Clinton spoke to a reporter Thursday before her arrival in the South Korean capital. She said the Obama administration is deeply concerned about the possible change in North Korea leadership. She warned that such a change could raise tension between North Korea and its neighbors. Earlier North Korea warned it is prepared for war with South Korea. The official Korean central news agency reported that North Korean military officials said their army is ready for battle.

Additional training

Finally, the number of American's collecting unemployment assistance rose to nearly 5 million last week. The labor department says this is the fourth week in a month that the number receiving assistance for more than a week has reached a record high. The number of jobless Americans seeking government aid for the first time remained unchanged at 627000. Also A new report says many factoring in part of eastern Unites States failed to an 18 year low. The report blamed the drop from fuel factory orders and rising unemployment.

Some business leaders say their information suggest the economy may begin to grow stronger later this year.

Part Two

1. Preview Exercises

(1) This is called QQ chatting software. It helps us communicate with each other. I like it because it is quite convenient.

The reasons why I like Baidu searching engine is as follows: First of all, it can help us find the materials I want. Secondly I can get some knowledge from it. Finally, it is quite convenient for us to operate.

(2) The ways of expressing my attitude toward network, such words as likes, dislikes , preference are:

I like…; I enjoy…; I love…; I'm fond of…; I'm keen on…;

I don't like…; I dislike…; I hate…; I can't stand…; I can't bear…

2. Warming up Exercises

(1) This picture tells us something about buying things on the net. I like it because I can buy something without going to supermarkets. However, I doubt what if I am cheated.

This picture shows us ATM by which people withdraw or save money. I enjoy it because I can deal with my money any – time and anywhere. However, if you don't care too much, thieves have the chances to steal money easily.

(2) Network can help us deal with many things quicker than we do it in a normal way. For example, we can search on the net, we can talk on the net, we can buy something on the net, even we can learn on the net. However, If you are addicted on the net, it is harmful to our eyes; you will be spoiled, even commit crimes.

3. Listening Material Review

Task 1

It tells us the Internet addiction and how to solve this issue.

Task 2

(1) They bought it for his son's birthday.

(2) John was addicted to the Internet.

(3) His parents took away his computer, and sought counseling for him.

Task 3

(1) Internet is a sword with double blades. It can both help us and spoil us, which depends on how you use it.

(2) John's parents bought a computer as a present for his birthday. However, John was addicted to the Internet so that his parents were very worried. They had to take away his computer and asked for help.

Task 4

(1) In a few months they began to notice that John wasn't coming out of his room as often.

(2) He became cranky and upset if his parents asked him to leave the computer.

(3) Abstaining completely from Internet usage will probably not solve the problem.

(4) The best way to overcome an addiction is to seek help or counseling if needed.

4. Video-aural Material Review

Task 1

This clip tells computers are widely used in agriculture, industry, home affairs, transportation and education.

Task 2

(1) "glass house" is a house controlled by computers to produce vegetables.

(2) The video phone is used to hold a conference.

(3) Yes. In the future the price will be so cheap that ordinary people can afford visiting outer space.

Task 3

(1) It can record the data. For example, patients with the same illness are now kept on computer. It is possible to have a group of these records selected or updated.

(2) The clip tells us computers which are used in different fields. For example, green house is used in agriculture; central computer is used in houses; transportation is also controlled by computer. It is not a dream that ordinary people can have a visit to outer space. Computer can also be used in education and research.

Task 4

(1) Through the world computers will be used more and more in the future. They are already be used in agriculture and industry.

(2) The idea that computers that recognize human voices surprises many people.

(3) Computers will be used more and more in transport.

(4) In the field of education, health and research, computers will continue to play an important part.

5. Additional Video-aural Material

Task 1

This clip tells us how network is formed and how to use the network.

Task 2

(1) Network can help us in finding a job, meeting new friends and finding parterners.

(2) This is because the connections are often hidden. If you can explore it, it has big potential.

(3) If you find a person you are interested in, you can find a button and says "Add as Friend", press it and you can contact with her or him.

Task 3

(1) From network you can know many strangers by the help of your friends and your friends' friends.

(2) This clip teaches us how the network is formed and how to make friends with each other on the net.

Task 4

(1) Networks get things down whether sending a letter or writing in your home.

(2) This is network of people, a social network.

(3) You know longer strangers, so you will contact them more easily.

(4) Your net work is suddenly more useful.

Listening Scripts

Part One

1. Preview Exercises

Computers have been used in teaching for more than twenty years. But a new book says that only now are they changing education. And it predicts that a lot more is about to happen.

The new book says the needed disruptive force in education is computer-based learning. Michael Horn, another author of "Disrupting Class", told us about a Boston public school that he visited. Every student at Lilla G. Frederick Middle School in Dorchester, Massachusetts, has a laptop computer.

Computer-based learning offers a way for students to take advanced courses not offered at their school, or to retake classes they failed. It also serves those who can not physically attend school, and students who receive home schooling or need tutoring.

2. Listening Material

On John's 10th birthday, his parents bought him a computer and put it in his room. They thought it would be wise to let him begin learning about the computer and the Internet. When John first started going online, his parents would monitor his online activities. After a trial period, his parents left him alone.

In a few months they began to notice that John wasn't coming out of his room as often. John liked the Internet, and thought it was a cool way to connect with virtual friends, and play online games. But as time went on, John became less connected to the real world around him, and more in time with the virtual world that existed 24 hours a day on the Internet. He became cranky and upset if his parents asked him to leave the computer. Finally, his parents took away his computer, and sought counseling for him.

John is not in a class of his own. There are many others who also struggle with what experts call Internet addiction. Everyone agrees that in this day and age, it is important that children have the opportunity to learn about the Internet. Thus, access to the Internet can be found in homes, offices, schools, and sometimes even shopping malls. However, the problem of Internet addiction begins when someone is more attached to a virtual online world than the world that exists around them.

Some may become so attached that they will spend more than 8 hours a day on the computer playing games or chatting. Abstaining completely from Internet usage will probably not solve the problem. It is wiser to gradually reduce the amount of time that is spent on the Internet. The Internet can be a wonderful tool that exposes one to many different worlds, but it can also become an addiction, just like caffeine, drugs or smoking. The best way to overcome an addiction is to seek help or counseling if needed.

3. Additional Listening Material

This is the VOA Special English Education Report.

Knowledge is free on the Internet at a small but growing number of colleges and universities.

About one hundred sixty schools around the world now offer course materials free online to the public. Recent additions in the United States include projects at Yale, Johns Hopkins and the University of California, Berkeley.

Berkeley said it will offer videos of lectures on YouTube. Free videos from other schools are available at the Apple iTunes store.

The Massachusetts Institute of Technology became an early leader with its OpenCourseWare project, first announced in 2001. Free lecture notes, exams and other resources are published at ocw. mit. edu. Many exams and homework assignments even include the answers. The Web site also has videos of lectures and demonstrations.

Today, OpenCourseWare offers materials from one thousand eight hundred undergraduate and graduate courses. These range from physics and linear algebra to anthropology, political science-even scuba diving.

Visitors can learn the same things M. I. T. students learn. But as the site points out, Open-CourseWare is not an M. I. T. education. Visitors receive no credit toward a degree. Some materials from a course may not be available, and the site does not provide contact with teachers.

Still, M. I. T. says the site has had forty million visits by thirty-one million visitors from almost every country. Sixty percent of the visitors are from outside the United States and Canada.

There are links to materials translated into Spanish, Portuguese, Chinese and Thai. Open-CourseWare averages one million visits each month, and the translations receive half a million more.

Students and educators use the site, including students at M. I. T. But the largest number of visitors, about half, are self-learners.

Some professors have become well known around the world as a result of appearing online. Walter Lewin, a physics professor at M. I. T. , is specially popular. Fans enjoy his entertaining demonstrations.

M. I. T. OpenCourseWare now includes materials for high school. The goal is to improve education in science, technology, math and engineering.

And that's the VOA Special English Education Report, written by Nancy Steinbach. Let us know if you have taken any free online courses through an American college or university. Tell us what you liked or disliked about your experience. Write to special@ voanews. com, and please include your name and where you are from. I'm Bob Doughty.

4. Video-aural Material

Throughout the world computers will be used more and more in the future. They are already be used in agriculture and industry. For example, many farms now use computers to control the growing condition of vegetables and other plants. In glass houses computers control the watering of the plants as well as the light and temperature. It is possible to work out whether you will save or lose money by increasing the temperature by 1 degree centigrade.

In their personal lives, people will also use computers more and more. Instead of going to the bank, they will use a computer and a telephone to change money and to pay their electricity bills and so on. House will be controlled by central computer. Lights will go off if no one in the room. The idea that computers can recognize human voices surprises many people. You will be able to telephone home half an hour before returning and by speaking into the telephone you will be able to tell the computer to turn on the heating and the hot water. The computer will recognize your voice and carry out the instruction. The possibility that the majority of the labour force will work at home is often discussed.

It will be much more convenient than spending a lot of time traveling to work every day. People will be able to use the video phone for conferences. They will be able to do drawing and send them by mail or by fax. Computers will be used more and more in transport. Railways in Japan already use them to work out to the best distance between trains. Trains will be operated by computer, and many of them will have no drivers. Space travel will become much cheaper. In 1993, a new space rocket with no wings was developed in the USA. This type of rocket is able to return to the earth and land on its legs. As a result, costs will be reduced by as much as 90 percent.

In the field of education, health and research, computers will continue to play an important part. It will be a part of everyone's education to learn computers skills and information record, for example, patients with the same illness are now kept on computer. It is possible to have a group of these records collected and printed. Computer programs for storing whole texts are already well developed. You can type the name of the subject, example, printing in China, and the computer will give you a worldwide list of magazine and book titles. The next step is to search the titles for more information. Finally you can choose certain text and read them on computer screen. If you want a copy of the article or a page, it can be printed out and sent to you.

5. Listening Skills

Sample practice

It is 23 : 30 universal time. And time for news in Special English on the Voice of America. I'm Will Whites in Washington.

China is reporting 11 more new deaths from SARS, severe acute respiratory syndrome. That disease has killed 97 people in China, and infected more than 2000 others. One of the new people infected in China is a visitor from New Zealand. He was taken to a hospital. after he attempted to get on a flight from Beijing from the city of Xi'an. In Hong Kong SARS has now killed 99 people. Singapore and Canada have reported 14 deaths each.

Additional training

American secretary of state Hillary Clinton, has expressed concern about north Korea and possible crisis, Kim Jong-Ⅱ is no longer in power. Mrs. Clinton spoke to a reporter Thursday before her arrival in the South Korean capital. She said the Obama administration is deeply concerned about the possible change in North Korea leadership. She warned that such a change could raise tensions between North Korea and its neighbors. Earlier North Korea warned it is prepared for war with South Korea. The official Korean central news agency reported that North Korean military officials said their army is ready for battle.

Finally, the number of American's collecting unemployment assistance rose to nearly 5 million last week. The labor department says this is the fourth week in a month that the number receiving assistance for more than a week has reached a record high. The number of jobless Americans seeking government aid for the first time remained unchanged at 627000. also A new report says many factoring in part of eastern Unites States failed to an 18 year low. The report blamed the drop from fuel factory orders and rising unemployment. Some business leaders say their information suggest the economy may begin to grow stronger later this year.

Part Two

Additional Video-aural Material

Networks get things done whether sending a letter or writing in your home. Network makes it happen. To get from Chicago to Santa Fe, we need to see the network or roads which would get us there. We see Chicago which is connected to St. Louis, connected to Dallas, connected to Santa Fe. Of course people networks can help us with finding jobs, meeting new friends and finding parterners. You know how it works. Bob is your friend and he knows Sally, and Sally's friend Joe has a job for you. This is network of people, a social network. The problems with networks in the real world most of the connections between people are hidden. Your network may have huge potential, but it is only as valuable as the people and the connections that you can see. This problem has been solved by a type of website called social network in site. These websites help you seek connections that are hidden in the real world. Here's how it works. You sign up for a free account and fill out your profile, then you look for the people you know. When you find someone, you could find a button and says "Add as Friend". Once you do this, you and that person have connection on website that others can see. They are a member of your network, and you are a member of theirs. What's really cool is you can see who your friends know, and who your friends' friends know. You know longer a stranger, so you can contact them more easily. This solves a real world problem because your network has hidden opportunity. Social networking makes these connections between people visible...Like a map for a highway, they show you the people network that help you get your next destination whether it's a job , a new parterner, or a great place to live. Your net work is suddenly more useful. You can get started at these sites, LinkedIn, Facebook and MySpace. I'm Lela Fever and this has been social networking in plain English on the common craft show.

IV Translation of the Listening Materials

Part one

1. Preview Exercises

电脑用于教学的历史已经超过 20 年。但是一本新书说只是现在它们才开始改变教育的格局。而且这本书预言到还有更多的事情发生。

这本新书提到在教育中必然产生的破坏因素是基于电脑的学习。"扰乱课堂"的另一作者 Michael Horn 告诉我们他访问了一个波士顿公立学校。马萨诸塞州，多尔切斯特 Lilla G. Frederrick 中学的每个学生都有一台便携式电脑。

基于电脑的学习为学生提供了一条途径，使他们可以利用学校无法提供的有用资源，或者重修他们不及格的课程。它还能服务于因为生理原因不能接受学校教育或需要家教的学生。

2. Listening Material

在 John10 岁生日的这天，他的父母给他买了一台电脑并安装在了他的房间。他们认为让孩子了解计算机和因特网是明智的。John 第一次开始上网，父母就监督其网上活动，一段考察时间之后，就让他独立上网了。几个月之后，父母开始发觉 John 经常不出自己的房间。John 非常喜欢网络，而且觉得与虚拟世界的朋友聊天，玩线上游戏是很酷的事情。但是随着时间的推移，John 变得与现实中他身边的人接触越来越少，他几乎 24 小时都泡在网上。当他父母要求他离开电脑的时候他变得怪癖和失落。最终他的父母拿走了他的电脑，并为他寻找咨询服务进行心理咨询。

John 不再上学了。有很多同样的学生在与专家称为的"网瘾"奋斗。所有人都认同在当今时代，让孩子们有机会认知网络是很重要的。因此，在家里、办公室、学校、甚至有时候在购物广场都能使用到网络。然而，当一部分人过多的接触虚拟网络世界而忽视了现实身边的世界的时候，网瘾这一问题就出现了。

有的人会非常入迷以至于他们会每天花多于 8 个小时的时间用电脑玩游戏或者聊天。完全拒绝使用网络的自制力可能解决不了这个问题。逐渐减少使用网络的时间才是比较明智的方法。网络是一个把一件事物展示在多个不同世界的美好工具，但是它也可以成为一种瘾，就像咖啡因、毒品和香烟。戒瘾的最好方法是在必要的时候寻求帮助和咨询。

3. Additional Listening Material

这里是美国之音教育报道栏目。

大专院校的资源免费上网，目前数量不多，但正在增长。世界上大约有 160 个学校免费为大众上传学校的课程资料。目前美国的 Yale 大学，Johns Hopkins 大学以及 California 的 Berkeley 大学都纷纷加入了行列。

Berkeley 大学说他们将在 YouTube 网站上传上课录像。其他学校的免费音频资料在 Apple iTunes store 上也能找到。

Massachusetts 技术学院早在 2001 年就率先进行了公开课件工程。教案、试卷等其他资源都公布在 ocw.mit.edu 网站上。很多考试试卷、作业布置，甚至还有答案。网站还有上课录像和演示。

现在，公开课件函盖了 1 800 个专科和本科课程的资料。课程从物理、线性代数到人类学、政治科学——甚至深水潜水不等。

来访者能学到 Massachusetts 技术学院学生同样的内容。但是，正如网站指出，公开课件不是 Massachusetts 技术学院的教学。来访者不能通过学分来获得学位。课程的有些材料在网上查不到。网站也不负责联系老师。

Massachusetts 技术学院还说，网站已经有 4 000 万人来访，其中 3 100 万是来自世界其他国家。60% 的来访者来自美国和加拿大以外地区。

网上的材料都可以链接到翻译出来的西班牙版、葡萄牙版、汉语版以及泰国版。公开课件每月有平均 100 万人光顾，而浏览这些翻译版网页的人数就有 50 多万。

使用这个网站的有学生和教育工作者，也包括 Massachusetts 技术学院的学生。但是大量的来访者，有一半是来自学的。

由于进行在线授课或答疑，有些教授们已经在世界上非常出名。Walter Lewin 是 Massachusetts 技术学院的物理教授，他就特别出名。他的追随者非常喜欢他生动有趣的演示课。

Massachusetts 技术学院的公开课件现在也提供高中的资料。其目的就是提高在科学、技术、数学和工程等教育水平。

这里是美国之音特别节目为您播出的教育报道栏目，由 Nancy Steinbach 撰写。如果你已经通过美国大专院校的网站免费学习课程，请告诉我们。告诉我对于这种学习经历的看法。来信请发给 special@voanews.com，并写上你的名字，来自哪里。我是主持人 Bob Doughty。

4. Video-aural Material

世界的未来电脑会越来越多的被应用。它们已经被应用于工农业了。比如，许多农场现在都开始用电脑来控制蔬菜以及其他庄稼的生长情况。在温室大棚，电脑控制着植物的水分以及灯光、温度。计算出由于增加一度的温度，而使你省钱还是亏损成为了可能。

在生活中，人们也会越来越多地利用电脑。他们可以不去银行，他们会用电话和电脑来存取款、付电费等。房屋将由中央电脑来控制。房间里没人的时候灯会自动关闭。电脑识别人声的创意震惊了很多人。你将可以在到家前半个小时往家里打电话，通过电话告诉电脑让它打开热水器烧好热水。电脑将识别出你的声音并接受指令。人们经常讨论大部分的劳动者在家里工作的可能性。

比起每天搭车上班这将变得方便很多。人们将可以用可视电话开会。他们将可以做画并用电子邮箱和传真来发送。电脑会被越来越多地应用于交通运输。日本的铁路已经利用计算机计算出火车运行区间的最佳距离。火车将由电脑操作，许多火车可以不用司机。太空旅行可以变得更加便宜。1993 年，新式没有机翼的火箭在美国被开发出来。这种火箭可以返回地球并用其轮子着陆，其结果花费减少了 90%。

在教育、健康和研究界，电脑一直扮演着很重要的角色。学习电脑技巧将成为每个人的学习任务，信息记录，例如，患有相同疾病的病人记录到电脑中，收集这些记录并打印输出成为了可能。储存整个文本的程序已经成功地开发出来。你可以输入主题名称,案例,中国打印,电脑会给出世界各国的杂志书籍目录。接着就是根据标题搜索更多的信息了。最后你可以选择某一个文档进行网上阅读。如果你想复制一篇文章或者页面,电脑会打印出来发给你。

5. Listening Skills

Sample practice

现在是美国时间 23:30,这是美国之音特别英语的新闻节目。我是 Will Whites 在华盛顿播报。

据报道中国新发现超过 11 例 SARS 病毒感染死亡病例,这一病毒在中国夺走了 97 人的生命,2000 多人受感染。新一例感染者是从新西兰归来的游客。当他准备乘航班从西安飞往北京的时候被带往了医院。在中国香港 SARS 已经致死了 99 人。新加坡和加拿大分别报告了 14 例死亡病例。

Additional practice

美国国务卿希拉里·克林顿夫人在周四抵达韩国首都之前对记者表达了对朝鲜危机的关注,金正日不再掌权。她是在星期四抵达韩国首都之前向记者说这番话的。她说奥巴马政府非常关注朝鲜领导层可能发生改变。她警告道这样的改变会加深朝与其邻国之间的紧张局势。早些时候朝鲜宣告随时准备好应对与韩国的战争。韩国政府新闻中心报告了朝鲜军方宣布了他的部分随时准备投入战斗。

最后,美国失业救济人数在上周达到了将近 500 万人。劳动部说这是这个月连续第四周来救济人数的新高。美国失业人数首次在寻求政府帮助的时候一直保持在 627000 人。最新消息还报道了许多美国东部工厂 18 年来产量最低。报道指责了石油工厂定单下降和失业率的升高。一些工商界领导人说他们得到信息称,经济在今年晚些时候恢复增长。

Part Two

Additional Video-aural Material

不管是发送信件还是在家写作,网络可以帮你搞定,网络使其运转。从芝加哥到圣菲,我们需要通过浏览网络,来知道如何到达那里。我们可以看到先从芝加哥到圣路易斯,再到达拉斯,最后到达圣菲。当然,人际关系网能帮助我们找到工作,会见新朋友或者找到新的伙伴。你知道它是如何运作的，Bob 是你的朋友，并且他认识 Sally，而 Sally 的朋友 Joe 帮你找到了工作，这就是人们之间的关系网，一个社会关系网络。在现实世界中的大多数人之间的联系是隐藏的，你的关系网络可能潜在的数量非常大，但是对你来说，你可能只能看到对你有价值的人，以及他们的关系网。这个问题因为一种叫作社会网络的网站出现而得以解决，这个网站帮助你寻找现实生活中隐藏的关系。这是它的工作流程：你先免费注册然后填写自己的资料。然后寻找你认识的人，当你找到某个人时，你可以看到一个按钮，上面写着"加为好友"。这样，别人就能看到你和他之间的关系。他们是你的关系网，你也是他们的关系网。非常酷的是，你能看到你的好友认识哪些人，或者你的好友的好友认识哪些人，这样，你和陌生人进行联系就会方面很多。这解决了现实中的问题，因为，你的网络有隐藏的机会。社会网络站点让人们之间的关系变得可见。这就像一个高速公路地图，你的人际关系网，能帮助你找到下一个目的地，或许是一份新工作，或者一个新的伙伴，或者是一个好的住处。你的人际关系网会突然变的非常的有用，你可以看看这些站点，比如，Linkedln，Facebook 和 MySpace，我是 Lela Fever，这是由我主持的用简明英语交流的社会型网络通络节目。

I Background Knowledge

1. Language Points

Preview Exercises

It has become a non-religious holiday.

non- adj. [prefix] indicating negation/表示非，无，不

    e. g. non-automatic/ 非自动的, non-governmental/非政府性的

Listening Material

(1) **give birth to to** bear (a child) to/生产，分娩

    e. g. On October 17, at 9：25am, Jane gave birth to a beautiful baby girl.

    initiate, originate/引起，造成

    e. g. It is said that James Watt's observation of steam issuing from a kettle gave birth to the idea of the steam engine.

(2) **stand for** to represent; symbolize/代表

    e. g. What does ESL stand for?

    to tolerate; allow/忍受

    e. g. I won't stand for this insolence.

Additional Listening Material

…surviving their first year

survive v. continue to live; endure or last/生存

    e. g. You need to be tough to survive in the jungle.

    continue in existence after (an adversity, etc.)/幸存

    e. g. These birds are able to survive the perils of the Arctic winter.

    live longer than/比……活得长

    e. g. The old lady has survived all her children.

Video-aural Material

(1) **give away** to reveal or betray (esp. in the phrases give the game or show away)/泄露，背叛

        e. g. He was given away by one of his accomplices.

        to give up or abandon (something)/放弃

        e. g. He decided to give away everything he possessed and became a monk.

(2) **take on** (no passive) begin to have (a particular quality, appearance, etc)/呈现(某种性质，样子等)

        e. g. Her eyes took on a hurt expression.

2. Cultural Background

(1) Christmas

The roots of Christmas

No one knows exactly when Jesus Christ was born. For many years, local Christian churches celebrated Christ's birth at different times. Then, in the AD 300s, the Roman Catholic Church set the birth date on December 25.

At that time, older non-Christian festivals were celebrated around Christmas. The Romans celebrated Saturnalia, a festival honoring their god of harvest and god of light. Other Europeans held festivals in mid-December marking the end of the harvest season. The Roman Catholic Church probably chose December 25 to give a Christian meaning to these older festivals.

Christmas gifts

The custom of exchanging gifts at Christmas came from the ancient Romans. During Saturnalia, the Romans exchanged tokens of good luck. Later, it became customary for Romans to exchange more valuable gifts, such as clothes or jewelry. The Biblical story of the Three Wise Men who presented gifts to baby Jesus also shaped this Christmas custom.

Christmas trees

The tradition of the Christmas tree came to North America from Germany. Long ago, Germans began decorating evergreen trees in their homes at Christmas. They trimmed their trees with fruits, cookies, and lighted candles. German immigrants to the United States brought this custom with them in the 1800s.

Before Christian times, ancient people used evergreens for decoration and religious ceremonies. Because evergreens do not die in the winter, they came to symbolize eternal life.

Christmas dinner in the United States

Many Christmas customs in the United States have been adopted from those in the United Kingdom, although customs from other countries are also found. Accordingly, the mainstays of the English table are also found in the United States: roast turkey (or other poultry), beef, ham, or pork; stuffing or dressing, corn, squash, green beans, and mashed potatoes are common. Dessert often reflects the ethnic background of the participants, but examples include pumpkin pie, sugar cookies, fruitcake, apple pie, carrot cake, mince pie and so on. Children often help their parents in the kitchen making the meal and often get special sweet rewards, like popcorn balls.

The centerpiece of a sit-down meal varies on the tastes of the host but can be ham or roast beef, particularly since turkey is the mainstay at dinner for the American holiday of Thanksgiving in November, almost exactly one month earlier. Regional meals offer incredible diversity. For example, Hawaii has Turkey teriyaki and pork dishes, the latter a carryover from Polynesian and Asian traditions, and often seasoned accordingly with fresh pineapple or soy sauce concoctions. Virginia has oysters, ham pie, and fluffy biscuits, a nod to its very English 17th century founders. In some rural areas, game meats like wapiti or quail may grace the table, often prepared with recipes that are extremely old: it is likely that similar foodstuffs graced the tables of early American settlers on their first Christmases.

In the United States, it is increasingly not unheard of for people of very different ethnic backgrounds to gather around the table, especially on Christmas Eve when it is common to receive friends as guests and have parties. Thus, dishes that have been handed down over generations often mix at the table; a feast can include an old Neapolitan recipe for eel as a dish, a plate of black eyed peas (African-American origin) and desserts of French-Canadian origin. As the Christmas season often runs very close to Hannukah and the U.S. has an extremely large Jewish population, many Christian and Catholic Americans often invite their Jewish neighbors and friends over for dinner as a sign of goodwill and love: sometimes (and especially in families where more than one religion exists) one shall see a plate of latkes on the table and small bags of chocolate coins for the children alongside the candy canes.

(2) Thanksgiving Day

The earliest observance of Thanksgiving on this continent was with special services in Virginia as early as 1607. The first Thanksgiving Festival began on December 13th in 1621 at Plymouth, Massachusetts. It started as a harvest festival with the people thanking God for giving them sufficient crops. That first Thanksgiving celebration lasted three days with the people enthusiastically participating. On June 20, 1676 the town of Charlestown, Massachusetts issued the First Thanksgiving Proclamation. By unanimous vote the governing council instructed the clerk, Edward Rawson, to proclaim June 29th as a day of thanksgiving. George Washington issued the first national Thanksgiving proclamation in 1789, the year of his inauguration as President of the United States of America. He called for another Thanksgiving Day in 1795. With other presidents and state governors proclaiming days of thanksgiving at various times there was no effort to organize a yearly Thanksgiving Day until Mrs. Sarah Joseph Hale started her crusade in 1827. It took thirty-six years to achieve victory when, in 1863, President Abraham Lincoln made his Thanksgiving Day Proclamation. The nation has celebrated the special day ever since. Today Thanksgiving Day is a legal holiday with most government and private employees being given the day off. Some companies and most schools also shut down the following Friday. Yes, the United States of America, for most purposes, observes Thanksgiving Day. But, it appears that Thanksgiving Day, like most other national and religious holidays, has been highly commercialized, to the point that many people forget what we are supposed to be celebrating. As we approach Thanksgiving Day, let's not focus on the food, which are gifts. Let's focus on the giver. Let's thank God for all He has provided. Let's call on his name and invite him to be present at our table. Let's celebrate Thanksgiving Day with grateful hearts.

Part One

1. Preview Exercises

(1) Dictation

In the west today, the real meaning of Christmas is often forgotten. It has become a non-religious holiday! More children believe in Santa Claus than in Jesus. Christmas Day is a time for eating and drinking too much and watching television.

As a matter of fact, this biggest and best-loved holiday in the west is for celebrating the birth of Jesus Christ, the Savior of the world. According to the Bible, the holy book of Christians, God decided to allow his only son, Jesus Christ, to be born to a human mother and live on earth so that people could understand God better and learn to love God and each other more. "Christmas", meaning "celebration of Christ", honors the time when Jesus was born to a young Jewish woman, Mary.

(2) Questions

① Christmas has become a non-religious holiday! It is a time for eating and drinking too much and watching television.

② A young Jewish woman, Mary gave birth to Jesus.

2. Warming up Exercises

(1) See Cultural Background

(2) See Dictation in Preview Exercises

(3) Thanksgiving, Valentine's Day, Easter, etc.

3. Listening Material

Task 1

B   A

Task 2

A C A

Task 3

(1) was engaged to be married (2) virgin (3) pregnant

(4) righteous (5) break the engagement (6) disgrace

(7) go ahead with your marriage to Mary

(8) for he will save his people from their sins

(9) fulfill the Lord's message

(10) give birth to

4. Additional Listening Material

Task 1

B C

Task 2

D B B

Task 3

(1) Pilgrims (2) feast (3) surviving their first year in America

(4) being good citizens (5) what they are each thankful for

(6) organizes (7) share with those in need (8) preschool

(9) teach about the importance of sharing (10) strengthen

5. Video-aural Material

Task 1

B A

Task 2

B A C

Task 3

(1) universal memory

(2) the tree with all of the presents underneath it

(3) vivid images

(4) master of ceremonies of this visual feast

(5) more than 2000 years

(6) real figure

(7) kindness, help children and the poor

6. Listening Skills

Short conversations

(1) A　(2) B　(3) B　(4) B　(5) C　(6) D　(7) C　(8) B　(9) C　(10) B

Long conversations

Conversation 1 (1) D　(2) C　(3) B

Conversation 2 (1) B　(2) A　(3) C

Compound dictation

Passage 1

(1) quality　(2) investigated　(3) value　(4) familiar

(5) recommend　(6) perhaps　(7) additional

(8) Equivalent German models tend to be heavier and slightly less easy to use

(9) Similarly, it is smaller than most of its competitors, thus fitting easily into a pocket or a handbag

(10) The only problem was the slight awkwardness in loading the film

Passage 2

(1) mysterious　(2) coupled　(3) ruining　(4) percent

(5) species　(6) ensure　(7) average

(8) When you consider that equal a quarter of the world catch, you begin to see the sides of the problem

(9) some countries are beginning to deal with this problem

(10) it would make sense to give the fish enough time to recover, grow to full sizes and reproduce

Passage 3

(1) focused　(2) emotionally　(3) distant　(4) cancer

(5) retirement　(6) crossed　(7) increasingly

(8) Regardless of your age, you can make a number of important changes in your current lifestyle

(9) We know much more about preventive health today than our parents and grandparents

did in the past

(10) And this new knowledge can be transmitted to our children to help them become healthier than our generation

Part Two

1. Preview Exercises

(1) I think Christmas is one of the most important festivals in the western countries.

In my opinion, Christmas is a religious holiday.

My view is that Christmas in the west is as important as the Spring Festival in China. It is a great moment of people gathering and celebration for the birth of Jesus Christ.

First of all, I'll buy the presents for my family members.

Secondly, I'll decorate my house with different things, such as Christmas tree, flowers etc.

Finally, I'll have Christmas dinner with my family members to celebrate this important festival.

(2) Some people think we should attach more importance to Chinese traditional festivals rather than Christmas and other western festivals.

Others are willing to celebrate Christmas because they think Christmas is an important occasion on which people can get together with family members and exchange gifts and they can know more about western culture.

2. Warming up Exercises

(1) See *Cultural Background-Christmas Dinner*

(2) Christmas in America means different things to different people. To some people, Christmas means brightly wrapped packages under a decorated tree. To others, it means family reunions and a wonderful meal together. To Christians, it means Jesus' birthday. Christmas also means lending a helping hand to people in need. Along with all the hubbub of shopping for presents and sending Christmas cards, many people in America take time to help others.

(3) Both of them are very important traditional festivals. On both occasions, people will get

together with family members to have a grand dinner and make wishes for the next year. The ways of celebration are different. On Christmas Eve, parents will decorate the Christmas tree and put lots of presents under it, but on New Year's Eve, the elders will give money to children as a lunar New Year gift. The foods they have for dinner are different. In America, the main dish is turkey, but in China, it varies. For example, dumplings in the north.

3. Listening Material Review

Task 1

It is mainly about the birth story of Jesus Christ.

Task 2

(1) Joseph was a righteous person. Yes. When he knew his fiancée was pregnant, he decided to break the engagement quietly so as not to disgrace her publicly.

(2) It means he is the son of God.

(3) In the year 354, church leaders chose December 25 as his birthday.

Task 3

(1) Through listening to it, I have known something about Jesus' birth and meanings of AD and BC...

(2) "Joseph, son of David," the angel said, "Do not be afraid to go ahead with your marriage to Mary, for the child within her has been conceived by the Holy Spirit. And she will have a son, and you are to name him Jesus, for he will save his people from their sins. "

Task 4

(1) Mary was engaged to be married to Joseph, but while she was still a virgin, she became pregnant by the Holy Spirit.

(2) When Joseph woke up, he did what the angel of the Lord commanded.

(3) All returned to their towns to register for this census.

(4) And while they were there, the time came for her baby to be born.

4. Video-aural Material Review

Task 1

This clip is mainly about people's memory for Christmas.

Task 2

(1) Fat, jolly, chubby, big, generous and a good listener.

(2) Saint Nicholas, a 4th century monk in what is now Turkey, who is famous for his kindness. It's said that he gave away his wealth to help children and the poor.

(3) Some French nuns decided one year, baked some little treats, went by all the homes, put treats in the shoes of the little children and told them that Nicholas brought them for being good.

Task 3

(1) People's sweet memories for Christmas and the origin of Christmas.

(2) See *Scripts*

Task 4

(1) I really remember the lights, because that to me was the most magical.

(2) It's said that he gave away his wealth to help children and the poor.

(3) The date of Nicholas'death, December 6th, was honored every year with a popular feast.

(4) Saint Nicholas gradually became associated with the holiday as did the notion of a phantom gift giver who doled out rewards to the worthy.

5. Additional Video-aural Material

Task 1

The clip is mainly about the family's gathering at Thanksgiving Dinner and how to express their thanks to each other.

Task 2

(1) Thanksgiving was about Pilgrims, the first settlers in America who had the first harvest with the local Indians to give thanks to them.

(2) Because the Indians helped them to survive the first winter.

(3) All the family members showed thanks to others, such as Michelle, Susan, Robbie, Marilyn etc.

Task 3

(1) The family members on Thanksgiving Day. They all thanked other people for different reasons.

(2) Grandpa said, "I give thanks for being here with my family and for being well, so I can enjoy you all. " Susan said, " I'd like to give thanks for a healthy year, a good job, and for meeting Harry and Michelle. " Robbie said, " I'd like to give thanks for Grandpa coming to live with us. And I'd also like to thank my math teacher for giving me a passing grade. " And other family members expressed their thanks as well.

Task 4

(1) But first, I think we should take a moment and remember the meaning of Thanksgiving.

(2) I give thanks for being her with my family and for being well, so I can enjoy you all.

(3) I'd like to give thanks for a healthy year, a good job, and for meeting Harry and Michelle.

(4) I should thank you for encouraging me to keep working on my fashion designs.

Listening Scripts

Part One

1. Preview Exercises

In the west today, the real meaning of Christmas is often forgotten. It has become a non-religious holiday! More children believe in Santa Claus than in Jesus. Christmas Day is a time for eating and drinking too much and watching television.

As a matter of fact, this biggest and best-loved holiday in the west is for celebrating the birth of Jesus Christ, the Savior of the world. According to the Bible, the holy book of Christians, God decided to allow his only son, Jesus Christ, to be born to a human mother and live on earth so that people could understand God better and learn to love God and each other more. "Christmas", meaning "celebration of Christ", honors the time when Jesus was born to a young Jewish woman, Mary.

2. Listening Material

Now this is the story of how Jesus the "Messiah" was born. In Nazareth, a village in Galilee, his mother, Mary, was engaged to be married to Joseph. But while she was still a virgin, she became pregnant by the Holy Spirit. Joseph, her fiancé , being a righteous man, decided to break the engagement quietly, so as not to disgrace her publicly. As he considered this, he fell asleep, and an angel of the Lord appeared to him in a dream. "Joseph, son of David," the angel said, "Do not be afraid to go ahead with your marriage to Mary, for the child within her has been conceived by the Holy Spirit. And she will have a son, and you are to name him Jesus, for he will save his people from their sins. All of this happened to fulfill the Lord's message through his prophet: Look! The virgin will conceive a child! She will give birth to a son. And he will be called Immanuel. "

When Joseph woke up, he did what the angel of the Lord commanded.

At that time the Roman emperor, Augustus, decreed that a census should be taken throughout the Roman empire. All returned to their own towns to register for this census. And because Joseph was a descendant of King David, he had to go to Bethlehem in Judea, David's ancient home. He traveled there from the village of Nazareth in Galilee. He took with him Mary, who was obviously pregnant by this time. And while they were there, the time came for her baby to be born. She gave birth to her firstborn son, and wrapped him in swaddling cloths, and laid him in a manger, because there was no room for them in the inn.

Although the exact date of the birth of Jesus nearly 2000 years ago is not known, the calendar on the supposed date divides all time into B. C. , standing for "Before Christ" and A. D. , a Latin phrase, standing for "in the year of our Lord". For the first 300 years, Jesus' birthday was celebrated on different dates. Finally, in the year 354, church leaders chose December 25 as his birthday.

3. Additional Listening Material

This is the VOA Special English Education Report.

The fourth Thursday in November is Thanksgiving Day in the United States. Tradition says early English settlers known as the Pilgrims held the first celebration in 1621 in Plymouth,

Massachusetts. They invited local Indians to a feast to thank them for help in surviving their first year in America.

So what are schoolchildren learning these days about Thanksgiving?

Sharon Biros is a first-grade teacher in Clairton, Pennsylvania. Her students learn about the holiday as they discuss being good citizens. They read stories about the Indians and the Pilgrims. And the children tell what they are each thankful for.

Many of the families are poor. The school organizes a project in which students bring food and money to share with those in need.

Brook Levin heads a preschool in Broomall, Pennsylvania. She says the kids learn about native culture Thanksgiving, she says, is a good time to teach about the importance of sharing. The children make bread and other foods and invite their parents to school to enjoy them.

Thanksgiving is used as a time to strengthen a sense of community.

And that's the VOA Special English Education Report, written by Nancy Steinbach.

4. Video-aural Material

For most of us, the season evokes a kind of universal memory. My strongest memory of Christmas is the tree with all of the presents underneath it.

And usually in the morning I wake up really early like at five o'clock. And when you come downstairs Christmas morning and the trees lit up, there is piles of presents, there might be a bicycle, there are skis, there is all... there's stuff all over the place. I really remember the lights, because that to me was the most magical. And hearing just the Christmas music that you only hear that one time a year. There is just lots to be happy for. Is that what you ask from Santa? Yeah. Christmas comes with a host of vivid images that bombard us from all directions for entire season: candy canes and carolers, stockings and store windows, Nativity scenes and nutcrackers, not to mention entire neighborhoods that explode in a kaleidoscope of light and colors. Then on top of all that, throwing the art character who's the master of ceremonies of this visual feast. Santa Claus.

I'd describe him as fat and jolly.
Big, chubby.
A loving, very generous kind of guy.
A good listener, listens to requests.
I used to think that Santa Claus was probably one of the greatest people in the world. Merry Christmas!

Santa's origins go back more than 2000 years, but it took centuries of poetic embellishment and a few things lost in translation before the Santa that we know today emerged. The legend begins with a real figure, Saint Nicholas, a 4th century monk in what is now Turkey, who is famous for his kindness. It's said that he gave away his wealth to help children and the poor. He believed in, in helping others and doing it secretly, secret giving.

Tim Connaghan, who plays Santa in movies and TV, has studied the evolution of Saint Nicholas from monk to myth. Nicholas was a bishop by the time he died around 350 AD, he was later canonized as a saint and became a revered symbol of generosity throughout Europe and beyond.

There were so many churches, cathedrals and religious locations named after Nicholas. It was a very remarkable thing. The Greek adopted him as a patron saint. The Russians adopted him as a patron saint.

The date of Nicholas' death, December 6th, was honored every year with a popular feast. But in 12th century France, the celebration took on a new twist that quickly became part of the tradition.

Some French nuns decide one year, bake some little treats, go by all the homes, put treats in the shoes of the little children and tell them that Nicholas brought them for being good. And over the next hundred, two hundred years, more people pick up on this idea of giving something to the children.

Because of the proximity of his feast day to Christmas, Saint Nicholas gradually became associated with the holiday as did the notion of a phantom gift giver who doled out rewards to the worthy.

5. Listening Skills

Short conversations

(1) W: Carol told us on the phone not to worry about her. Her left leg doesn't hurt as much as it did yesterday.

M: She'd better have it examined by a doctor anyway. And I will call her about it this evening.

Q: What does the man think Carol should do?

(2) M: Excuse me, I am looking for the textbook by a Professor Jordon for the marketing course.

W: I am afraid it's out of stock. You'll have to order it. And it will take the publisher 3 weeks to send it to us.

Q: Where did this conversation most probably take place?

(3) W: I ran into Sally the other day. I could hardly recognize her. Do you remember her from high school?

M: Yeah, she was a little out of shape back then. Well, has she lost a lot of weight?

Q: What does the man remember of Sally?

(4) M: Did you really give away all your furniture when you moved into the new house last month?

W: Just the useless pieces, as I am planning to purchase a new set from I taly for the sitting room only.

Q: What does the woman mean?

(5) M: In my opinion, watching the news on TV is a good way to learn English. What do you think?

W: It would be better if you could check the same information in English newspapers afterwards.

Q: What does the woman say about learning English?

(6) W: You've sold your car. You don't need one?

M: Not really. I've never liked driving anyway. Now we've moved to a place near the subway entrance. We can get about quite conveniently.

Q: What do we learn from the conversation?

(7) M: What do you think of the prospects for online education? Is it going to replace the traditional school?

W: I doubt it. Schools are here to stay, because there are much more than just book learning. Even though more and more kids are going online, I believe fewer of them will quit school altogether.

Q: What does the woman think of the conventional schools?

(8) M: Mary, would you join me for dinner tonight?

W: You treated me last weekend. Now, it's my turn. Shall we try something Italian?

Q: What do we learn from the conversation?

(9) W: Listen to me, Joe, the exam is already a thing of the past. Just forget about it.

M: That's easier said than done.

Q: What can we infer from the conversation?

(10) M: Do you still keep in touch with your parents regularly after all these years?

W: Yes, of course. I call them at weekends when the rates are down fifty percent.

Q: What do we learn about the woman from the conversation?

Long conversations

Conversation 1

W: Hey, Bob, guess what? I'm going to visit Quebec next summer. I'm invited to go to a friend's wedding. But while I'm there I'd also like to do some sightseeing.

M: That's nice, Shelly. But do you mean the province of Quebec, or Quebec City?

W: I mean the province. My friend's wedding is in Montreal. I'm going there first. I'll stay for five days. Is Montreal the capital city of the province?

M: Well, Many people think so because it's the biggest city. But it's not the capital. Quebec City is. But Montreal is great. The Saint Royal River runs right through the middle of the city. It's beautiful in summer.

W: Wow, and do you think I can get by in English? My French is OK, but not that good. I know most people there speak French, but can I also use English?

M: Well, People speak both French and English there. But you'll hear French most of the time. And all the street signs are in French. In fact, Montreal is the third largest French speaking city in the world. So you'd better practice your French before you go.

W: Good advice. What about Quebec City? I'll visit a friend from college who lives there now. What's it like?

M: It's a beautiful city, very old. Many old buildings have been nicely restored. Some of them were built in the 17th or 18th centuries. You'll love there.

W: Fantastic. I can't wait to go.

Q: What's the woman's main purpose of visiting Quebec?

What does the man advise the woman to do before the trip?

What does the man say about the Quebec City?

Conversation 2

M: Sarah, you work in the admission's office, don't you?

W: Yes, I'm, I've been here for 10 years as an assistance director.

M: Really? What does that involve?

W: Well, I'm in charge of all the admissions of post graduate students in the university.

M: Only post graduates?

W: Yes, post graduates only. I have nothing at all to do with undergraduates.

M: Do you find that you get a particular... sort of different national groups? I mean you get larger numbers from Latin America or...

W: Yes, well, of all the students enrolled last year, nearly half were from overseas. They were from the African countries, the far east, the middle east and Latin America.

M: Ehm, but have you been doing just that for the last 10 years or have you done other things?

W: Well, I've been doing the same job, ehm, before that I was a secretary of the medical school at Birmingham, and further back I worked in the local government.

M: Oh, I see.

W: So I've done different types of things.

M: Yes, indeed. How do you imagine your job might develop in the future? Can you imagine shifting into a different kind of responsibility or doing something...

W: Oh, yeah, from October 1st I'll be doing an entirely different job. There is going to be more committee work. I mean, more policy work, and less dealing with students unfortunately. I'll miss my contact with students.

Q: What is the woman's present position?

What do we learn about the post graduates enrolled last year in the woman's university?

What will the woman's new job be like?

Compound dictation

Passage 1

There are a lot of good cameras available at the moment-most of these are made in Japan but there are also good quality models from Germany and the USA. We have investigated a range of different models to see which is the best value for money. After a number of different tests and interviews with people who are familiar with the different cameras being assessed, our researchers recommend the Olympic BY model as the best auto-focus camera available at the moment. It costs $200 although you may well want to spend more-perhaps as much as another $200-on buying additional lenses and other equipment. It is a good Japanese camera, easy to use. Equivalent German models tend to be heavier and slightly less easy to use, whereas the American versions are considerably more expensive. The Olympic BY model weighs only 320 grams which is quite a bit less than other cameras of a similar type. Indeed one of the other models we looked at weighed almost twice as much. Similarly, it is smaller than most of its competitors, thus fitting easily into a pocket or a handbag. All the people we interviewed expressed almost total satisfaction with it. The only problem was the slight awkwardness in loading the film.

Passage 2

It's difficult to imagine the sea ever running out of fish. It's so vast, so deep, so mysterious. Unfortunately, it's not bottomless. Over-fishing, coupled with destructive fishing practices, is killing off the fish and ruining their environment.

Destroy the fish, and you destroy the fishermen's means of living. At least 60 percent of the world's commercially important fish species are already over-fished, or fished to the limit. As a result, governments have had to close down some areas of sea to commercial fishing.

Big, high-tech fleets ensure that everything in their path is pulled out of water. Anything too small, or the wrong thing, is thrown back either dead or dying. That's an average of more than 20 million metric tons every year.

When you consider that equal a quarter of the world catch, you begin to see the sides of the problem.

In some parts of the world, for every kilogram of prawns (对虾) caught, up to 15 kilograms of unsuspecting fish and other marine wildlife die, simply for being in the wrong place at the wrong time.

True, some countries are beginning to deal with this problem, but it is vital we find rational ways of fishing. Before every ocean becomes a dead sea, it would make sense to give the fish enough time to recover, grow to full sizes and reproduce, then catch them in a way that doesn't kill other innocent sea life.

Passage 3

If you are a young college student, most of your concerns about your health and happiness in life are probably focused on the present. Basically, you want to feel good physically, mentally, and emotionally now. You probably don't spend much time worrying about the distant future, such as whether you will develop heart disease, or cancer, how you will take care of yourself in your retirement years, or how long you are going to live. Such thoughts may have crossed your mind once in a while. However, if you are in your thirties, forties, fifties, or older, such health related thoughts are likely to become increasingly important to you.

Regardless of your age, you can make a number of important changes in your current lifestyle, that will help you feel better physically and mentally. Recently researchers have found that , even in late adulthood, exercise, strength training with weights, and better food can help elderly individuals significantly improve their health and add happiness to their life. We know much more about preventive health today than our parents and grandparents did in the past, giving us the opportunity to avoid some of health problems that have troubled them. And this new knowledge can be transmitted to our children to help them become healthier than our generation.

Part Two

Additional Video-aural Material

Philip: OK, everybody.

I want to welcome Harry and his daughter Michelle to Thanksgiving with us.

Harry: Thank you, Dr. Stewart.

Philip: Call me Philip.

Harry: OK.

Philip: But first, I think we should take a moment and remember the meaning of Thanksgiving.

Harry: Philip, I took Michelle to a school play about the first Thanksgiving.

Philip: Well, why don't you tell us about that, Michelle?

Michelle: Thanksgiving was about the Pilgrims, the first settlers in America. They shared the first harvest with the Indians and gave thanks.

Philip: All right. Then in that spirit let each of us give thanks. Each in his own way. Who wants to begin?

Grandpa: I will. I give thanks for being here with my family and for being well, so I can enjoy you all.

Robbie: All right! We love you, Grandpa.

Susan: I'd like to give thanks for a healthy year, a good job, and for meeting Harry and Michelle.

Harry: We'd like to give thanks for meeting Susan and the Stewart family.

Michelle: I love you, Daddy.

Susan: Thanks, Harry. That was very kind of you.

Robbie: I'd like to give thanks for Grandpa coming to live with us.
  And I'd also like to thank my math teacher for giving me a passing grade. And call me, Alexandra.

Ellen: Oh, Robbie! She'll call.

Richard: You go first, Marilyn.

Marilyn: I'm thinking. You go first.

Richard: Well, you all know I'm working on my photo album. It's not finished yet. And I'd like to thank Marilyn for being so patient.

Marilyn: Thanks, Richard. I should thank you for encouraging me to keep working on my fashion designs. I'm lucky to have a husband with an artistic eye.

Ellen: Oh, we have a lot to be thankful for. For the food on this table. Just like the Pilgrims.

Philip: I'll go along with that, Ellen.

Ellen: Well, help me serve, Robbie.

Translation of the Listening Materials

Part One

1. Preview Exercises

在今日的西方社会，圣诞节的真正涵义已逐渐被人们遗忘。它已变成了一个非宗教的节日！比之基督，更多的孩子们信仰圣诞老人。圣诞节是一个让人们大吃大喝，看电视的日子。

事实上，这个西方社会最大且最受欢迎的节日是为了庆祝耶稣·基督——救世主的诞生的。根据《圣经》——基督徒的圣书记载，上帝决定让他唯一的儿子，耶稣·基督由人类母亲生产并住在凡间，从而使人们更了解上帝，学会去敬爱上帝和彼此。"圣诞"，指的是"庆祝基督"，是对年轻的犹太母亲玛丽产下基督这一时刻的敬意。

2. Listening Material

现在这个就是"救世主"耶稣如何诞生的故事。在拿撒勒，加利利的一个村庄里，他的母亲玛丽与约瑟夫订婚了。但当她还是个处女的时候，她已因圣灵而怀有身孕。约瑟夫，她那正直的未婚夫，决定偷偷的废除婚约，为的是不让她在公众面前受辱。正当他考虑这个的时候，他睡着了，在梦中，一个上帝的天使出现了。"约瑟夫，大卫之子，"天使说道，"不要害怕去兑现你与玛丽的婚约，因她肚里的孩子是拜圣灵所赐。她将会有个儿子，而你将给他取名耶稣，因他将会把人们从他们的罪孽中解救出来。所有这些发生的事是通过上帝的先知来实现的他的旨意：看哪！处女将怀有身孕！她将诞下男婴，而这孩子将被称作以马利。"

约瑟夫醒来后，他按照上帝的天使所要求的去做了。

与此同时，古罗马君主奥古斯塔斯宣布，整个古罗马帝国应进行人口普查。所有居民需回到所属市镇做人口普查登记。而因为约瑟夫是大卫国王的后裔，他不得不回到大卫的老家，位于朱迪亚的伯利恒。他从加利利的拿撒勒出发。带着此时已明显怀有身孕的玛丽。当他们到达伯利恒时，她的孩子要出生了。因为旅店里没地方了，她产下第一个儿子，将他裹在褓褓中并放在马槽里。

尽管 2000 多年前耶稣诞生的具体日子无人知晓，但日历上还是根据假定的日期将所有时间分为代表"耶稣诞生前"的公元前和在拉丁短语中代表"上帝之年"的公元。

在刚开始的 300 年间，耶稣的生日在不同的日子里被庆祝着。最终，在 354 年，教堂领袖选择 12 月 25 日作为他的生日。

3. Additional Listening Material

这里是美国之音慢速英语教育报道。

美国十一月的第四个周四是感恩节。传统记载，英国早期移民者，即被人们所认知的朝圣者于 1621 年在马萨诸萨州的普利茅斯举行了第一次庆祝。他们邀请了当地的印第安人来到盛宴上以感谢他们帮助自己度过在美国的第一年。

那么现在学校的孩子们在学习感恩节的什么呢？

莎伦·拜勒斯是宾夕法尼亚州 Clairton 的一位一年级老师。她的学生在讨论做模范市民时了解到这个节日。她们阅读了关于印度人和朝圣者的故事。然后孩子们说出了她们每个人感到感激的事情。

许多家庭都很贫困。学校组织了一次活动，让孩子们带着食物和钱去分享给那些需要它们的人分享。

布鲁克·拉文掌管一所位于宾夕法尼亚州 Broomall 的幼儿园。她说孩子们了解了当地的感恩节文化，她说，这是个好机会去教育孩子们，使其懂得分享的重要性。孩子们做了面包和其他食物，然后邀请他们的家长来到学校与他们共享这些食物。

感恩节被视为是加强人们集体荣誉感的一个节日。

以上是由南茜·斯丁拜斯撰写的美国之音慢速英语教育报道。

4. Video-aural Material

对于大多数人，这个季节能唤起一种的普遍性的记忆。我最强烈的圣诞节记忆是圣诞树下会是礼物。

通常我都会在清晨五点的样子就早早地醒来。当你在圣诞节的早晨下楼来时，圣诞树已被点亮，那儿有成堆的礼物，也许会有辆自行车，也会有滑雪板，无所不有……整个地方都堆满了东西。我真切地记得那些灯，只因为那对我来说是最神奇的。也会听到那每年才听得到一次的圣诞音乐。有很多值得高兴的东西。那是你向圣诞老人要的东西吗？是啊。圣诞节带来了一大群各方面的生动景象，足以让我们整整狂轰一个季节：糖果，袜子和商店的橱窗，基督诞生的景象和胡桃钳，更别说整个邻里都被千变万化的灯和色彩围爆了。还有，最高潮的环节，就是这场视觉盛宴的始作俑者——对诞老人的登场。

我会将他描述成为肥肥的，开心的，

巨大的，胖嘟嘟的。

一个有爱心的，大方善良的人。

一个绝佳的倾听者，听人们的要求。

我时常想圣诞老人大概算得上是这世上最伟大的人之一了吧。圣诞快乐！

圣诞老人的源头可追溯到 2000 多年前，但却花了几个世纪的诗词润饰，还有部分翻译失传才有了我们今天所熟知的圣诞老人形象的出现。传说始于一个真人，圣尼古拉斯，他是在现今土耳其的一个以善心闻名的四世纪时期的僧人。传说他将自己的财产都布施给了孩子和穷人。他信仰帮助别人并且是悄悄地做善事，悄悄地给予。

提姆·康那根，在电影和电视中出演圣诞老人的演员，研究了圣尼古拉斯从僧人到传奇人物的发展路程。在约公元 350 年尼古拉斯逝世时他是当时的大主教，不久后他被封为圣人并成为整个欧洲及其他地区尊崇的慷慨精神的象征。

有很多的教会，教堂和宗教机构都以他的名字命名。这确实是件不寻常的事。希腊人和俄国人都奉其为守护神圣者。

尼古拉斯逝世的日子，12 月 6 日，每年都会举办宴会以缅怀。但是在 12 世纪的法国，这种庆祝呈现出了一种新的形态并迅速成为法国的传统。

一些法国修女决定每年都烘烤一些甜食，走访到每家每户，将甜食放进小孩子们的鞋子里并告诉她们尼古拉斯因为她们表现的好给他们带来了这些东西。在接下来的一百年，两百年间，越来越多的人沿袭了这个给孩子们东西的传统。

因为举行盛宴的日子和圣诞节很接近，圣尼古拉斯逐渐因其向值得奖励的人发放奖品的神圣的幽灵礼物赠送者的身份而与这个节日联系起来。

Part Two

Additional Video-aural Material

Philip：好啦，各位。我想对 Harry 和他女儿 Michelle 来参加我们的感恩节晚餐表示
　　　　欢迎。

Harry：谢谢你，Stewart 大夫。

Philip：叫我 Philip。

Harry：好的。

Philip：不过首先，我想我们应该用一两分钟来追忆一下感恩节的意义。

Harry：Philip，我带 Michelle 看过学校演出的第一次感恩节历史剧。

Philip：那好，能否给我们讲一讲，Michelle？

Michelle：感恩节是关于清教徒的，他们是第一批来美国定居的移民。他们与印第安人

分享首次收获并向他们表示感激。

Philip：很正确。现在本着同样的心意让我们开始感恩。每个人用自己的方式来表达。谁先开始？

Grandpa：我来。我感谢能在这里和家人同住而且很健康，让我享受到你们大家的温馨。

Robbie：太好了！我们爱你，爷爷。

Susan：我感谢这一年来身体健康，工作顺利，并且认识了 Harry 和 Michelle。

Harry：我们要感谢认识了 Susan 和 Stewart 一家人。

Michelle：我爱你，爸爸。

Susan：谢谢你，Harry。你真好。

Robbie：我感谢爷爷到这儿和我们一起生活。我还要感谢我的数学老师给我及格分数。还有，打电话给我，Alexandra。

Ellen：啊，Robbie！她会打的。

Richard：你先讲，Marilyn。

Marilyn：我还在想。你先来。

Richard：好吧，你们都知道我正在进行我的影集。现在还没有完成。我要感谢 Marilyn 没有不耐烦。

Marilyn：谢谢你，Richard。我应该感谢你一直鼓励我继续我的服装设计工作。我很庆幸，我丈夫具有艺术的眼光。

Ellen：啊，我们有很多需要感谢的事情。感谢这桌上的丰盛食物。就像早年清教徒那样。

Philip：我也有同感，Ellen。

Ellen：好，帮我分菜，Robbie。

I Background Knowledge

1. Language Points

Preview Exercises

(1) **environmentalist** n. people who are enthusiastic about environ-mental protection/环保主义者

e. g. The environmentalist launched out at great length on energy preservation.

(2) **Palo Alto City** n. a small city of America in western California, southeast of Sanfrancisco/帕洛阿图市

e. g. The world famous university Stanford is located in the Palo Alto City.

Listening Material

(1) **guideline** n. a light drawn as a guide for further writing, action, opinion, etc./准则,指导方针

e. g. The government should issue clear guideline on the control of milk product.

(2) **beneficial** adj. promoting or enhancing well-being/有益的

e. g. I am sure, China will be more powerful than it is to-day, and that will be beneficial to world peace.

Additional Listening Material

(1) **purify** v. remove impurities from / increase the concentration of / and separate through the process of distillation/使纯净, 洁净

e. g. They open the windows to purify the air of the room.

(2) **convert** v. change/转化为

e. g. Let sadness convert to joy.

(3) **evaporate** v. lose or cause to lose liquid by vaporization leaving a more concentrated residue/使……蒸发

e. g. The water soon evaporated in the sunshine.

(4) **transform into** change or alter in form, appearance, or nature/把……转变成……

e. g. The sofa can transform into a bed.

(5) **release**   v.   let (something) fall or spill a container/释放

　　　　　　　　e. g. After my examination I had a feeling of release.

(6) **be incorporated into**   make into a whole or make part of a whole incorporate/被吸纳
进入；被合为一体

　　　　　　　　e. g. Many of your suggestions have been incorporated in the
new plan.

(7) **in a mad rush**   a strong passion for doing sth/疯狂地追求……

　　　　　　　　e. g. Many girls are in a mad rush to lose weight.

Additional Video-aural Material

(1) **pop in**   to visit sb suddenly/突然出现

　　　　　　　　e. g. She often pops in for coffee.

(2) **chock-full**   packed full to capacity/充满，塞满

　　　　　　　　e. g. A report, chock-full of errors, failed to get high marks.

(3) **once and for all**   in a conclusive way/一劳永逸的

　　　　　　　　e. g. John's back home once and for all.

2. Cultural Background

(1) The causes and consequences of Global Warming

Scientists have determined that a number of human activities are contributing to global war-ming by adding excessive amounts of greenhouse gases to the atmosphere. Greenhouse goses such as carbon dioxide accumulate in the atmosphere and trap heat that normally would exit into outer space.

Greenhouse Gases and Global Warming

While many greenhouse gases occur naturally and are needed to create the greenhouse effect that keeps the earth warm enough to support life, human use of fossil fuels is the main source of excess greenhouse gases. By driving cars, using electricity from coal-fired power plants, or heating our homes with oil or natural gas, we release carbon dioxide and other heat-trap-ping gases into the atmosphere. Deforestation is another significant source of greenhouse ga-ses, because fewer trees means less carbon dioxide conversion to oxygen.

During the 150 years of the industrial age, the atmospheric concentration of carbon dioxide has increased by 31 percent. Over the same period, the level of atmospheric methane has risen by 151 percent, mostly from agricultural activities such as raising cattle and growing rice.

The Consequences of Global Warming

As the concentration of greenhouse gases grows, more heat is trapped in the atmosphere and less escapes back into space. This increase in trapped heat changes the climate and alters weather patterns, which may hasten species extinction, influence the length of seasons, cause coastal flooding, and lead to more frequent and severe storms.

(2) Green roof

A green roof is a roof of a building that is partially or completely covered with vegetation and soil, or a growing medium, planted over a waterproofing membrane. This does not refer to roofs which are merely colored green, as with green roof shingles. It may also include additional layers such as a root barrier and drainage and irrigation systems.

The term green roof may also be used to indicate roofs that use some form of "green" technology, such as solar panels or a photovoltaic module. Green roofs are also referred to as eco-roofs, vegetated roofs, living roofs, and green roofs.

(3) Famous movies about environmental protection:

An Inconvenient Truth 《不能被掩盖的真相》

An Inconvenient Truth is a 2006 documentary film about global warming directed by Davis Guggenheim, presented by former United States Vice President Al Gore. The film premiered at the 2006 Sundance Film Festival and opened in New York and Los Angeles on May 24, 2006. The film was released on DVD by Paramount Home Entertainment on November 21, 2006. A companion book by Gore, *An Inconvenient Truth*: The Planetary Emergency of Global Warming and What We Can Do About It, reached on the paperback nonfiction New York Times bestseller list on July 2, 2006. The documentary won Academy Awards for Best Documentary Feature and for Best Original Song.

Earning $49 million at the box office worldwide, An Inconvenient Truth is the fourth-highest-grossing documentary film to date in the United States (in nominal dollars, from 1982 to the present), after Fahrenheit 9/11, March of the Penguins, and Sicko.

Erin Brockovich《永不妥协》

Erin Brockovich—Ellis (born June 22, 1960) is an American legal clerk and environmental activist who, despite the lack of a formal law school education, was instrumental in constructing a case against the Pacific Gas and Electric Company (PG&E) of California in 1993. Since the release of the movie that shares her story and name, she has hosted Challenge America with *Erin Brockovich* on ABC and Final Justice on Lifetime. She is the president of Brockovich Research & Consulting, a consulting firm. She is currently working as a consultant for the New York law firm Weitz & Luxenberg, which has a focus on personal injury claims for asbestos exposure.

(4) Sasakawa

The UNEP Sasakawa Prize was established in 1982, upon the initiative and with funds provided by Mr Ryoichi, Chairman of the Japan Shipbuilding Industry Foundation and President of the Sasakawa Memorial Health Foundation.

The Sasakawa Health Prize consists of a statuette and a sum of the order of US $ 200000 to be given to one or more persons, institutions or nongovernmental organizations having accomplished outstanding innovative work in health development, in order to encourage the further development of such work.

联合国环境规划署（UNEP）环境奖　已经设立了 20 余年，由联合国和日本 Sasakawa 同名基金会共同推出的。按照联合国的年度生态大事记计划，用 20 万美金来奖励那些有关环保各方面主题项目的创意。

(5) Some useful websites on environmental protection
　　http://www.ep.net.cn 中国环保网
　　http://www.epa.gov 美国官方环保网
　　http://www.environmental-protection.org.uk 英国官方环保网

Reference Key

Part One

1. Preview Exercises

1. Dictation: (See *scripts*)

2. Questions:

(1) My family and I usually take bus /subway/light rail/ferry/taxi/private car/motor to go to school/work.

I think public transportation should be advocated because it is environmental-friendly, as well as economic. If we have an advanced public transportation system, then everyone will feel great to take buses instead of private cars.

I think private transportation should be advocated because it is comfortable and time-saving. What's more, applying private transportation is an important feature of modern life. If we want to live a casual, efficient and convenient life, why not use cars instead of buses?

(2)

	Public Transportation	Private Transportation
Advantages	cheap, economic, safe, environmental-friendly, space-saving...	convenient, comfortable, time-saving, fast ...
Disadvantages	noisy, crowded, tiring, inconvenient, time-consuming...	expensive, dangerous, contaminative, no place for parking...

2. Warming up Exercises

A brief introduction to environmental protection

(1) Common natural disasters and their causes.

NAME	CAUSES	EXAMPLES
Earthquakes	The discharge of stress accumulated along geologic faults	① The 2004 Indian Ocean earthquake, the second largest earthquake in recorded history which cost the lives of at least 229000 people. ② The 7. 9 magnitude May 12, 2008 Sichuan earthquake in Sichuan Province, China. Death toll at over 61150.
Floods	Tropical cyclones	① The Great Flood of 1993 was one of the most costly floods in the history of United States. ② The 1998 Yangtze River Floods, also in China, left 14 million people homeless.
Tsunamis	Undersea earthquakes	Ao Nang, Thailand (2004). The 2004 Indian Ocean Earthquake created the Boxing Day Tsunami and disaster at this site.
Droughts	Depletion of precipitation over time	① 1928-30, northwest Chinaresulting in over 3 million deaths by famine. ② 1900, India, killing between 250000 and 3. 25 million.
Heat waves	Long Hours of Sunshine Reduction of Atmospheric Moisture Dry landscape High Humidity at the Earth's surface	The worst heat wave in recent history was the European Heat Wave of 2003.

(2) Famous modern environmental protection movements in America.

1952		David Brower became the first Executive Director of the Sierra Club. Under his leadership, the Club became America's foremost environmental protection organization.
1965		The Sierra Club brought suit to protect New York's Storm King Mountain from a power project. The case established a precedent, allowing the Club standing for a non-economic interest in the case.

1969		Santa Barbara Oil Spill-Oil from Union Oil's offshore wells fouled beaches in Southern California and aroused public anger against pollution.
1969		National Environmental Policy Act passed and Environmental Protection Agency created.
1970		Clean Air Act passed, greatly expanding protection began by the Air Pollution Control Act of 1955 and the first Clean Air Act of 1963.
1970	April 22	Earth Day
1978	August	President Carter declared an emergency at Love Canal. The Love Canal scandal alerted the country to the long-term, hidden dangers of pollution of soil and groundwater.
1997	Dec. 10	A 23-year-old woman named Julia Butterfly Hill climbed into a 55-meter (180 foot) tall California Coast Redwood tree. Her aim was to prevent the destruction of the tree and of the forest where it had lived for a millennium.
2005	Feb. 16	Kyoto Protocol comes into effect. Almost all countries in the world are now pledged to reduce the emission of gasses that contribute to global warming.

3. Listening Material

Task 1

A   D

Task 2

C   B   D

Task 3

(1) guidelines   (2) lessen   (3) quantities

(4) tube   (5) electrical   (6) treasure

(7) Giving away items not only helps another person but also helps the environment.

(8) batteries   (9) recyclable   (10) beneficial

4. Additional Listening Material

Task 1

B   A

Task 2

D   B   C

Task 3

(1) pressing   (2) deforesting   (3) global warming

(4) ecosystem   (5) purify   (6) convert

(7) evaporate   (8) vital   (9) transformed

(10) resulting in the release of greenhouse gases into the atmosphere

5. Video-aural Material

Task 1

B   A

Task 2

B   C   D

Task 3

(1) natural building resources

(2) continue the tradition; environmental advantages

(3) tied around the edges of the house

(4) 150 square meters of grass roofing; oxygen

(5) new art style; old fashion

6. Listening Skills

Sample practice

Who: Huey Johnson

What: The United Nations Sasakawa Environment Prize

When: 2001

How and why: Protect the earth's natural resources; create

programs designed to save water, reduce energy

use and car pollution.

Additional training

Who: Mr. Johnson

Identity: An official in charge of natural resources in California

When: Early 1980s

What programs: Statewide programs to save natural resources such as water, forest

and soil

One of them is called Investing for Prosperity

Details of this program :

Function: To invest money to protect California's natural resources

Influence: A model for other countries

Major success: The development of Renewable Energy Technologies

Honor: President's Award for Sustainable Development in 1996

Part Two

1. Preview Exercises

(1)

For the purpose of protecting environmental / reducing air pollution/ diminishing water pollution...I think:

We are not allowed to cut down trees which can help purify the air.

Human beings can't neglect the present environmental problems which are mostly caused by ourselves.

People shouldn't build inefficient factories which may release gas /waste water into the air/river.

It's wrong for us to cut down trees only for short-term profits.

In order to protect our environment/ purify the air/ clean our rivers and lakes, I think we can do as follows:

We have to pay much attention to/ focus on/ face the environmental problems without any delay.

Human beings are supposed to invent more high-efficient/ energy-saving/ environmental-friendly equipments.

People must say no to / refuse those inefficient factories or industries.

It's compulsory for us to take relevant measures immediately to redeem what we have done in the past.

(2) Permission: may/ can/ be permitted/allowed to...

Obligation: must, have to, be supposed to, need to, it's necessary/compulsory for sb to...

Prohibition: can't, mustn't, shouldn't, be not allowed/permitted/supposed to, Absence of obligation: needn't, don't have to, it's not compulsory for sb. to

2. Warming up Exercises

(1) With an age of around 4. 5 billion years accepted by scientists, our mother earth is seriously ill now. In the past, the earth mother with the sweet milk fed on numerous children and grandchildren. However, for human self-interest, she is and will be tortured. The Earth is facing severe environmental crisis. "Save the Earth" has become the people's strongest voices of the world.

(2) Everything we do in everyday life is connected with the environment. The waste of energy: usually, some small habits lead to the waste of energy. For example, we keep the water on when we're brushing our teeth. We keep the lights on sometimes even if we can see things clearly or there's nobody at home. Some unnecessary household appliances were launched always. These are all waste of resources.

(3) To protect the environment, governments of many countries have done a lot. Legislative steps have been introduced to control air pollution, to protect the forest and sea resources and to stop any environmental pollution. Therefore, governments are playing the most important role in the environmental protection today.

In my opinion, to protect environment, the government must take even more effective measures. First, it should let people fully realize the importance of environmental protection through education. Second, much more efforts should be made to put the birth control policies into practice, because bigger population means less clean water and fresh air or worse environment for us to live. Finally, those who destroy the environment intentionally should be severely punished. We should let them know that destroying environment means destroying mankind themselves.

3. Listening Material Review

Task 1

Reduce, Reuse, Recycle.

Task 2

(1) —Being informed about the negative influence on environment caused by the products.

—Bulk buying when possible, but don't buy more than you can use.

—Choose products with less packaging.

—Choose products with recyclable or reusable packaging.

—Carry reusable shopping bags or boxes.

—Say "no" to unnecessary plastic bags and other packaging.

—Reuse plastic bags and all types of containers over and over again.

—Buy goods with good and endurable quality.

—Warn manufacturers of their responsibilities for environmental protection.

(2) —Look for products in reusable, refillable or recyclable packaging when you shop.

—Donate unwanted clothing, furniture and white goods to charities.

—Enquire if goods can be repaired rather than replaced.

—Hold a garage sale.

—Use rechargeable batteries rather than single-use batteries and ask your local council about how to dispose of batteries properly.

—Use retreaded tires if they are appropriate to your driving.

—Use glass bottles and jars, plastic bags, aluminum foil and take away food containers over and over again before recycling or disposing of them.

—Carry your lunch in a reusable container rather than disposable wrappings.

—Reuse envelopes and use both sides of paper.

(3) Yes, I have recycled glass/plastic/paper/aluminum and other metals before. We can save paper by using old newspaper, to use it for wrapping gifts: The Sunday comics for kids presents, style section for housewarming, bridal section for a shower gift or financial section for a graduation gift.

Task 3

(1) I think it is very impressive. Environmental protection is not something far away that people needn't worry about. Actually, it is something we can do through daily efforts.

(2) This passage tells us how to protect our environment through daily efforts. If we all pay attention to what we do in daily life, we can simply reduce the waste by 50%. The key words are "reduce, reuse, recycle", which means to reduce how much we use, and make full use of what we already have. In general, wisely using the things we have will not only help us save money but also help to save our earth.

Task 4

(1) By following the simple guidelines-"Reduce, Reuse, Recycle", we can make good use of what we have and lessen the amount of waste and pollution.

(2) For example, buying a large tube of toothpaste or a large bottle of dish soap instead of a small one helps reduce waste.

(3) Secondly, we should reuse what we have. Instead of throwing something away, we might give it away.

(4) Reducing, reusing, and recycling are not only beneficial to us but will also be for the generations to come.

4. Video-aural Material Review

Task 1

It is about how and why people build grass roofs in Faroe Island.

Task 2

(1) Maybe the grass-roofs are brought by Vikings or monks, but we have no ideas about it.

(2) The grass-roofs can protect the environment. For example, it can filter pollutants and CO_2 out of the air and produce more oxygen. What's more, they are very beautiful.

(3) Bill Clinton admired the grass-roofs very much and highly praised it. He thought Faroe

Island has set a good example for the rest of world. Because the climate change can't be avoided by everyone on the earth.

Task 3

(1) I think people in Faroe Island are full of responsibilities and wisdom. They can combine environmental protection with beauty together. If I have a chance, I'd like to have my own green grass roof too.

(2) People in Faroe Island keep the tradition of building houses with grass roofs. It is said that because of rare natural building resources, the Vikings used grass on their roofs to provide stability and extra insulation. However, young people there are still interested in green grass roofs, not only because it is beautiful, but also for the purpose of protecting the environment. Even the former US president Bill Clinton praised it highly.

Task 4

(1) Walk through any town or village in the Faroe Islands, located between Iceland and Scotland, and it will be hard not to notice the green grass roofed houses on every street.

(2) Yore says having a grass roof is a way for people on the islands to take responsibility for the environment.

(3) Last fall, former U. S. president Bill Clinton visited the Faroe's capital for a conference, and spoke on the effects of climate change.

(4) All over America we're in a mad rush to green all of our roofs, to put vegetation on our roofs, to cut down on the electric cost and the CO_2 emissions that come from having inefficient buildings.

5. Additional Video-aural Material

Task 1

The causes of Global warming.

Task 2

(1) Susie's ice-cream was melted because of the high temperature caused by global warming.

(2) The phrase "pop in" means to visit someone occasionally or suddenly.

  e. g. She often pops in for coffee.

(3) Literally it means that the problem can be resolved in a conclusive way. No, the problem of global warming can't be solved simply by constantly putting giant ice cube into the sea. If we want to get rid of greenhouse gases, we have to take many measures from

now on. For example, we should plant more trees, use less heat and air conditioning, drive less and drive smart, buy energy-efficient products, use less hot water, use the "Off" switch, encourage others to conserve, etc.

Task 3

(1) I think it is very impressive. Before that, I really don't know how global warming is formed. However, what the man said about solving the matter of global warming is very ridiculous.

(2) A little girl named Susie bought an ice cream. However, it was so hot that the ice cream melted soon. A man told her it was because of global warming. The sunbeam visited earth every day to give it light and warmth, but trapped by greenhouse gases. As a result of that, the temperature was getting higher and higher. According to the man, we could solve the problem forever simply by dropping a giant ice cube into the ocean every now and then.

Task 4

(1) Hello, Earth. Just popping in to brighten your day.

(2) Pretty soon, Earth is chock-full of Sunbeams. Their rotting corpses heating our atmosphere.

(3) Fortunately, our handsomest politicians came up with a cheap, last-minute way to combat global warming.

(4) Of course, since the greenhouse gases are still building up, it takes more and more ice each time.

Listening Scripts

Part one

1. Preview Exercises

Several years ago, I was very lucky to have an opportunity to live in the United States for about 2 years. I not only enjoyed the beautiful environment there, but also appreciated the American people's active way of protecting their environment. In some states of America, in order to decrease air pollution, save energy and reduce traffic jams, state governments encourage people to take buses to work or to share a car among several people. They even set special "diamond lanes" in some main streets which are only for the vehicles for 2 or more people.

2. Listening Material

Reduce, Reuse, Recycle

Did you know that there is a simple way we can reduce our waste by almost 50%? This is an important question to consider because the more waste that is burned, the more pollution we have. Reducing waste, therefore, is the key to reducing pollution. By following the simple guidelines-"Reduce, Reuse, Recycle", we can make good use of what we have and lessen the amount of waste and pollution.

First of all, we should reduce how much we use. We should only buy what we will use and use what we have bought. Also consider that buying products in larger quantities can reduce garbage. For example, buying a large tube of toothpaste or a large bottle of dish soap instead of a small one helps reduce waste. Try also to reduce our energy use. Turning off lights in the house when we are not using them helps save electrical energy.

Secondly, we should reuse what we have. Instead of throwing something away, we might give it away. There is an expression, "One man's trash is another man's treasure. " Giving away items not only helps another person but also helps the environment. In addition, we can reuse plastic bags from the supermarket. Of course, instead of throwing away a broken item, we should fix it!

Finally, we can protect our world by recycling the products we have. Many materials can be used again to make something else. Soda bottles, paper products, plastic bags, batteries, jars, and tires are just a few examples of recyclable items.

Protecting our world is the responsibility of every person. Reducing, reusing, and recycling are not only beneficial to us but will also be for the generations to come. Wisely using the things we have will not only help us save money but also help to save our earth.

3. Additional Listening Material

(*Dr. McKinley of Awareness Magazine interviews a group of experts on environmental issues.*)

M : Hello, Dr. Semkiw. In your research, what environmental issues do you find most pressing?

W : Two environmental issues that we find most pressing are deforesting and global warming. Mankind has now cut down half of the trees that existed 10000 years ago. The loss of trees upsets the ecosystem as trees are necessary to build topsoil, maintain rainfall in dry climates, purify underground water and to convert carbon dioxide to oxygen. Trees bring water up from the ground, allowing water to evaporate into the atmosphere. The evaporated water then returns as rain, which is vital to areas that are naturally dry. Areas downwind of deforested lands lose this source of rainfall and are transformed into deserts. Global warming results from the burning of fossil fuels, such as petroleum products, resulting in the release of greenhouse gases into the atmosphere. Carbon dioxide and other greenhouse gases then trap heat, resulting in warming of our atmosphere.

4. Video-aural Material

Walk through any town or village in the Faroe Islands, located between Iceland and Scotland, and it will be hard not to notice the green grass roofed houses on every street. A local historian says, because of the lack of natural building resources on the islands, the Vikings used grass on their roofs to provide stability and extra insulation.

"The grass is something that roofs here when the Viking came and started it, or maybe even the monks started it with the grass roof. We don't know. "

He says young people on the islands continue to build their houses with traditional grass roofs, not only to continue the tradition, but also because there are environmental advantages. Grass roofs filter pollutants and CO_2 out of the air.

"Here, you have this waterproof membrane, and the first you have to do that, the, actually, grass is against this waterproof membrane. The root is up. To keep holding this made mechanical, and then you have to put this fishnet here, and this will be tied around the edges of the house. Afterwards you take the second lay of the grass and put it over. "

Yore says having a grass roof is a way for people on the islands to take responsibility for the environment. He says, if a house has 150 square meters of grass roofing, the grass would produce enough oxygen for one person per day. Jacob Mittyord has incorporated a grass roof into his new house design.

"There are two reasons. The first is the aesthetic, we want it to look nice. And the second is the tradition. It's an old tradition in the Faroe Islands, so we asked our architect to get some solutions, where we could combine this new art style, that (went) well together with this old fashion. "

Last fall, former U. S. president Bill Clinton visited the Faroe's capital for a conference, and spoke on the effects of climate change.

"I look at the old-fashioned roofs with the grass on it, and I was thinking how far ahead of us you're now. All over America we're in a mad rush to green all of our roofs, to put vegetation on our roofs, to cut down on the electric cost and the CO_2 emissions that come from having inefficient buildings. "

The Prime Minister of the Faroe Islands has a grass roof on his house. "First of all, I think it's very important that we all, very all, we are in the society, politicians, or a school teacher, or a fisherman, that we're putting the climate in focus, that we're thinking about the climate change all the time. "

5. Listening Skills

Sample practice

An American environmental activist Huey Johnson won the United Nations Sasakawa Environment Prize in 2001, this prize is worth $ 200000. It is considered one of the most important environmental awards in the world. Mr. Johnson won the award for his efforts to protect the earth's natural resources. He helped create programs designed to save water, reduce energy use and car pollution.

Additional training

Mr. Johnson was an official in charge of natural resources in California in the early 1980s. He developed statewide programs to save natural resources such as water, forest and soil. One program is called Investing for Prosperity. This 100-year plan invests money to protect California's natural resources. The plan became a model for other countries. One of the program's major successes was the development of Renewable Energy Technologies. Experts say these efforts have saved Californian's thousands of millions of dollars and have helped the state's economy grow. For his efforts in this area, Mr. Johnson received the President's Award for Sustainable Development in 1996.

Part Two

Additional Video-aural Material

Global Warming or None Like It Hot!

Man: You're probably wondering why your ice cream went away. Well, Susie, the culprit isn't foreigners. It's global warming.

Susie: Global...

Man: Yeah. Meet Mr. Sunbeam.

He comes all the way from the sun to visit Earth.

(Mr. Sunbean) Hello, Earth. Just popping in to brighten your day. Lalalala ...And now I'll be on my way.

(Greenhouse gases) Not so fast, Sunbeam. We're greenhouse gases. You aren't going nowhere.

(Mr. Sunbean) Oh, ah ...Oh, God, it hurts.

Pretty soon, Earth is chock-full of Sunbeams. Their rotting corpses heating our atmosphere.

Susie: How do we get rid of the greenhouse gases?

Man: Fortunately, our handsomest politicians came up with a cheap, last-minute way to combat global warming. Ever since 2063, we simply drop a giant ice cube into the ocean every now and then.

Susie: Just like Daddy puts in his drink every morning. And then he gets mad.

Man: Of course, since the greenhouse gases are still building up, it takes more and more ice each time. Thus, solving the problem once and for all.

Susie: But...

Man: Once and for all!

Translation of the Listening Materials

Part One

1. Preview Exercises

几年前，我有幸在美国生活了 2 年。在那里，我不仅享受到了美丽的环境，也很欣赏美国民众对于环境保护的积极参与。在美国一些州，为了减少空气污染，节约能源，缓解交通堵塞，州政府鼓励民众乘坐公汽上下班，或者几人共用私家车。他们甚至在一些主干道设立了特别的"钻石通道"，专供乘客人数在 2 人以上（包括 2 人）的车辆通行。

2. Listening Material

缩减降低，反复使用，回收利用

你知道用一种简单的方式就能够让我们将身边的浪费减少几乎 50% 吗？这是一个值得我们深思的问题，因为被焚烧的垃圾越多，污染就越大。因此，减少污染的关键在于减少浪费。只要遵循一条简单的原则——"缩减降低，反复使用，回收利用"，我们就能好好利用自己已有的东西，减少浪费和污染。

首先，我们应该减少对于物品的使用量。只买需要的东西，也只用已买的东西。同时，也应该考虑到，购买大数量装的产品能够减少垃圾。比如，我们可以选择购买大支装的牙膏或者大瓶装的洗碗剂，从而减少浪费。除此之外，也应该减少能源浪费。在不需要用灯的时候，我们可以把它关掉，这样可以节省电。

其次，应当尽量重复使用已有的物品。我们可以把自己不需要的东西送给别人，而不是随意扔掉。有一句话这么说"一个人的垃圾，可能是另一个人的宝藏。"将东西赠人不仅能帮到他，同时也能保护环境。此外，我们也可以将从超市带回来的塑料袋重复使用。当然了，如果东西坏了，别扔掉，应该修好它！

最后，我们也能通过循环再利用已有的物品来爱护环境。很多材料经过再加工可以变成别的东西。汽水瓶，纸制品，塑料袋，电池，罐子以及轮胎都是可循环再用的例子。

保护环境，人人有责。"缩减降低，反复使用，回收利用"不仅仅能造福我们自身，也会造福我们的下一代。学会聪明地使用身边的物品可以使我们节省金钱，更能节约能源。

3. Additional Listening Material

（来自于《意识》周刊的麦克尼先生正在就环境问题采访一群专家）

M：您好，Semkiw 博士。请问在你的研究中，让你感到最迫切的环境问题是什么？

W：我们感到最迫切的环境问题是砍伐山林和全球变暖。人类现在已经将始于 1 万年
前的树木砍伐近半。树木的消失打乱了生态系统，因为树木在修整表土层，锁住
干旱季节里的降雨，净化地下水，以及将二氧化碳转化为氧气等方面必不可少。
树木能够将水从地下带出，并让其蒸发在空气里。然后水蒸气会转化成雨，这对
于是自然干旱地区至关重要的。而处于无森林区顺风方向的地区，就会失去雨源，
从而变成沙漠。全球变暖是由化石燃料（如石油制品）的燃烧引起的，它会导致温
室气体释放入大气层。然后，二氧化碳以及其他的温室气体会将热度封锁起来，
引发大气升温。

4. Video-aural Material

法罗岛位于冰岛与苏格兰之间，当你漫步于该岛的任何城镇村庄时，很难不去注
意到大街小巷里无处不在的绿色草屋顶。据当地一位历史学家说，由于该岛缺乏建筑
资源，北欧海盗们就用草屋顶来加固房屋，同时也起到了额外的隔离作用。

"使用草屋顶可能始于北欧海盗，也有可能是修道士。对于这一点我们并不
清楚。"

他说岛上的年轻人们仍然沿用草屋顶来修建房屋，这样做不仅仅是为了延续传
统，也是因为对环境有益。草屋顶能够将空气中的污染物及二氧化碳过滤。

"看这儿，准备好一张防水薄膜，然后首先要这样做，事实上，要把草皮根朝上，
放在薄膜上。为了保持其技术性，接下来一层放置渔网，并沿着房屋的边缘将渔网固
定住。之后再开始放第二层草皮，就大功告成了。"

约尔说当地居民将草皮屋顶看做是爱护环境的一份责任。他说，如果一栋房子的
草皮屋顶面积达到了 150 平方米，那么它就能产生处足够一个人一天所需的氧气量。

"有两个原因。第一个是为了美观，我们想让屋顶看起来更漂亮。第二个原因是
为了传统，（建造草皮屋顶）是法罗岛的一个悠久传统。所以我们请建筑设计师找出解
决的办法，如何将古老的传统和现代的艺术形式结合在一起。"

去年秋天，前美国总统比尔克林顿曾到法罗岛首都出席一项会议，期间谈到了由
于气候变化所带来的影响。

"看着这些老式的草皮屋顶，我不禁想，你们现在已经遥遥领先于我们了。现在

全美国人民都在忙于绿化屋顶，在上面种菜，同时减少用电和低效能产业排放的二氧化碳排放物。"

法罗岛首相家也使用草皮屋顶。"首先，我认为社会各界人士，无论你是政客，还是教师，或是渔民，都应该关心气候问题，应该一直保持对气候变化的关注。"

5. Listening Skills

Sample practice

美国活动家修伊·约翰逊于 2001 年获得了联合国 Sasakawa 环保大奖，奖金 20 万美元。此奖被认为是当今世界上最重要的环保奖项。因为其对地球自然资源保护的不懈努力，约翰先生被授予了这一荣誉。他协助发起了多项旨在节约水资源，减少能源使用和汽车尾气污染的活动。

Additional training

20 世纪 80 年代初期，约翰先生是加利福尼亚州一名负责自然资源的官员。他在全州范围内发起了多项活动，号召大家节约自然资源，如水，森林，土壤等。其中一项名为"为繁荣投资"的百年计划，将投入资金用以保护加利福尼亚州的自然资源，这已经成为其他国家的典范和榜样。该计划主要的成就之一在于促进了"可回收能源技术"的发展。专家说，这些举措为加州政府节省了成百上千万美元，同时也促进了该州经济发展。由于他在这一领域的努力，约翰先生于 1996 年被授予了"可持续性发展"总统勋章。

Part Two

Additional Video-aural Material

"全球变暖"或"不喜欢这么热！"

Man：你一定很想知道你的冰激凌怎么没了。好吧，苏茜，我们的敌人不是外国侵略者，是全球变暖。

Susie：全球……

Man：是的。来看看阳光先生，他大老远的从太阳那儿来访问地球。

（阳光先生）你好啊，地球。我只是顺便来访，照亮你的一天。现在我得继续旅行了。

（温室气体）且慢，阳光先生！我们是温室气体，你哪儿都别想去！

（阳光先生）噢，天哪，疼死了！

不久，地球周围就被阳光先生们塞满了。他们那些腐烂的尸体加热了我们的大气层。

Susie：那我们怎样才能赶走那些温室气体呢？

Man：幸运的是，我们高明的政治家们找到了一个便捷的应急措施来对抗全球变暖。从公元 2063 年一直到现在，我们只需不停地把大块冰投入海洋降温就行了。

Susie：就像爸爸每天往酒里放冰一样么？然后他就会发酒疯。

Man：当然，由于温室气体在不断产生，所以每次需要越来越多的冰块。从而，一劳永逸地解决了这个问题。

Susie：可是……

Man：一劳永逸！

Ⅰ Background Knowledge

1. Language Points

Preview Exercises

(1) **scroll** n. a long roll of paper or other material with writing on it/卷轴

      e. g. The Tibetan art of scroll painting, or Tangka, is well preserved.

(2) **printing press** /印刷术

      e. g. The invention of the printing press announced the diffusion of knowledge.

(3) **contemporary** adj. existing now or at the time you are talking-about/当代的,同时代的

      e. g. contemporary Western political thought

(4) **metaphor** n. a figure of speech by referring to something else which has the qualities that you want to express/比喻

(5) **project** v. to show and display/呈现

      e. g. He just hasn't been able to project himself as the strong leader.

Warming up Exercises

(1) **trace back** find out or describe how something started or developed/追溯

      e. g. He can trace his jealousy back to when he was age two.

(2) **event** n. any of the contests in a program of sports/项目

      e. g. The current Olympic Games programme includes 33 sports and nearly 400 events.

(3) **host city**/主办城市

      e. g. The host city of the 2008 Olympic Games has been working to create a greener environment.

Listening Material

(1) **embody** v. express or give visible form to (ideas, feelings, etc.)/体现,代表

e. g. Jack Kennedy embodied all the hopes of the 1960s.

(2) **take up** (informal) accept (a challenge, a bet, an offer, etc.) from sb. /欣然接受

e. g. Since she had offered to babysit, I took her up on it.

(3) **in accordance with** (formal) according to a rule, system etc. /根据

e. g. In accordance with his father's wish, he gave the money to the school.

Additional Listening Material

(1) **be taken with** to be attracted by a particular idea, plan, or person/被吸引

e. g. She seems very taken with the idea.

(2) **town hall** a public building used for a town's local government/市政厅

Video-aural Material

up to date modern or fashionable/最近的,最新的

e. g. The most up to date electric power station is located on that hill.

Additional Video-aural Material

(1) **come to somebody's attention**

if something such as a problem comes to the attention of someone in authority, they find out about it/引起关注

e. g. Nowadays, the drug abuse has already come to people's attention.

(2) **usher** n. someone who shows people to their seats at a theatre, cinema, wedding etc. /引座员

e. g. His father works as an usher in the cinema.

(3) **acquit** v. if you acquit yourself in a particular way, other people feel that you behave in that way/表现

e. g. Most officers and men acquitted themselves well.

2. Cultural Background

(1) the differences between the ancient Olympic Games and the modern Olympic Games

The ancient Olympic Games differ greatly from the modern Games. There were fewer e-vents, and only free men who spoke Greek could compete, rather than athletes from any other countries. Slaves, women and dishonored persons were not allowed to compete. Many thousands of spectators gathered from all parts of Greece, but no married woman was admitted even as a spectator. The Games were always held at Olympia instead of moving around to different sites every time.

(2) the Olympic flag

Eight people carry the Olympic flag during opening and closing ceremonies. Five people represent the five continents: Africa, America, Asia, Oceania, and Europe. Three people represent the three Olympic ideals: sport, environment and culture.

(3) the Olympic Charter

The Olympic Charter is the official constitution of the Olympic Movement. It contains the Fundamental Principles, Rules and Bylaws adopted by the International Olympic Committee (IOC). It governs the organization and running of the Olympic Movement and sets the conditions for the celebration of the Olympic Games.

(4) the volunteers

The volunteers serve as sport official and organizers, as messengers and mailers, as clerks, collators and crowd-controllers, as typists and timing officials, as judges and juries. They are unknown to the world because they work behind the scenes, helping to ensure that the Olympic Games run smoothly.

(5) This Is Your Life

This Is Your Life was a television documentary series hosted by its producer, Ralph Edwards. It originally aired in the United States from 1952 to 1961, and again in 1972 on NBC. It originated as a radio show airing from 1948 to 1952 on NBC Radio. A version of it continues a very long run in the United Kingdom starting in 1955, and another version is still running in Australia. It has also been broadcast from time to time in New Zealand and Scandinavia.

(6) the introduction of opening ceremony of 2008 Beijing Olympic Games

Welcoming Ceremony

Presidential Arrival

A military band welcomes the arrival of the Presidents of China and the IOC at the north end of the National Stadium.

Countdown

A dazzling light activates an ancient sundial, and a special multimedia production kicks off the Opening Ceremony.

Welcome Fireworks

Fireworks burst from the National Stadium's exterior trusses, making the entire stadium look like a blossoming flower.

Welcome

2008 performers beat ancient Chinese fou drums, chanting "Friends have come from a-far, how happy we are," a famous Confucian saying.

Performances

Footprints of History

Emitted one per second in the final 30-second countdown to the Opening Ceremony, 29 burning footprints rise into the sky above Beijing, travelling along the axis of the ancient capital city in a series of firework explosions.

Dream Rings

Mythical Buddhist goddesses, float above the stadium floor. Clustering gracefully around the Olympic rings, their costumes glow with light.

Entry of the Chinese National Flag

56 children from China's 56 ethnic groups cluster around the Chinese national flag.

Raising of the National Flag

Members of China's 56 ethnic minority groups come together to sing the Chinese national anthem in the National Anthem Chorus.

Art Performance

A short artistic film depicts the process of Chinese scroll painting-from papermaking and coloring to the mounting of the final painting.

Painting Scroll

A Chinese painting scroll opens on the floor of the stadium, marking the beginning of the evening's performances.

Chinese Writing

The 3,000 disciples of Confucius chant a famous line from Confucius' Analects—"All those within the four seas can be considered his brothers."

Peking Opera

Percussionists accompany a performance of traditional Peking Opera. Peking Opera is just one of the hundreds of forms of traditional Chinese opera, many of which are still performed today.

Silk Road Performance

This is the percussion performance of traditional Peking Opera of China. As China has a vast territory with numerous dialects, hundreds of traditional operas have been derived.

Musical Performance

The actor is singing Kunqu, which is an ancient and traditional art and has been selected into world intangible cultural heritage list.

Parade of Athletes

For the 2008 Summer Olympics, instead of using either French or English, the countries were ordered by how many strokes it takes to write the country's name in Simplified Chinese.

Lighting of Flame Cauldron

Former Chinese gymnastics star Li Ning carries the Olympic flame as he is lifted to the air during the Opening Ceremony of the Beijing Olympic Games in the National Stadium in north Beijing, China, Aug. 8, 2008.

 # Reference Key

Part One

1. Preview Exercises

Dictation

Catherine: "The way the people performed was fantastic but I think the ideas behind it were astonishing, especially things such as when the dancers were drawing the characters with their own bodies on the scroll, we thought that was particularly good. "

Razia: "I love the opening of the scroll. I love the imagine of the printing press. All the history of China was being presented in a very contemporary high-tech way. I thought that was a fantastic metaphor for what China was trying to project on that day. Visually I just thought it was masterful. I thought it was the work of the genius film maker. I love it, it was great. "

Questions

Sample words used in the description are: fantastic, astonishing, particularly good, masterful, great...

2. Warming up Exercises

Brief introduction to Olympic Games

(1) The ancient Olympic Games

The history of the ancient Olympic Games can be traced back over 3,000 years to ancient Greece. In ancient Greece sports played a very important part in the life of the people. While celebrating physical excellence, they were mainly held for religious purpose, that is, athletic contests were regarded by the ancient Greeks as a way to show their respects to their gods, especially Zeus. They eventually chose a place called Olympia to hold the festival, partly because of its many religious temples. The first recorded ancient Olympics were held in Olympia in 776 BC, and had only one event, a race of about two hundred yards. These early Olympics each lasted between one and three days, but from around 400 BC on, the festival was a full five days as more and more events were added. Many of these events are still held today, like running race, javelin and discus throws, wrestling and boxing.

(2) The modern Olympic Games

The modern Olympic Games are an international multi-sport event, occurring every four years, organized by the International Olympic Committee. The first modern Olympic Games were held in Greece in 1896. Just over 200 men, representing 14 countries, competed in a total of 43 events. Winners received a silver medal, a certificate and a crown of olive leaves. Runners-up were given bronze medals and a crown of laurel, while those who finished third went home empty-handed. The Olympic Games are held every four years with one country being responsible for the organization of the event. There is often fierce competition to be the host city. In 2008, Beijing hosts the Games and in 2012 they will be held in London.

3. Listening Material

Task 1

C   B

Task 2

B   C   D

Task 3

(1) expresses   (2) in accordance with   (3) Olympians

(4) improvement

(5) urging man to surpass himself in the essence of his very being

(6) mental and physical improvement of man's natural qualities

(7) priority

(8) striving for personal excellence

(9) strides

(10) philosophy

4. Additional Listening Material

Task 1

D   C

Task 2

B   D   C

Task 3

(1) 2. 06m long   (2) 60cm high

(3) The top three circles, form left to right, are blue, black and red.

(4) The bottom two circles, from left to right, are yellow and green.

(5) peace and truth

(6) Blue representing Europe

(7) Black representing Africa

(8) Red representing America

(9) Yellow representing Asia

(10) Green representing Australia(Oceania)

5. Video-aural Material

Task 1

C　D

Task 2

B　D　C

Task 3

(1) peaceful environment

(2) good organization; Was the athlete happy at the Games? Was the athlete well cared for? Was the Olympic village up to date? Was transportation OK?

(3) the promotion of the Games

(4) personal issues; security and the care of the athletes

6. Listening Skills

Sample practice

(1) actor

(2) July 2nd, 194?

(3) started school

(4) moved to Lane End Secondary School

(5) went to the London School of Drama

(6) left the London School of Drama

(7) went to Hollywood

(8) were in a movie

Additional training

(1) a lecture to look up a new word or an unfamiliar sentence pattern

(2) the meaning of words from the context

(3) concentrating solely on the most important points

(4) accurately and completely

(5) many of the major points

(6) "This is, of course, the crunch" or "Perhaps you'd like to get it down"

(7) The sentences are delivered quickly, softly, within a narrow range of intonation and with short or infrequent pauses

(8) abbreviation

(9) verbs or adjectives

(10) only one point on each line

(11) "Moreover" , "furthermore" , "also"

(12) new and perhaps unexpected information is going to follow

(13) underlining

(14) conventional symbols

(15) numbering

Part two

1. Preview Exercises

Comments on opening ceremony

(1) Sentence structure:

I think … / In my opinion … / … left me the deepest impression. / The most impressive scene is…

(2) Words and phrases:

It showed parts of the long history of China. It was a good way to show the Chinese culture to the foreigners. It was a perfect combination between tradition and modernity. Many people will want to know more about China and Chinese after the Olympic Games. There are many elements in the event that shows the romantic side of typically regarded as "serious" Chinese characteristics.

The students are required to find some relevant information about comparison which will be used in the class discussion. Some tips about comparison will be introduced in exercise II.

2. Warming up Exercises

	Ancient Olympic Games	Modern Olympic Games
Purpose	Show respects to gods	Develop individual, promote world peace
Place	In Olympia	In different host cities
Events	Few	Many
Duration	1 or 3 days	About half a month

Useful expressions in comparison:

Although the modern Olympic Games are originated from the ancient Olympic Games,...

According to my understanding, ...

First, ... ; second, ... ; third, ...

Useful connections in comparison:

however, but, otherwise, although, though, while, on the other hand, compared with

3. Listening Material Review

Task 1

It introduces the content, meaning and the sense of the Olympic Motto and Creed in the recording.

Task 2

(1) The abbot Father Didon, a Dominican priest and school teacher, used these words first. He used these words to describe the great achievements of the athletes at his school.

(2) The phrase means to do something better than you have ever done before.

(3) The sentence means the development of human ability should base on the mental and physical improvement of human being.

Task 3

(1) The sense of the motto is that being first is not necessarily a priority, but that giving one's best and striving for personal excellence is a worthwhile goal.

(2) Participation is the most important thing in the Olympic Games instead of the triumph. Although you are not the champion, your excellent performance makes the game more wonderful.

Task 4

(1) The Olympic Motto supposes the progress of human capacity on the basis of mental and physical improvement of man's natural qualities.

(2) The sense of the motto is that being first is not necessarily a priority, but that giving one's best and striving for personal excellence is a worthwhile goal.

(3) The most important thing in the Olympic Games is not to win but to take part, just as the most important thing in life is not the triumph but the struggle.

(4) The essential thing is not to have conquered but to have fought well.

4. Video-aural Material Review

Task 1

It talks about the factors of the successful Olympic Games.

Task 2

(1) Jacques Rogge is a Belgian sports functionary. He is the eighth president of the IOC.

(2) The sentence means which level does the athletes'sports performance reach?

(3) The security and the care of athletes.

Task 3

(1) Good organization includes athletes' mood, the care of athletes, the facilities and services in Olympic village, and the transportation.

(2) Mr. Rogge introduces some factors which influence the success of the Olympic Games.
They are the organization of the Games, the promotion, the sports performance, and the
personnal issues. Among them, the personnal issues are the most important which includes the security and the care of the athletes.

Task 4

(1) First of all, the Games are held in security and peaceful environment.

(2) Was the athlete well cared for?

(3) Was the Olympic village up to date?

(4) But believe me, the personal issues come first, the personal issues are security and the
care of the athletes.

5. Additional Video-aural Material

Task 1

It makes a brief introduction about the history of volunteers and the importance of volunteers
in the Games.

Task 2

(1) It was during the 1912 Stockholm Games that volunteers first came to people's attention.
Most of them were military soldiers.

(2) Flag escort is the person who holds and protects the flag.

(3) The volunteer has played a very important role in the Games. They serve for the Games

in different ways.

Task 3

(1) Volunteers are the people who make the Games happen, supporting every athlete, spectator, visitor and functional area in all competition and non-competition venues.

(2) The volunteers play a very important role in the Olympic Games. They first served as ushers and security guards in 1912 Stockholm Games. Nowadays, the volunteers supply the support to the Games in different ways. Mr. Rogge thinks highly of the contribution of the volunteers.

Task 4

(1) In the 1992 Barcelona Olympics, volunteers were written in the official report.

(2) The volunteer is someone who devotes his time or her time during the Olympic Games to welcome the visitors, to help the athletes, to support the organization.

(3) When the modern Olympics returned to its origin in 2004, Athens welcomed it with great enthusiasm.

(4) IOC president Jacques Rogge was so impressed that on several occasions he put on the uniform and stood among them.

Listening Scripts

Part One

1. Preview Exercises

Catherine: "The way the people performed was fantastic but I think the ideas behind it were astonishing, especially things such as when the dancers were drawing the characters with their own bodies on the scroll, we thought that was particularly good."

Razia: "I love the opening of the scroll. I love the imaging of the printing press. All the history of China was being presented in a very contemporary high-tech way. I thought that was a fantastic metaphor for what China was trying to project on that day. Visually I just thought it was masterful. I thought it was the work of the genius film maker. I love it, it was great. "

2. Listening Material

The spirit of the modern Olympic Games is embodied in the Olympic Motto "Citius, Altius, Fortius", Latin for "Faster, Higher, Braver" and the modern interpretation as "Swifter, Higher, Stronger".

In 1886, in the early days of modern Olympics, the abbot Father Didon, a Dominican priest and school teacher, used these words to describe the great achievements of the athletes at his school. These words were taken up with enthusiasm by de Coubertin and became the official Olympic Motto later, expressing the athlete's ambition to run faster, jump higher, and throw more strongly.

According to the Olympic Charter, it expresses the message which the IOC addresses to all who belong to the Olympic Movement, inviting them to excel in accordance with the Olympic Spirit. This phrase has been inspiring modern Olympians since its introduction at the 1920 Games. But these words should not be understood simplistically as a call for unfettered improvement of man's physical performances, but rather as urging man to surpass himself in the essence of his very being. The Olympic Motto supposes the progress of human capacity on the basis of mental and physical improvement of man's natural qualities.

The sense of the motto is that being first is not necessarily a priority, but that giving one's best and striving for personal excellence is a worthwhile goal. It can not only apply to the individual athlete who makes great strides in his or her chosen field, but also apply to sports bodies, clubs, organizations and even states committed to the philosophy of modern Olympics.

In a way, the IOC has a second motto, which is called the Olympic Creed. Pierre de Coubertin got the creed from a speech given by Bishop Ethelbert Talbot at a service for Olympic champions during the 1908 Olympic Games.

The Olympic Creed reads: "The most important thing in the Olympic Games is not to win but to take part, just as the most important thing in life is not the triumph but the struggle. The essential thing is not to have conquered but to have fought well. "

The creed and motto are meant to spur the athletes to embrace the Olympic Spirit and perform to the best of their abilities.

3. Additional Listening Material

Pierre de Coubertin is said to have found the original five-ring symbol engraved on an altar-stone unearthed at Delphi. The colorful Olympic rings are one of the most widely recognized symbols in the world today.

The founder of the modern Olympic Games, Pierre de Coubertin, wanted to memorialize the 20the anniversary of the revival of the Olympic Games. He decided to create a banner, an emblem to represent the Olympic Spirit, to present at the 1914 Paris Congress. For his design, Coubertin chose a five-ring symbol that came from an altar-stone discovered at Delphi. The number five refers to the five continents. He chose six colors (white, red, yellow, green, blue and black) because each flag of the countries that were part of the Olympic Movement contained at least one of those colors. The Paris Congress in 1914 was so taken with the design that they adopted it as the official flag of the Olympic Movement. The new flag made its debut at the 1920 games in Antwerp, Belgium. It was here that the rings became the official Olympic symbol.

The Olympic flag measures 2.06m long, 60cm high and is completely white with five circles in the center. The top three circles, from left to right, are blue, black and red. The bottom two circles, from left to right, are yellow and green. The white background symbolizes peace and truth. The five rings represent the five continents of the world:

Blue representing Europe
Black representing Africa
Red representing America
Yellow representing Asia
Green representing Australia (Oceania)

The opening and closing ceremonies incorporate the Parade of the flags. During the opening ceremony, each team parades into the stadium behind their flag. The first flag to enter the stadium is the flag of Greece, the birthplace of the Olympics. The rest follow in alphabetical order according to the language of the host country. The flag and team of the host country close the parade.

At the end of each Olympic Games, the mayor of the host city presents the Olympic flag to the mayor of the nest host city. It then rests in the town hall for four years until the next opening ceremony.

The original Olympic flag, created by Pierre de Coubertin and presented to the mayor of Antwerp in 1920, traveled from Olympic city to Olympic city for 68 years. Finally, in 1988, it found its resting place in Lausanne, Switzerland, where it holds a place of honor in the Olympic museum.

4. Video-aural Material

For me and many of my colleagues, the success of the Games, first of all the Games held in security in peaceful environment, that is our first criteria. And then after that, you look at good organization, centered around the athletes, was the athlete happy at the Games? Was the athlete well cared for? Was the Olympic village up to date? Was transportation OK? Where the sports performances of the highest possible level? When all of that is been achieved, then you look at a promotion for sport around the world and then you look at the audience of some television. But believe me, the personal issues come first, the personal issues are security and the care of the athletes.

5. Listening Skills

Sample practice

Terry: Good evening and welcome to "This is Your Life". This is Terry Donovan speaking. We're waiting for the subject of tonight's programme. He's one of the world's leading actors, and he thinks he's coming here to take part in a discussion programme ... I can hear him now ... yes, here he is! Jason Douglas ... This is your life!

Jason: Oh, no ... I don't believe it! Not me ...

Terry: Yes, you! Now come over here and sit down. Jason, you were born at number 28 Balaclava Street in East Ham, London on July 2nd, 1947. You were one of six children, and your father was a taxi driver. Of course, your name was then Graham

Smith.

Terry: Now, do you know this voice? "I remember Jason when he was two. He used to scream and shout all day."

Jason: Susan!

Terry: Yes ... all the way from Sydney, Australia ... She flew here specially for this pro-gramme. It's your sister, Susan Fraser!

Jason: Susan ... Why didn't you tell me ... oh, this is wonderful!

Terry: Yes, you haven't seen each other for 13 years ... take a seat next to him, Susan. You started school at the age of five, in 1952, and in 1958 you moved to Lane End Secondary School.

Terry: Do you remember this voice? "Smith! Stop looking out of the window!"

Jason: Oh, no! It's Mr. Hooper!

Terry: Your English teacher, Mr. Stanley Hooper. Was Jason a good student, Mr. Hooper?

Mr. Hooper: Eh? No, he was the worst in the class ... but he was a brilliant actor, even in those days. He could imitate all the teachers?

Terry: Thank you, Mr. Hooper. You can speak to Jason, later. Well, you went to the London School of Drama in 1966, and left in 1969. In 1973 you went to Hollywood.

Terry: Do you know this voice? "Hi Jason ... Can you ride a horse yet?"

Jason: Maria!

Terry: Maria Montrose ... who's come from Hollywood to be with you tonight.

Maria: Hello, Jason ... it's great to be here. Hello, Terry. Jason and I were in a movie to-gether in 1974. Jason had to learn to ride a horse ... Well, Jason doesn't like horses very much.

Jason: Like them! I'm terrified of them!

Maria: Anyway, he practiced for two weeks. Then he went to the director ... it was Charles Orson ... and said, "What do you want me to do?" Charles said, "I want you to fall off the horse". Jason was furious. He said, "What? Fall off! I've been practicing for two weeks ... I could fall off the first day ... without any practice!"

Additional training

Lectures and Note-taking

Note-taking is a complex activity which requires a high level of ability in many separate skills. Today I'm going to analyze the four most important of these skills.

Firstly, the student has to understand what the lecturer says as he says it. The student cannot stop the lecture in order to look up a new word or check an unfamiliar sentence pattern. This puts the non-native speaker of English under a particularly severe strain. Often – as we've already seen in a previous lecture – he may not be able to recognize words in speech which he understands straight away in print. He'll also meet words in a lecture which are completely new to him. While he should, of course, try to develop the ability to infer their meaning from the context, he won't always be able to do this successfully. He must not allow failure of this kind to discourage him however. It's often possible to understand much of a lecture by concentrating solely on those points which are most important. But how does the student decide what's important? This is in itself another skill he must try to develop. It is, in fact, the second of the four skills I want to talk about today.

Probably the most important piece of information in a lecture is the title itself. If this is printed (or referred to) beforehand the student should study it carefully and make sure he's in no doubt about its meaning. Whatever happens he should make sure that he writes it down accurately and completely. A title often implies many of the major points that will later be covered in the lecture itself. It should help the student therefore to decide what the main point of the lecture will be.

A good lecturer, of course, often signals what's important or unimportant. He may give direct signals or indirect signals. Many lecturers, for example, explicitly tell their audience that a point is important and that the student should write it down. Unfortunately, the lecturer who's trying to establish a friendly relationship with his audience is likely on these occasions to employ a colloquial style. He might say such things as "This is, of course, the crunch" or "Perhaps you'd like to get it down". Although this will help the student who's a native English-speaker, it may very well cause difficulty for the non-native English speaker. He'll therefore have to make a big effort to get used to the various styles of his lecturers.

It's worth remembering that most lecturers also give indirect signals to indicate what's important. They either pause or speak slowly or speak loudly or use a greater range of intonation, or they employ a combination of these devices, when they say something important. Conversely, their sentences are delivered quickly, softly, within a narrow range of intonation and with short or infrequent pauses when they are saying something which is incidental. It is, of course, helpful for the student to be aware of this and for him to focus his attention accordingly.

Having sorted out the main points, however, the student still has to write them down. And he has to do this quickly and clearly. This is, in fact, the third basic skill he must learn to develop. In order to write at speed most students find it helps to abbreviate. They also try to select only those words which give maximum information. These are usually nouns, but sometimes verbs or adjectives. Writing only one point on each line also helps the student to understand his notes when he comes to read them later. An important difficulty is, of course, finding time to write the notes. If the student chooses the wrong moment to write he may miss a point of greater importance. Connecting words or connectives may guide him to a correct choice here. Those connectives which indicate that the argument is proceeding in the same direction also tell the listener that it's safe time to write "moreover" , "furthermore" , "also" , etc., are examples of this. Connectives such as "however" , "on the other hand" or "nevertheless" usually mean that new and perhaps unexpected information is going to follow. Therefore, it may, on these occasions, be more appropriate to listen.

The fourth skill that the student must develop is one that is frequently neglected. He must learn to show the connections between the various points he's noted. This can often be done more effectively by a visual presentation than by a lengthy statement in words. Thus the use of spacing, underlining, and of conventional symbols plays an important part in efficient note-taking. Points should be numbered, too, wherever possible. In this way the student can see at a glance the framework of the lecture.

Part Two

Additional Video-aural Material

It was during the 1912 Stockholm Games that volunteers first came to people's attention. Most of them were military soldiers, who served as ushers and security guards. In the 1992 Barcelona Olympics, volunteers were written in the official report. And as a mark of respect, two of them served as flag escorts.

"The volunteer is someone who devotes his time or her time during the Olympic Games to welcome the visitors to help the athletes to support the organization. They are not professionals and they are not paid by the organizing committee. They are not working for the organizing committee. But they are very important because they are the people that the athletes, the tourist and the media people need. So they are very important and they are very helpful in many aspects of the organization."

When the modern Olympics returned to its origin in 2004, Athens welcomed it with great enthusiasm. The number of people who were willing to be volunteers were three times the 60 thousand needed. They acquitted themselves well during the event. IOC President Jacques Rogge was so impressed that on several occasions he put on the uniform and stood among them.

 # Translation of the Listening Materials

Part One

1. Preview Exercises

凯瑟琳:"人们表演的方式非常梦幻而理念更是令人惊讶,尤其像舞者用自己的身体在画卷上写字那一幕,特别好。"

纳琪娅:"我喜欢画卷打开的时候,我喜欢印刷术的创意。中国历史通过一种现代高科技的方式完全呈现出来。我认为那正是中国所要传达的。从视觉上来说,我认为非常专业,不愧是出色的电影导演的作品。我喜欢,非常好。"

2. Listening Material

现代奥运会的精神体现在奥林匹克格言"Citius, Altius, Fortius"中,在拉丁语中它的含义是"更快,更高,更勇敢",目前更为普遍的译法是"更快,更高,更强"。

1886 年,在现代奥林匹克的早期,多米尼加传教士兼教师迪东用这三个词来形容他所在的学校的运动员们所取得的优异成绩。这三个词被顾拜旦积极采纳并成为后来正式的奥林匹克格言,它表达了运动员希望跑得更快、跳得更高、掷得更远的雄心壮志。

根据奥林匹克宪章,奥林匹克格言表达了国际奥委会对一切隶属于奥林匹克运动的人们的号召,鼓励他们本着奥林匹克精神超越奋进。自 1920 年奥运会奥林匹克格言被使用以来,它就一直激励着现代奥运健儿。但这些词语不能被简单地理解为号召人们毫无节制地提高人类的体能,而是激励着人们超越自己生命的本质。奥林匹克格言认为应以提高人类精神和身体自然品质为基础来使人类的能力进步。

奥林匹克格言的意义在于,夺取第一并不是要优先考虑的事,但全力以赴并为取得个人最好成绩而奋力拼搏却是值得追求的目标。奥林匹克格言不仅适用于那些在各自领域内取得巨大成就的运动员,也同样适用于那些奉行现代奥林匹克宗旨的体育团体、俱乐部、组织甚至国家。

在某种程度上,国际奥委会还有第二条格言,被称为奥林匹克信条。1908 奥运会期间,埃希尔贝特·塔尔博特主教在为运动员布道时的讲话被顾拜旦采用,成为奥林匹克信条。

奥林匹克信条的内容是:在奥运会上最重要的不是取胜而是参与,正如在生活中最重要的不是凯旋而是奋斗。最重要的不是已经征服,而是曾经奋力拼搏。

奥林匹克格言和信条激励着运动员实践奥林匹克精神,并且在比赛中表现出他们最好的一面。

3. Additional Listening Material

据说皮埃尔·德·顾拜旦是在德尔菲出土的一块祭祀用的石头上,发现了雕刻在其上的最早的五环标志。五颜六色的奥运五环,是当今世界上尽人皆知的标志之一。

为了纪念奥运复兴 20 周年,现代奥林匹克之父顾拜旦决定设计并创作一面旗帜和一枚徽章来代表奥运精神,并呈送给 1914 年的巴黎奥林匹克代表会议。在他的设计里,顾拜旦选择了一个五环标志,这个标志来自于在德尔菲发现的一块祭祀用的石头。五环中的“五”代表五大洲。顾拜旦之所以选择六种颜色(白、红、黄、绿、蓝和黑色),是因为所有参加奥林匹克运动的国家的国旗上都至少包括了这六种颜色中的一种。1914 年的巴黎奥林匹克代表大会非常喜欢这个设计,于是将其定为奥林匹克运动的正式会旗。这面新的旗帜在 1920 年比利时安特卫普奥运会上首次亮相。正是在这次奥运会上,五环正式成为了奥林匹克的象征。

五环旗长 2.06 米,宽 60 厘米。纯白的底色中央有五个环。上边的三个环从左至右分别是蓝、黑和红色。底部的两个环从左至右分别是黄色和绿色。白底象征和平和真理。五环代表着世界上的五大洲:

蓝色代表欧洲

黑色代表非洲

红色代表美洲

黄色代表亚洲

绿色代表澳洲(大洋洲)

开幕式及闭幕式上都有五环旗的环场展示。开幕式上,每个国家的代表队都跟随各自的旗帜进场。第一个进场的旗帜是奥运会的诞生地——希腊的国旗。其他国家按照举办国所用语言的字母顺序依次入场。主办国的国旗和代表队最后一个入场。

每次奥运会闭幕时,主办城市的市长都会把五环旗交给下一届奥运会主办城市的市长。五环旗将在市政厅存放四年,直到下一届奥运会开幕。

最初那面由皮埃尔·德·顾拜旦设计创作,并在 1920 年奥运会上呈送给安特卫普市市长的五环旗在奥运城市间整整旅行了 68 年。最终,它在 1988 年安身于瑞士洛桑的奥林匹克博物馆。在那里,五环旗拥有着自己光荣的一席之地。

4. Video-aural Material

对于我和我的同事来说,成功的奥运会首先应该是在和平的环境中举行,这是第一个标准。其次就是以运动员为中心的组织工作。运动员是否满意? 运动员是否受到良好的照顾? 奥运村是否现代化? 交通情况好不好? 体育用品如何? 当这些标准都达到了,还有向全世界观众做奥运会的宣传工作。但请相信我,人身问题是放在第一位的,即运动员的安全和对运动员的照顾。

5. Listening Skills

Sample practice

特里:晚上好,欢迎收看《这就是生活》。我是特里·多诺万。我们在等待今天节目的嘉宾。他是世界著名演员,他以为今天来这是上一档话题讨论节目……我可以听到他的脚步了……没错,他来了! 詹森·道格拉斯……这就是你的生活!

詹森:哦,我简直不敢相信!

特里:是你! 快过来坐下。詹森,1947 年 7 月 2 日,你出生在伦敦东三区巴拉克拉瓦街28 号。你是六个孩子中的一个,你的父亲是位出租车司机。当然,那时候你叫格雷厄姆·史密斯。

特里:你认识这个声音吗? "詹森两岁的时候我就知道他了。他那时候整天哭闹。"

詹森:苏珊!

特里:对,她为了今天的节目特地从澳大利亚的悉尼飞过来。你的妹妹苏珊·弗拉瑟。

詹森:苏珊,你怎么没有告诉我呢? 哦,太好了!

特里：你们有 13 年没有见面了。苏珊，坐到他旁边。詹森，1952 年在你 5 岁的时候开始上学。1958 年你进入雷恩德中学学习。

特里：你还记得这个声音吗？"史密斯，不要看窗外！"

詹森：不会吧！那是霍伯先生！

特里：霍伯先生是你的英语老师。老师，詹森是个好学生吗？

霍伯：嗯……不算是，他是班上最调皮的，但是在那个时候他就是一位出色的演员了。他可以模仿所有的老师。

特里：谢谢您，霍伯先生。待会儿您可以和詹森聊聊。接着，1966 年你去了伦敦戏剧学院学习，1969 年离开那里。在 1973 年，你去了好莱坞。

特里：你认得出这个声音吗？"你好，詹森。你还骑马吗？"

詹森：玛利亚！

特里：玛利亚·蒙特罗斯，专从好莱坞过来参加你的节目。

玛利亚：你好，詹森！很高兴来这里。特里，你好！1974 年，我和詹森在一部电影里演出。那时詹森不得不学习骑马。但是，他根本不喜欢马。

詹森：喜欢他们？我害怕都来不及！

玛利亚：不管怎样，他练习了两个星期。然后他去导演查尔斯·奥森那儿并对他说："你想我怎么做？"查尔斯说："我想要你从马上摔下来。"詹森非常气愤，他说："什么？摔下来！我练习骑马练了两个星期……我第一天就可以摔下来不需要任何的练习！"

Additional Training

笔记是一项综合技能，对许多专门技能的要求较高。今天，我将说说这些技巧中的四项最重要的。

第一，在老师讲课过程中，学生必须听懂老师所说的内容。学生不可能为了查找一个生词或是不熟悉的句式而去打断老师的讲课。这会给那些不说英语的人带来压力。正如我们在前面一讲里面所提到的，书本上认识的单词，在听的时候他可能不懂，认为遇到了生词。当然，他会试着结合上下文内容推断生词的意思，可这种方法不可能总是奏效。但是，他也不能因这种失败而沮丧。通常来讲，有时关注那些重要信息可以明白许多讲话内容。但是学生如何知道哪些是重要内容呢？那么他需要掌握另外一种技巧。这就是我说的四种技巧中的第二种。

讲课中最重要的信息可能就是标题本身了。如果事先写出（或者提到）题目，学生就会仔细研究题目并且保证对其意思没有疑问。无论怎样他都应当准确无误地写下标题。题目往往包含有许多后面讲话会涉及到的重点。因此这可以帮助学生判断讲话中的重点内容。

当然，认真的老师通常会示意哪些是重点和哪些是非重点。他会给出一些直接或间接信号。比如，有老师会明白地告诉他们的学生重点并要求他们写下来。不幸的是，在这种时候，想和学生建立友好关系的老师很可能会使用口语化的语言。他可能会说："当然，这个很重要"或是"可能你想把它记下来"。这对英语为母语的学生说很有用，但是对于母语不是英语的学生来说则很难理解。于是，他必须尽力去习惯他的老师们的各种各样的说话方式。

值得注意的是大多数老师也会间接地给出信号暗示重点。当他们说重要的事情的时候，他们或是暂停一下或是放慢讲话速度或是大声说话或是使用更重的语气和语调，又或者综合运用这几种方法。反之，当他们说一下非重点内容时，他们会说得很快，放低音量，语调平和以及没有停顿。当然，知道这个对学生很有用并且学生也可以集中注意力。

虽然找到了重点，但是学生还必须将它们记录下来，而且要快速和清楚。事实上，这是他们要掌握的第三种基本技巧。为了写得快，很多学生发现缩写很有用。他们也试着只选用那些能给出最多信息量的词语。这些词语通常是名词，但有时也有副词或形容词。每一行只写一个重点也便于学生日后看笔记的时候好理解他们记录的内容。当然，主要的困难是找出做笔记的时机。如果学生选择错误的时机做记录，他可能会错过更重要的内容。连接性的词语可以帮助他们做出正确的时机选择。那些表示讲话内容正朝着一个方向进行的连接词告诉听众现在非常适宜做记录。而这样的词语有"而且"、"此外"、"同样"等等。而像"可是"、"另一方面"、"不过"这样的连接词则常常意味着接下来将会出现新内容。因此，这些时候最好是仔细听。

第四种学生要掌握的技巧经常被学生忽略。学生必须学会指出他们所记录下的各种内容之间的联系。栩栩如生的表述往往比记流水账更奏效，因而在速记中，使用空格、下划线以及一些常用符号则变得非常重要。当然无论什么情况下，应当给重点内容编号。这样，学生就可以对内容结构一目了然了。

Part Two

Additional Video-aural Material

志愿者第一次引起人们的注意是在1912年斯德哥尔摩奥运会上。他们大多是军人，主要是当引座员和警卫。在1992年巴塞罗那奥运会上，志愿者被载入官方报告中，并且为了表达对志愿者的敬意，他们其中的两位担任了护旗手。

"在奥运会期间，志愿者贡献出自己的时间来接待游客，给运动员提供帮助，为组委会提供支持。虽然他们不是专业人士,不为奥委会工作,也没有酬劳,但是他们非常重要,因为运动员、游客以及媒体都需要他们。他们很重要并且在组织工作的许多方面都提供帮助。"

    2004 年,当现代奥运会回到它的发源地的时候,雅典以极大的热情迎接它。志愿者报名人数是实际需要志愿者60000 人的三倍。他们在运动会上表现得非常出色。奥委会主席雅克罗格非常感动以至于有几次他都穿上制服成为志愿者中的一员。

I Background Knowledge

1. Language Points

Listening Material

(1) **hectic** adj. a hectic situation involves a lot of rushed activity/兴奋的

e. g. Because of his hectic work schedule, he cancelled the family outing on the weekends.

(2) **sort of** kind of, often used orally/有点

Additional Listening Material

(1) **prospective** adj. You use prospective to describe a person who wants to be the thing mentioned or is likely to be the thing mentioned/角度

e. g. The report should act as a warning to other prospective buyers.

(2) **brochure** n. a brochure is a booklet with pictures that gives you information about a product or service /小册子

e. g. Please have a look at our holiday brochures.

Video-aural Material

(1) **leadership** n. kind of charisma needed to be in charge of a group of people /领导力

e. g. There will be times when firm leadership is required.

(2) **for sure** definitely true/肯定的

e. g. One thing is for sure, they will not be calling him James.

2. Cultural Background

(1) All-inclusive scholarship

Many government-funded universities in the United States and HKSAR provide all-inclusive scholarship, which covers generally the tuition fees and basic living expenses during the program schedule, to both home and overseas students. It's actually difficult for prospective undergraduate students to get such a scholarship. For most of them, they can get a scholarship which at most can offset half of their tuition fees. All-inclusive scholarship is generally open to research master and PhD students. In HKSAR universities, such a scholarship is known as Postgraduate Studentship (PGS).

(2) Dental insurance

Dental insurance, like medical insurance, is coverage for individuals to protect them against dental costs. In the U. S. , dental insurance is often part of an employer's benefits package, along with health insurance.

II Reference Key

Part One

1. Preview Exercises

Dictation (1):

Ladies and gentlemen, have you solved the problem of paying the tuition fees? I guess a lot of people may just make the tuition by parents and a lot of people would just have got scholarship or tuition-ship. But I think it's not the most fashionable way to solve the problem. I want to say that, what is the most fashionable and what is the most effective way to solve this problem is paying the tuition by installment plan.

Questions(1):

There are multiple ways to pay tuition fees. Generally speaking, the majority of college students have their tuition fees paid by their parents. A handful student, those from rural areas in particularly, afford their tuition fees with the help of study loans. But more and more students nowadays choose to have their tuition fees paid by their parents, while involving themselves in some study-work programs in their spare time to subsidize their daily expenses.

Dictation(2):

Some students are good at managing school and work and they don't mind the problems that are at rise. Let's find out how.

How do you balance work and school?

School is in the week, and work is for the weekends.

You know it's not really that hard and I don't work too often.

It's difficult sometimes. On the weekdays I only work like maybe one weekday. But I just have to balance my time.

Questions(2):

Disadvantages and advantages of taking a part-time job as a university student:

The main advantage of taking a part-time job is to enable students to gain social experience, apply what they have learned to practice. College students can also learn how difficult it is to earn money, so they will cherish more time on campus and spend their money more wisely. The main disadvantage of taking a part-time job is the encroachment on spare time. As a result, students' study schedule may be affected.

2. Listening Material

Task 1

D C

Task 2

B C A

Task 3

(1) room   (2) breathe   (3) crazy   (4) graduate   (5) started
(6) changing   (7) through
(8) I'm on four-year scholarship that pays may tuition.
(9) I work on weekends for a travel agency.
(10) That seems a little perfect experience for you.

3. Additional Listening Material

Task 1

D A

Task 2

C D C

Task 3

(1) type   (2) focus   (3) supervisor   (4) assistant   (5) prospective

(6) compensation   (7) annual   (8) two weeks paid vacation

(9) I will commend you to a follow-up interview with the sales manager.

(10) feel free to call me if you have any questions.

4. Video-aural Material

Task 1

D C

Task 2

B   D   D

Task 3

(1) than real leadership skills   (2) creatively and confidently

(3) communication skills   (4) separate

(5) wait for the results of handwriting test before we decide

5. Listening Skills

Sample practice

Symbols：

Ts 士

　志

　　…救

　　　　Mon

　　　　　sw 中

　Ts

　　　　埋　_Π_

官：

　　死 ↗ 50t

Fr

胡 → sc

支　救

Explanation：

（1）Symbols

"…" stands for "continue".

" ⌷ " symbolizes "buildings".

" ↗ " means "rise, increase".

" → " signifies "to, towards".

（2）Abbreviations

"Ts" represents "thousands of".

"Mon" and "Fr" are short for "Monday" and "Friday".

"sw" is the abbreviation for "southwest".

Additional training

China says no abnormalities have been discovered in the Three Gorges Dam after Monday's powerful earthquake in Sichuan province.

China's Three Gorges Project Corporation says the dam, as well as the main structures in the project, including the five-tier ship lock were not affected by the quake.

Authorities say installation of the remaining four turbo-generators on the right bank is under way and will go on as planned. The construction of the ship lifting facility was temporarily suspended due to concerns for worker safety. But construction work resumed on Tuesday.

Part Two

1. Preview Exercises

（1）There are different ways in paying one's college tuitions. Most of the students have their tuitions paid by their parents. Some other students utilize the government study loans to help them tide through the financial difficulties. Handful top students have their tuitions covered by scholarships.

(2) Maybe students can take a part-time in their spare time, especially the summer and winter vacations to support themselves financially. But the most effective way to help parents reduce their burden is to make the tuitions worthwhile. That means students should study hard to maximize the opportunity of learning on campus. If no, you can have your own answers.

(3) If you seek help through green channel, that means you are making a interest-free loan to help you afford college tuitions.

2. Warming up Exercises

The main advantage of taking a part-time job is to enable students to gain social experience, apply what they have learned to practice. College students can also learn how difficult it is to earn money, so they will cherish more time on campus and spend their money more wisely. The main disadvantage of taking a part-time job is the encroachment on spare time. As a result, students' study schedule may be affected.

3. Listening Material Review

Task 1

The interviewer and the interviewee are discussing about work type and position and other related matters.

Task 2

(1) "Compensation" means welfare here, including salary, vocation, health insurance, etc. "Feel free to" means "don't hesitate to do something".

(2) "Brochure" is a manual or catalogue that carries the information about products or services provided by a company.

(3) It means that "I will arrange for the next around of interview between the sales manager and you".

Task 3

(1) When seeking a job, you have to sit for an interview, during which, you need to know what kind of questions to be asked and how to answer interviewers'questions. This clip gives some enlightenment for students who are seeking a part-time job.

(2)（Omitted）

Task 4

(1) It's especially crazy when you are a freshman.

(2) What do you plan to do after you graduate?

(3) Pinding a job in an IT industry shouldn't be as difficult.

(4) Well, I am on four – year scholarship that pays my tuition.

4. Video-aural Material

Task 1

Two interviewers are comparing the three candidates they have just interviewed.

Task 2

(1) Candidate One.

(2) Leadership and communication skills.

(3) This sentence means "Compared with his charm, the first candidate seems to lack in leadership skill".

Task 3

(1) This clip tells us the evaluation standards for job candidates in most companies, namely, leadership and communication skills. So, while on campus, we need to strengthen our communication skills with other people and participate and organize some school activities to cultivate leadership quality.

(2) See *scripts*.

Task 4

(1) He seems very charming; don't you think?

(2) She's very serious and seems to be a hard-working person.

(3) What about the third candidate? I can't separate him from the second one.

(4) Perhaps we should wait for the result of the handwriting test before we decide.

5. Additional Video-aural Material

Task 1

First determine what kind of job is best for you. Organize yourself. Take a list. Be open-minded. Be honest about yourself.

Task 2

(1) Write down your expectations and desires for your job. Write down a few sentences which you realistically looking to accomplish at your job. Do you want experience, a high paycheck, a good time, chance for promotion, good hours, and convenient location? Make a list of what isn't important for you.

(2) Ask your school guidance councilors for advice what jobs they think would be appropriate for you. Visit the career section in your local library. Ask around. Find people you trust who can guide your career decisions.

(3) This sentence means "The best method to tackle this dilemma is to make your thoughts in order".

Task 3

(1) This clip gives us an elaborate list of steps for effective job hunting, thus it's very helpful.

(2) See *scripts*.

Task 4

(1) It means breaking down the processes into concrete steps which you can follow.

(2) Write down your expectations and desires for your job.

(3) You may want to be a celebrated sportscast some day. But try to be open-minded about your prospects today.

(4) Once you become organized and focused, you are in a much better position to move on in the job hunting process.

III Listening Scripts

Part One

1. Preview Exercises

Dictation (1)

Ladies and gentlemen, have you solved the problem of paying the tuition fees? I guess a lot of people may just make the tuition by parents and a lot of people would just have got scholarship or tuition-ship. But I think it's not the most fashionable way to solve the problem. I want to say that, what is the most fashionable and what is the most effective way to solve this problem is paying the tuition by installment plan.

Dictation (2)

Some students are good at managing school and work and they don't mind the problems that are at rise. Let's find out how.

How do you balance work and school?

School is in the week, and work is for the weekends.

You know it's not really that hard and I don't work too often.

It's difficult sometimes. On the weekdays I only work like maybe one weekday. But I just have to balance my time.

2. Listening Material

Boy: Hi, I saw you yesterday with John. We room together, I'm Michael.

Girl: Oh...hi, Mike! How are you doing?

Boy: I'm ok. But school's been really hectic since I came. I haven't even had a chance to breathe.

Girl: I know. It's especially crazy when you are freshman. Hey, what's your major?

Boy: Traveling tourism.

Girl: Wow, what do you plan to do after you graduate?

Boy: Um...I haven't really decided it. I think I like to work for a travel agency in this area. What about you?

Girl: Well, when I first started college, I majored in physics. But later I realized that I'd have a hard time in finding a job in that field. I ended up in changing to computer science. Finding a job in the IT industry shouldn't be as difficult.

Boy: Have you got a part-time job to support yourself through school?

Girl: Well, I'm on four-year scholarship that pays my tuition.

Boy: Wow, lucky you!

Girl: Yeah. How about you? Are you paying for school yourself?

Boy: Sort of...I work on weekends for a travel agency.

Girl: A travel agency. That seems a little perfect experience for you. What do you do there?

Boy: I'm a tour guide. I show tour groups around the city.

Girl: Wow! Your English must be pretty good then.

Boy: Actually. They are all Chinese tourists. That's why I got the job.

3. Additional Listening Material

Woman: I've asked you a lot of questions. Now do you have any questions about life type or the position?

Man: Yes. Can you tell me about the company's future plans?

Woman: Yes. Our big focus now is on the internet sales. It's all printed in our company brochure. Here.

Man: Thank you, and who will be my supervisor?

Woman: As a sale representative, you'll be working in a sales department. You report to the assistant sales manager.

Man: And does the job require much travel?

Woman: Yes. Our sales people are on the road a lot, visiting prospective customers. Any more questions?

Man: Um..., no, I can't think of things of any others at this time.

Woman: Well, let me give you some information about our compensation package. We offer our entry-level sales people an annual salary of 30000 dollars, physical health and dental coverage and, two weeks paid vacation.

Man: That sounds good.

Woman: Well, Sean, I so enjoy meeting you. You seem a strong candidate for this position. I will commend you to a follow-up interview with the sales manager.

Man: Thank you very much.

Woman: Good luck and feel free to call me if you have any questions.

4. Video-aural Material

Woman: Well, what do you think of the first candidate?

Man: Well, I thought his resume was good, but I don't really think he has all the skills we are looking for.

Woman: Yes, he seems very charming, don't you think?

Man: Mmmm, exactly. I think he has more charm than real leadership skills.

Woman: I see. Well, what about the second candidate?

Man: Oh, better, I thought. She answered the question we gave her creatively and confidently.

Woman: She did, didn't she? She's very serious and seems to be a hard-working person.

Man: Yes, but that may mean she doesn't have the communication skills that we are looking for.

Woman: Mmmm, but we don't know for sure, so we shouldn't consider that too much.

Man: Yes, I think you're right.

Man: Un, what about the third candidate? I can't separate him from the second one.

Woman: Yes, he was good. And I think you're right. It's a hard choice. Perhaps we should wait for the result of the handwriting test before we decide.

Man: Yes, that's a good idea. We'll wait.

5. Listening Skills

Sample practice

Thousands of soldiers and civilian volunteers continue rescue and relief efforts after Monday's huge earthquake in southwestern China. Thousands of people are believed to still be buried under collapsed buildings. Officials say the number of dead is expected to rise to more than fifty thousand. On Friday, Chinese President Hu Jintao arrived in Sichuan Province to support earthquake relief efforts.

Additional training

China says no abnormalities have been discovered in the Three Gorges Dam after Monday's powerful earthquake in Sichuan province.

China's Three Gorges Project Corporation says the dam, as well as the main structures in the project, including the five-tier ship lock were not affected by the quake.

Authorities say installation of the remaining four turbo-generators on the right bank is under way and will go on as planned. The construction of the ship lifting facility was temporarily suspended due to concerns for worker safety. But construction work resumed on Tuesday.

Part Two

Additional Video-aural Material

How can you find a part-time job? Finding the right job for you is critical. Let's talk about how to prepare for an effective job hunt.

Where do you begin a job-hunting process? By deciding what kind of job you like. So, let's talk about setting job objectives for yourself.

Even if you look for your first job or a part time job, you should first determine what kind of job is best for you.

Organize yourself. The first key to setting a job objective is to get organized. What does this mean? It means breaking down the processes into concrete steps which you can follow. It's common for job seekers to be a little confused when deciding what they really like to do as their careers or what sort of job they really like. The best way to break this ambivalence is to organize your thought.

Take a list. Write down your expectations and desires for your job. Write down a few sentences which you realistically looking to accomplish at your job. Do you want experience, a high paycheck, a good time, chance for promotion, good hours, convenient location? Make a list of what isn't important for you.

Be open-minded. You may want to be a celebrated sportscast some day. But try to be open-minded about your prospects today. If someone presents a job opportunity to you, you should be in a state of mind where you can seriously consider the possibilities. Realize that first jobs are often not very glamorous or high paid or even fun, but the only way to move to the job you really do like is to start with your first job.

Be honest about yourself. Make a list of your abilities. What areas are you good at? Where does your experience lie? What jobs you most likely to succeed in? Do research. Ask your school guidance councilors for advice what jobs they think would be appropriate for you. Visit the career section in your local library. Ask around. Find people you trust who can guide your career decisions.

Once you become organized and focused, you are in a much better position to move on in the job hunting process.

 Translation of the Listening Materials

Part One

1. Preview Exercises

Dictation (1)

女士们,先生们,你们都解决了怎么付学费的问题吗?我猜很多人会让他们的父母来帮着出学费,也有许多人申请到了奖学金或助学金。但我觉得这都不是解决问题最时尚的方法。我想说,解决这个问题最时尚、最高效的方法就是以贷款分期付款。

Dictation (2)

有些学生很擅于平衡兼职和上学,他们不担心兼职可能带来的问题。他们怎么做到的?我们来听听。

你是如何边读边工作的?

上学是在工作日,工作是在周末。

你知道其实这并不难,因为我不经常工作。

有时是挺难。但在上学的周一到周五,我只工作一天。是需要把时间安排好。

2. Listening Material

男:你好,我昨天看见你和约翰一块。我们是一个寝室的,我叫迈克。

女:哦,你好啊,迈克!你都还好吧?

男:还好。我一到学校,就感觉到非常地兴奋,我都没机会喘气了。

女:我知道。特别是你现在还是大一,会特别兴奋。你什么专业呢?

男:旅游。

女:哇哦,那你毕业了准备做什么?

男:呃,我还真没想好。不过我想在当地找个旅行社工作。你呢?

女:刚进大学时,我的专业是物理。后来我发现这个专业以后找工作会挺难,最后我转专业到了计算机科学。在 IT 业找工作应该不会那么难吧。

男:你有没有找兼职工作来帮你完成学业呢?

女:嗯,我得到了四年的奖学金,用来支付我的学费。

男:你好幸运哦!

女:是的。你呢?你得自己交学费吗?

男:差不多。周末我在旅行社工作。

女:旅行社呀。那应该是对你很有帮助的经验哦。你在那做什么呢?

男:我是个导游。我带团参观这座城市。

女:哇。那你英语挺好的呀。

男:其实,他们都是来自中国的游客。所以,我才得到这份工作。

3. Additional Listening Material

女:我问了您不少问题了。现在您对今后的工作方式或职位有什么疑问吗?

男:是的。您能告诉我公司将来的计划吗?

女:是的。我们公司现在关注的是网上销售。所有的东西都印在我们公司的宣传册上了。您看。

男:谢谢。请问谁是我的上司呢?

女:作为销售代表,你将来会在销售部工作。你向助理销售经理汇报工作。

男:这个工作要求经常出差吗?

女:是的。我们的销售代理经常要旅行,出去拜访潜在的顾客。您还有什么其他问题吗?

男:嗯,我暂时想不出有什么问题要问。

女:好,那让我给您讲讲我们的福利薪酬。新来的销售员工每年的收入是 3 万美元,医疗和牙医保险,再加上两周的带薪假。

男:听起来不错。

女:嗯,肖恩,很高兴能认识您。您是个很有竞争力的竞聘者。我会推荐您进一步和我们的销售经理面谈。

男:非常谢谢。

女:祝您好运,有问题随时给我打电话。

4. Video-aural Material

女：你觉得第一个竞聘者怎么样？

男：我觉得他的简历不错,但我不觉得他具备我们所想要的所有技巧。

女：是的。他看上去很有魅力,你觉得是不？

男：嗯,的确是。我觉得比起他的真实领导能力,他的魅力的确不少。

女：嗯,我觉得是。那第二个竞聘者你觉得怎么样呢？

男：哦,我觉得她强些。她所有的问题回答都很不错,比较新颖,比较自信。

女：是的。她很认真,看上去像是一个非常刻苦的人。

男：但是,那可能正说明她不具备我们想要的沟通技巧。

女：是的,但我们也不能确定,所以还是先不想那么多。

男：是的,我想你是对的。

男：嗯,那第三个应聘者怎么样呢？我无法把他和第二个应聘者区别开来。

女：嗯,他不错。我觉得你是对的。很难选择。也许我们还是得等到笔试结果出来了再决定。

男：不错。这个想法很好。我们就等着吧。

5. Listening Skills

Sample practice

成千上万的士兵和民间志愿者继续奋战在中国西南部周一发生特大地震的地区。还有成千上万人被埋在建筑物废墟下。中国官方称死亡人数可能将达到 5 万人。周五,中国主席胡锦涛抵达四川省指导救灾工作。

Additional training

政府表示三峡大坝在四川省周一的大地震后,未发现异常。

中国的长江三峡工程开发总公司表示,作为工程的主要项目的大坝以及包括五个层次船闸均未受到地震的影响。

当局负责人称,安装在右岸的其余四个汽轮发电机将继续按计划进行。由于担心工人的安全,建造船舶起重设施暂停。但建筑工程将于星期二恢复。

Part Two

Additional Video-aural Material

怎样找到一个兼职工作呢？找到合适的工作对你来说是很重要的。我们来谈谈如何做好找工作的准备。

你准备找工作的第一件事是什么呢？决定你喜欢的工作是什么。所以我们先来谈谈给自己树立一个工作目标。

即使你是在找第一份工作或是兼职工作，首先你应该想清楚哪种工作最适合你。

理清头绪。确立工作目标的第一个关键是理清头绪。这是什么意思呢？这意味着你要把这整个过程分解成切实的每个单步来让你可以继续下去。找工作的人在思考他们到底喜欢的职业或者工作是什么样子时，往往有点困惑。最好解决这一问题的方法就是理清思绪。

列一份单子。写下你对这份工作的期待和要求。写些东西，总结一下在工作中你希望获得的东西是什么。你想要的是工作经验，高收入，美好时光，晋升机会，还是交通方便。把你认为对自己不重要的东西也写下来。

思想豁达。也许某天你想成为一个著名的体育节目主持人。但对目前的期望你要看得开些。当你得到一个工作机会时，你应该认真地思考一下自己是不是要做这份工作。要认识到先开始的工作可能不是那么的辉煌，高薪和有趣。但如果你今后想真正做自己要做的工作就必须从这第一份工作开始。

诚实看待自己。理出自己的能力。哪些是你擅长的，而哪些是你有经验的方面。今后让你最有可能成功的工作是什么？做些研究。问一下学校里的就业指导方面的老师，让他们帮你参谋下哪种工作他们认为适合你。到当地图书馆中读些找工作的书。四处问问。找些可以信赖的人来帮你做些职业规划。

一旦你准备得非常有条理，重点突出，你就能以更佳状态进入找工作的阶段。

I Background Knowledge

1. Language Points

Preview Exercises

(1) **relief**　n.　a feeling of comfort when something frightening, worrying, or painful has ended or has not happened. /减轻,解除

　　　　　　e. g.　relief fund（救援基金）, relief workers（救援人员）and etc.

(2) **collapse**　v.　fall down suddenly, usually because it is weak or damaged. / 倒塌,崩溃,瓦解

　　　　　　e. g.　The wind caused the tent to collapse.

(3) **aftershock**　n.　a small earthquake that happens after a larger one. /（地震后的）余震

　　　　　　e. g.　Aftershocks are generally weaker than the main quake, but buildings that have already been damaged are prone to collapse in an aftershock.

(4) Blood is thicker than water. Our veins are bounded. /血浓于水,血脉相连。

(5) This is awful. I did not think the earthquake would have taken so many lives! /太恐怖了,我简直不敢相信这场大地震夺去了那么多人的生命!

(6) The Chinese people will never give in to the disaster. /中华民族从不会向灾难屈服。

(7) I sincerely hope that the people in the disaster area will soon overcome difficulties. /我衷心地希望灾区人民能早日渡过难关。

(8) This earthquake that has claimed thousands of lives in Sichuan. /这次四川地震造成成千上万人死亡。

Listening Material

(1) quake disaster areas　the place which earthquake happened /震区

(2) rock and mud slides/泥石流

(3) Roads in the mountainous area have been badly damaged by earthquake

and landslides. /山区里的路已经被地震和山崩严重破坏。

(4) China's Prime Minister Wen Jiabao has flown to the epicenter to see relief work, having met survivors elsewhere. /国家总理温家宝已经飞往灾区指挥救援工作并看望生还者。

(5) Soldiers have began to reach the isolated epicenter by helicopter. /士兵被空投到隔绝的震中地区。

(6) The confirmed national death toll reached 12300 by 2am Wednesday. / 在周三凌晨 2 点已经确认的死亡人数上升至 12300 人。

(7) Meteorologists are forecasting a small break in the bad weather that has hampered aid efforts. /气象学家预测坏天气将对救援工作产生妨碍。

Additional Listening Material

(1) **condolence books**　phrase books for showing sympathy for someone who has had something bad happen to them, especially when someone has died. /吊唁簿

　　　　e. g. China's missions abroad were ordered to observe the order of three – day national mourning and condolence books are to be opened in the Foreign Ministry.

(2) **disaster relief material**　phrase something useful for relieving after people suffered from the great misfortune/救灾物

　　　　e. g. Around 4:00 pm Wednesday, May 14, China's air force dropped 5 tons of disaster relief materials, including mineral water, milk, instant noodles, into Mianzhu City in quake – stricken Sichuan.

(3) **air – drop**　n.　the action of delivering supplies to people by dropping them from a plane. It can be divided into three types, low – Velocity Air – drop (低速空投,一般用于易碎或者大件物品);High – Velocity Air – drop(高速空投,一般用于耐用品);and Free Fall Air – drop(自由降落空投,此类空投不用降落伞,常用于人道主义救援)。

(4) **silent tribute**　n.　something given or done as an expression of esteem quietly/默哀

　　　　e. g. President Hu Jintao, who just returned from a three – day visit to the quake – hit areas, paid a three – minute silent tribute to victims of the quake in the central government compound of Zhong Nanhai in Beijing.

(5) Let us stay together to overcome this strong earthquake. /让我们携手共进,一起渡过这个难关。

(6) Our hearts are with the citizens of China touched by this tragedy. /情系灾民。

(7) We're collecting for victims of the earthquake – stricken area, please give generously. /我们在为地震灾区的灾民募捐,请慷慨捐助。

Video – aural Material

The earthquake made everybody jump. /突如其来的地震让每个人都吓了一跳。

2. Cultural Background

A brief introduction to earthquake

(1) The cause of earthquake:

An earthquake (also known as a tremor or temblor) is the result of a sudden release of energy in the Earth's crust that creates seismic waves. Earthquakes are recorded with a seismometer, also known as a seismograph. The moment magnitude of an earthquake is conventionally reported, or the related and mostly obsolete Richter magnitude, with magnitude 3 or lower earthquakes being mostly imperceptible and magnitude 7 causing serious damage over large areas. Intensity of shaking is measured on the modified Mercalli scale.

(2) The effects of earthquake

There are many effects of earthquakes including, but not limited to the following:

Shaking and ground rupture

Shaking and ground rupture are the main effects created by earthquakes, principally resulting in more or less severe damage to buildings or other rigid structures. The severity of the local effects depends on the complex combination of the earthquake magnitude, the distance from epicenter, and the local geological and geomorphologic conditions, which may amplify or reduce wave propagation.

Landslides and avalanches

Landslides and avalanches are a major geologic hazard because they can happen at any place in the world, much like earthquakes. Severe storms, earthquakes, volcanic activity, coastal wave attack, and wildfires can all produce slope instability. Landslide danger may be possible even though emergency personnel are attempting rescue.

Fires

Fires of the 1906 San Francisco earthquake

Following an earthquake, fires can be generated by break of the electrical power or gas lines. In the event of water mains rupturing and a loss of pressure, it may also become difficult to stop the spread of a fire once it has started. For example, the deaths in the 1906 San Francisco earthquake were caused more by the fires than by the earthquake itself.

(3) Wenchuan earthquake

A strong earthquake measured 8 magnitude struck Wenchuan county in Sichuan Province at 2: 28 pm. On May 12th 2008, the areas around Wenchuan are seriously affected and destroyed. A large number of buildings collapsed, traffic and telecommunication broke down, and some counties even lay in ruins. The suffering of the people is extreme. Until May 20th, 2008 the number of people who died of the disaster has reached over 40000. More than 240000 people have injured and another over 30000 have declared missing.

(4) Pan Zhihua Earthquake

Relief workers are scrambling after a 6. 1 magnitude earthquake hit southwest China's Sichuan and Yunnan provinces on Saturday. Authorities are working to ensure relief workers and supplies reach those in need. 32 people have been killed and more than 400 others are injured.

The quake's epicenter was about 50 kilometers southeast of Panzhihua city in Sichuan province. More than 800000 people in Sichuan and Yunnan provinces have been affected. 250000 houses have been destroyed. Traffic has been disrupted and electricity—cut off in some of the worst hit areas.

On Sunday afternoon, a 5. 6 magnitude aftershock occurred in the same area as Saturday's quake.

The China Earthquake Administration has dispatched a team to offer assistance, and the Ministry of Civil Affairs has launched a class four emergency response.

II Reference Key

Part One

1. Preview Exercises

(1) Dictation

In1989, the Loma Prieta Earthquake shook the San Francisco and Monterey Bay regions. This major earthquake caused dozens of deaths, thousands of injuries and an estimated 6 billion dollars in property damage. It was the largest earthquake to occur on the San Andreas Fault since the great San Francisco earthquake in April 1906.

The Loma Prieta quake was similar to Monday's earthquake in China in depth, but its magnitude was just 7.1 on the Richter scale, compared to the Sichuan earthquke at 7.9. Seismology experts in Japan also compared the earthquake to the Kobe quake of 1995 in Japan, in which more than 5000 were killed.

(2) Questions

① Earthquake, quake, shock, hit, shake, damage, destroy, natural, disaster, tragedy, survivor, victim.

② It's a kind/type/sort of disaster. / It's the one that has (a terrible trembling).

2. Listening Material

Task 1

A D

Task 2

D C A

Task 3

(1) 7.8   (2) efforts   (3) disaster   (4) epicenter

(5) Tremors   (6) Thailand   (7) collapsed

(8) The telecom networks in Chengdu and Chongqing were down after the quake.

(9) Meanwhile, another earthquake measuring 3.9 on the Richter scale jolted Tongzhou district in east Beijing minutes later

(10) The quake was also felt in neighboring Tianjin.

3. Additional Listening Material

Task 1

A B

Task 2

D C D

Task 3

(1) Meanwhile   (2) Netherland   (3) benefit   (4) denoated
(5) studying   (6) rescue   (7) survivors   (8) wallets

4. Video-aural Material

Task 1

C A

Task 2

A D B

Task 3

(1) a keen observation   (2) subtle or abrupt shifts   (3) crashed into the coastline
(4) prior to   (5) Fund-sponsored   (6) epicenter   (7) the death toll

5. Listening Skills

Sample practice

(1) Notes

    <u>W2</u>   →——60

    US：

        ↗   生%

儿 +

20y > ⌐

☺ 名

bb

↙

。

(2) Explanation

W2 代表第二次世界大战,下面画线,表示在第二次世界大战末;60 是 20 世纪 60 年代,中间画线代表中期;儿代表 baby; +代表更多;20Y 是 20 年;⌐ 和 ∟ 分别表示过去和将来;☺表示有趣的;bb 是 baby 的缩写;°代表人,比如中国人,可以记录为中°

Additional training

See *scripts*

Part Two

1. Preview Exercises

Some sentences of earthquake and people's feeling on it.

(1) It's a kind of disaster.

(2) It's the one that has (a terrible trembling).

(3) I am concerned/ apprehensive about the people who are suffering from the earthquake.

(4) I am nervous/ worried about the survivors' lives after the earthquake.

2. Warming up Exercises

(1) See *Background Knowledge*

(2) Yes. There are more ways of expressing your attitude toward earthquake.

How sad!

How miserable!

What a pity!

I'm sorry to hear that.

I feel sad today.

I feel awful about it.

I can't help crying.

I hope this had never happened.

(3) See *Preview Exercises*

3. Listening Material Review

Task 1

It's about a disastrous earthquake measuring 7.8 on the Richter scale hitting Wenchuan county in southwest China's Sichuan province.

Task 2

(1) The epicenter of Wenchuan county lies in the Tibetan-Qiang Autonomous Prefecture of Aba.

(2) Yes, it's the task to alleviate pain or distress after the earthquake.

(3) Meanwhile, another earthquake measuring 3.9 on the Richter scale jolted Tongzhou district in east Beijing minutes later.

Task 3

(1) It was terrible. We can't describe the scene what we saw with any words.

(2) Omitted

Task 4

(1) The epicenter of Wenchuan county lies in the Tibetan-Qiang Autonomous Prefecture of Aba, about 100 kilometers northwest of the provincial capital Chengdu.

(2) Cracks were seen on walls of some residential structures in downtown Chengdu, but no buildings collapsed.

(3) An underground water pipe was broken underneath a viaduct close to Chengdu's southern railway station, and a road was flooded.

(4) Meanwhile, another earthquake measuring 3.9 on the Richter scale jolted Tongzhou county in this district in east Beijing just minutes later.

4. Video-aural Material Review

Task 1

Pandas could indicate that the earthquake was coming before it hit.

Task 2

(1) Some animal species have a greater awareness than humans of vibrations in the ground.

(2) Low frequency sound waves: low sound waves of complete cycles of a periodic process occurring per unit time.

(3) The members were visiting the Panda Reserve in Wolong when the earthquake struck.

Task 3

(1) People can make full use of some species of animals to help us find some important information, in order to avoid big problems.

(2) Omitted.

Task 4

(1) Some scientists say animals can sense impending danger by detecting subtle or abrupt shifts in the environment.

(2) Some animal species have a greater awareness than humans of vibrations in the ground.

(3) Twelve Americans, part of a World Wildlife Fund-sponsored tour of China, were visiting the Panda Reserve in Wolong when the earthquake struck.

(4) Wolong's 86 pandas were reported safe on Tuesday.

5. Additional Video-aural Material

Task 1

Scientists are working hard to deal with disasters, such as earthquake.

Task 2

(1) He was inspecting the damage.

(2) weather the storm: to experience something and survive it.

(3) Because better buildings will suffer less damage and be less likely to cause loss of life.

Task 3

(1) We're expecting that scientists can bring good news to our people about dealing with earthquake.

(2) Omitted.

Task 4

(1) The cracking at the base is actually minor and the building is structurally sound.

(2) We know we have the technology to design better buildings, buildings that will suffer less damage and be less likely to cause loss of life.

(3) Engineers also need to invent ways to strengthen existing buildings.

(4) And the ultimate quake-proofing technology is hiding beneath the oldest skyscraper in Los Angeles—City Hall.

6. Pronunciation Tips

Tips

(1)2　(2)1　(3)4　(4)2　(5)3　(6)5　(7)5　(8)3　(9)2　(10)3

(11)9　(12)9　(13)11　(14)15　(15)9

Listening Scripts

Part One

1. Preview Exercises

In1989, the Loma Prieta Earthquake shook the San Francisco and Monterey Bay regions. This major earthquake caused dozens of deaths, thousands of injuries and an estimated 6 billion dollars in property damage. It was the largest earthquake to occur on the San Andreas Fault since the great San Francisco earthquake in April 1906.

The Loma Prieta quake was similar to Tuesday's earthquake in China in depth, but its magnitude was just 7.1 on the Richter scale, compared to the Sichuan earthquake at 7.9. Seismology experts in Japan also compared the earthquake to the Kobe quake of 1995 in Japan, in which more than 5000 were killed.

2. Listening Material

A major earthquake measuring 7.8 on the Richter scale has hit Wenchuan county in southwest China's Sichuan province.

President Hu Jintao has ordered all-out efforts to rescue quake-hit victims. Premier Wen Jiabao was on his way to the hit area to direct the rescue work. Chengdu Military Area Command has dispatched troops to help with disaster relief work in the earthquake-stricken county.

The incident happened at 2:28 p. m. on Monday. The epicenter of Wenchuan county lies in the Tibetan-Qiang Autonomous Prefecture of Aba, about 100 kilometers northwest of the provincial capital Chengdu. Tremors were also reported in many other parts of China, including Ningxia, Qinghai, Gansu, Chongqing, Hunan, Hubei, Shanxi, Shanxi and Shanghai, and as far away as Thailand and Vietnam. Cracks were seen on walls of some residential structures in downtown Chengdu, but no buildings collapsed.

The telecom networks in Chengdu and Chongqing were down after the quake. An underground water pipe was broken underneath a viaduct close to Chengdu's southern railway station, and a road was flooded. Meanwhile, another earthquake measuring 3. 9 on the Richter scale jolted Tongzhou county in this district in east Beijing minutes later. The quake was also felt in neighboring Tianjin.

3. Additional Listening Material

Meanwhile overseas Chinese, including businesses and students, are showing their concern by pledging donations, and making donations.

Chinese businesses in the Netherlands raised the equivalent of over 360000 yuan in an hour. They will hold more fundraising performances to benefit Sichuan province.

In Belgium, over the past two days, Chinese students have donated in many ways, saying they will help in any way they can.

(Chinese student in Brussels Ren Tao said,) "I'm studying medicine and if my country needs my help, I would love to come back now. I'd like to do my best to rescue and treat patients. "

The Chinese Students Scholars Association in Britain has called for all overseas Chinese to donate money to the earthquake survivors. At the University of London, not only the Chinese, but people from all walks of life have opened their wallets. (Gu Xiaozeng, CCTV)

4. Video-aural Material

Did the pandas in China's Wolong Reserve know that Monday's earthquake was coming before it hit? A British tourist watching the pandas as the quake struck offered a keen observation.

"They had been really lazy and just eaten a little bit of bamboo and, and all of a sudden they were sort of parading around their pair. And, looking back, they must have sensed something was wrong."

Some scientists say animals can sense impending danger by detecting subtle or abrupt shifts in the environment. When the tsunami hit in 2004, there were reports that elephants in Sri Lanka fled to higher ground well before the waves crashed into the coastline. National Geographic grantee and Panda researcher Marc Brody says some animal species, such as elephants that are known to hear low frequency sound waves, hear things sonically and may get an early warning.

Some animal species have a greater awareness than humans of vibrations in the ground. And they may sense smaller tremors prior to a bigger earthquake. A group of tourists was airlifted to safety from Wolong and taken to the provincial capital of Chengdu on Thursday morning.

"We were looking forward then to moving onto the larger panda, where we were not sure whether that panda was going to come out of the enclosure or whether that someone was going into an enclosure just to be with that panda. So we were waiting for that to happen and then suddenly we had this horrendous noise which is just what you can't describe out what it's like, it's just a huge, huge noise and the land shaking underneath."

Twelve Americans, part of a World Wildlife Fund-sponsored tour of China, were visiting the Panda Reserve in Wolong when the earthquake struck.

"Certainly it was a surreal experience to be standing there going through a, whatever was 7.9 Richter earthquake surrounded by 25 pandas all sort of reacting to that as well."

Wolong's 86 pandas were reported safe on Tuesday. The 7.9 magnitude earthquake hit on Monday with the epicenter near Wolong Reserve. Rescuers are still making their way to the more remote areas affected. So far the death toll stands at almost 20000 and is expected to climb higher as rescue efforts progress.

5. Listening Skills

Sample practice

Thousands of soldiers and civilian volunteers continue rescue and relief efforts after Monday's huge earthquake in southwestern China. Thousands of people are believed to still be buried under collapsed buildings. Officials say the number of dead is expected to rise to more than fifty thousand. On Friday, Chinese President Hu Jintao arrived in Sichuan Province to support earthquake relief efforts.

Additional Listening

China says no abnormalities have been discovered in the Three Gorges Dam after Monday's powerful earthquake in Sichuan province.

China's Three Gorges Project Corporatinon says the dam, as well as the main structures in the project, including the five – tier ship lock were not affected by the quake.

Authorities say installation of the remaining four turbo – generators on the right bank is under way and will go on as planned. The construction of the ship lifting facility was temporarily suspended due to concerns for worker safety. But construction work resumed on Tuesday.

Part Two

Additional video-aural Material

Engineers inspect the damage. The cracking at the base is actually minor and the building is structurally sound. This new construction model of more concrete and less rebar provides e-nough flexibility and strength to weather the storm. The test results are clear. If this had been a real earthquake, the building survives, and the people walk away.

We know we have the technology to design better buildings, buildings that will suffer less damage and be less likely to cause loss of life.

This experiment is one small step in protecting earthquake zones around the world. But cities like Tokyo, Istanbul and Los Angeles can't be torn down and rebuilt. Engineers also need to invent ways to strengthen existing buildings. And the ultimate quake-proofing technology is hiding beneath the oldest skyscraper in Los Angeles—City Hall. This 80-year-old granddame is over 30 floors high, covers an entire city block and is irreplaceable. Built in 1926, this aging tower could be the first to crumble. But engineer Nabi Userf claims City Hall would be up and running, even after the big one.

VI Translation of the Listening Materials

Part One

1. Preview Exercises

1989 的洛克庞马大地震袭击了旧金山和蒙特雷湾地区。这个大地震造成数十人死亡,数千人受伤,估计有 60 亿美元的财产损失。这是自 1906 年 4 月旧金山大地震爆发以来,圣安德列斯断层发生的最大规模的地震。

洛克庞马大地震在程度上类似中国周一发生的地震,但其规模只有 7.1 级,而四川地震为 7.9 级 。日本的地震专家也比较了 1995 年在神户发生的比较大地震,其中超过 5000 人丧生。

2. Listening Material

四川省西南的汶川县发生了 7.8 级大地震。

国家主席胡锦涛已下令全力救援地震灾区的受害者。温家宝总理正前往灾区指挥救援工作。成都军区已派出部队,以帮助救灾工作中的地震灾区县。

事件发生在下午 2 点 28 分,星期一。震中汶川县位于阿坝藏族羌族自治州,离省会成都约 100 公里。地震还波及了许多其他地区,包括宁夏,青海,甘肃,重庆,湖南,湖北,山西,陕西,上海,以及泰国和越南。在市中心成都,一些住宅楼的墙壁上看到裂缝,但没有房屋倒塌。

成都和重庆的电信网络在地震之后崩溃。在高架桥下方,接近成都南部地铁站的地下供水管道被打破,并在道路被水淹没。与此同时,另一个地震台网测定,北京东部的通州区也在数分钟后发生了 3.9 级地震。这次地震还波及邻近的天津。

3. Additional Listening Material

海外华人向地震幸存者捐赠

同时,海外华人包括企业和学生,都纷纷捐赠,以表他们的关心。

荷兰的中国企业在一小时内捐赠价值超过 36 万元的财物,他们还将为四川举行更多的筹款演出。

过去两天里,比利时的中国学生通过种种途径捐赠,他们表示,会以任何方式帮助他们。

(华人学生任涛在布鲁塞尔说,)"我学医,如果我的国家需要我的帮助,我愿意回来。我愿意尽我最大的努力抢救和治疗病人。"

在英国,中国学生学术联谊会已呼吁所有海外华侨华人向地震幸存者捐款。在伦敦大学,不仅是中国人,而且社会各界人士都纷纷慷慨解囊。

4. Video-aural Material

我国卧龙自然保护区的大熊猫是否知道星期一的大地震即将袭击面前? 一名英国游客回忆地震来临时大熊猫的表现。

"他们变得很懒惰,只吃一点竹子,并突然绕圈走。现在看来,他们当时必然感觉到了什么。"

一些科学家说,动物可以感知即将发生的危险,探测隐蔽或突然改变环境。当 2004 年的海啸发生时,有报告称,斯里兰卡的大象在微波传到海岸线之前已逃往地势较高的地方。《国家地理》的熊猫研究员马克·布罗迪说,众所周知,一些动物物种,如大象,能听到低频声波后预警。

就地面震动而言,一些动物物种比人类更敏感。他们也许能感受到大地震前更小的震感。周四上午,一群游客从卧龙自然保护区被安全地转移到省会成都。

"我们期待向更大的熊猫靠近,但也不确定熊猫是否可以走出去,或是有人和熊猫一起走进去。所以,我们等待着,突然我们听到一种难以形容的可怕声响,一个巨大的噪音和摇晃的地面……"

12 个美国人,来自世界野生动物基金会,参观地震后卧龙自然保护区的大熊猫。

"当然这是一个可怕的经历,无论是里氏 7.9 级地震还是被 25 只大熊猫包围都反映了这一点。"

据报道,卧龙自然保护区的 86 只大熊猫周二是安全的。而周一 7.9 级地震的震中在卧龙保护区附近。搜救人员仍在以他们的方式探测受影响的偏远地区。到目前为止,死亡人数近两万,预计随着救援工作的进展仍会攀升。

5. Listening Skills

Sample practice

成千上万的士兵和民间志愿者继续奋战在中国西南部周一发生特大地震的地区。还有成千上万人被埋在建筑物废墟下。中国官方称死亡人数可能将达到 5 万人。周五,中国主席胡锦涛抵达四川省指导救灾工作。

Additional training

政府表示三峡大坝在四川省周一的大地震后,未发现异常。

中国的长江三峡工程开发总分司表示,作为工程的主要项目的大坝以及包括五个层次船闸均未受到地震的影响。

当局负责人称,安装在右岸的其余四个汽轮发电机将继续按计划进行。由于担心工人的安全,建造船舶起重设施暂停。但建筑工程将于星期二恢复。

Part Two

Additional video-aural Material

工程师正在检查损坏情况。根基的开裂实际上很轻微,建筑结构合理坚固。这种新的建筑模型,利用增加水泥,减少钢筋的方法提供足够的灵活性和强度,以渡过难关。测试结果是显而易见的。如果这是一次真正的地震,建筑幸存下来,人也可以逃离。

我们知道,我们有技术设计更好的建筑物,减少其受破坏程度和可能造成的生命损失。

这个实验对保护世界各地的地震带只是一小步。但是,像东京、伊斯坦布尔和洛杉矶等城市不能拆除和重建。工程师们还需要找到如何使现有的建筑物更坚固的方法。而且最终的防震技术是匿藏在洛杉矶摩天大楼——最古老的大会堂。这座大楼已80年的历史,30 多层高,不可替代地覆盖整个城高街区。大地震后,第一个可能坍塌的建筑就是这个建于 1926 年的老化大楼。但是,工程师那比·由瑟夫却坚信它能承受住。

I

Background Knowledge

1. Language Points

Preview Exercises

(1) **perceptual** adj. of or relating to the act of perceiving/感性的, 知觉的

(2) **quote** v. a passage or expression that is quoted or cited/引用

e. g. He quotes the Bible to support his beliefs.

(3) **exam-oriented** adj. exam-centered/以考试为中心

(4) **momentous** adj. of very great significance/重要的, 重大的

e. g. History bears evidence that each momentous political change is usually followed by an economic revival.

(5) **integrate practice into teaching** doing practice while teaching/讲练结合

e. g. The teachers are trying to integrate all the children into society.

Listening Material

(1) **hereby** adv. by means of this/因此, 据此

e. g. I hereby declare her elected.

(2) **milestone** n. turning point; stone post at side of a road to show distances/里程碑

e. g. Each birthday is a milestone we touch along life's way.

(3) **post-** a prefix meaning "after"/在……之后

e. g. postwar; post-flight check; postgraduate; post harvest....

(4) **vehicular** adj. of or relating to or intended for (motor) vehicles/车辆的

e. g. This is a period of time during which motor vehicular and pedestrian traffic is light.

Additional Listening Material

(1) **module** n.　detachable compartment of a spacecraft/（航天器上各个独立的）舱，太空舱

　　　　　　e. g. The two modules docked in outer space.

(2) **hatch** n.　the entrance of a module/舱口

　　　　　　e. g. She passed food through the hatch from the kitchen.

(3) **have faith in**　believe/相信，信任

　　　　　　e. g. She is a Party member and she has faith in communism.

(4) **bulgy** adj.　/膨胀的，凸出的

　　　　　　e. g. The spider has a bulgy abdomen.

2. Cultural Background

(1) The history of manned spacewalk project in China.

中国载人航天历史

The Chinese space program was put forward in 1956. Now it has a history of more than 50 years.

中国航天创建于 1956 年，已经走过了 50 多年的历程。

The successful trial launching of Dong Feng 1.

1960 年 11 月 5 日，东风一号近程导弹首次飞行试验成功。

The successful trial launching nuclear weapons.

1966 年 10 月 27 日，我国发射导弹核武器试验成功。

The successful launching of the first satellite called "Dong Fang Hong" at Jiuquan Launching Site.

1970 年 4 月 24 日，我国第一颗人造地球卫星"东方红"一号在酒泉发射成功。

The successful launching of carrier rocket.

1980 年 5 月 18 日，第一枚运载火箭发射成功。

The successful launching of Feng Yun Weather Satelite 1 launched by Long March 4 carrier rocket in Taiyuan.

1988 年 9 月 7 日，长征 4 号运载火箭在太原成功发射了风云一号 A 气象卫星。

The successful launching and landing of the first trial space shuttle of "Shenzhou".

1999 年 11 月 20 日，我国成功发射第一艘宇宙飞船"神舟"试验飞船，飞船返回舱于次日成功着陆。

The successful launching and landing of the second trial space shuttle of "Shenzhou".

2001 年 1 月 10 日，我国成功发射"神舟"二号试验飞船，于 1 月 16 日在内蒙古自

治区中部地区准确返回。

The successful launching and landing of the third trial space shuttle of "Shenzhou".

2002 年 3 月 25 日,我国成功发射"神舟"三号试验飞船。

The successful launching and landing of Shenzhou Ⅳ".

2002 年 12 月 30 日,我国成功发射"神舟"四号飞船。

The successful launching and landing of the manned space shuttle of "Shenzhou V".

2003 年 10 月 15 日至 16 日,我国首次载人航天飞行取得圆满成功。

The successful launching and landing of the manned space shuttle of "Shenzhou Ⅵ" with 2 astronauts for 5 days, which is the symbol for Chinese going into the space.

2005 年 10 月 12 日至 17 日,神舟六号飞船实现了两人五天的太空飞行,标志着我国跨入真正意义上有人参与的空间试验阶段,迈开了从航天大国走向航天强国的新步伐。

The Chinese astronaut Zhai Zhigang did the EVA in the space by the manned space shuttle of "Shenzhou Ⅶ", which means China has become a third country that can produce spacewalk module independently.

2008 年 9 月 27 日,中国航天员翟志刚从神舟七号飞船上进行了太空行走,中国成为世界上第三个航天员能从本国自主研制的航天器上独立进行太空行走的国家。

(2) Words for further study

Shenzhou Ⅶ	神舟七号
manned spaceship/ spacecraft	载人飞船
manned space flight	载人航天
manned space program	载人航天计划
space suit	航天服
unmanned spaceship/spacecraft	无人飞船
Experimental Spacecraft	试验太空船
multistage rocket	多级火箭
capsule	太空舱
recoverable satellite	返回式卫星
communication satellite	通信卫星
remote sensing satellite	遥感卫星
carrier rocket; rocket launcher	运载火箭
Long March II F carrier rocket	长征二号 F 运载火箭
low Earth orbit	近地轨道

weather satellite	气象卫星
orbital module	轨道舱
re-entry module	返回舱
propelling module	推进舱
command module	指令舱
service module	服务舱
space walk	太空行走
extra-vehicular activity(EVA)	舱外活动(即"太空行走")
launch pad	发射台
International Space Station	国际空间站
solar panel	太阳能电池板
outer space; deep space	外太空
Milky Way	银河系
Apollo	阿波罗号宇宙飞船
NASA(The National Aeronautics and SpaceAdministration)	美国航空航天管理局
launch a satellite	发射卫星
blast off	发射升空
artificial satellite	人造卫星
hatch	舱口
life support system	生命维持系统
ground operation system	地面操作系统
escape tower	逃逸塔
sterilized uniforms	消毒服
lead astronaut	领航宇航员
launch window	发射时限;发射窗

(3) Taikonaut

中国宇航员(由拼音太空(taikong)和 astronaut 合成,在 1998 年时由马来西亚籍华人科学家提出,后随着神舟飞船的不断发射成功,逐渐为国际认可。)

"Chinese astronauts" (combined "taikong" and "astronaut") was first used by Chinese-origin Malaysian in 1998. With the continous success in launching of Shenzhou space shuttles, this term is accepted in the world.

Reference Key

Part One

1. Preview Exercises

(1) Dictation

A primary school in Shanghai had suggested that all schools reduce or even postpone homework assignments to guarantee students enough time to watch the launch of China's Shenzhou VII space mission live on television.

An article in the Beijing News says that watching the live broadcast of the spacecraft's lift-off is meaningful homework.

The article points out that perceptual knowledge of Shenzhou VII can broaden and arouse students' interest in science and encourage them to be serious about their studies.

A teacher was quoted as saying that the manned space mission is a vivid science lesson for students to make up for the holes in China's exam-oriented educational system.

The Beijing News says encouraging students to watch such a momentous event is a good example of integrating practice into teaching.

(2) Questions

① Teachers regard such activity as a good chance for the students to get perceptual knowledge of science. This is a good example of integrating practice into teaching.

② Yes. While watching, I am feeling very proud of our country because it is the first manned spacewalk in the history of China. It shows our country is becoming stronger.

2. Listening Material

Task 1

B   D

Task 2

C   C   D

Task 3

(1) symbolizes   (2) behalf   (3) Commission   (4) gratitude

(5) representative   (6) challenge   (7) higher   (8) planning

(9) spacecraft

(10) I hope that everyone here would be very serious and have a careful attitude towards all the post-launch activities to ensure its complete success.

3. Additional Listening Material

Task 1

C   C

Task 2

C   A   D

Task 3

(1) greetings   (2) faith   (3) float   (4) waving   (5) stage

(6) actually

(7) the astronauts entered the module first with the feet and this process involved closing the module's door.

4. Video-aural Material

Task 1

A   D

Task 2

C   D   A

Task 3

(1) released   (2) approaching   (3) physiological   (4) weightless

(5) capsule   (6) accomplished   (7) checkups

5. Listening Skills

Dictation

The President of Iran said his country will carefully consider an international offer of aid in return for limits on Iran's nuclear pangram. President Mohamed Afar Dinajudge spoke in Shanghai China. He is there to observe a meeting of the Shanghai Cooperation Organization. In Washington Secretary of State said the international community needs an answer to the offer soon. The five permanent members of the United nations security council and Germany developed the plan that have offered Iran aid if it will stop its uranium enrichment work and return to nuclear talks. The United States and other countries believe Iran is trying to make a nuclear weapon. Iran denies this.

Fill in the blanks

(1) blamed; Iraq; supervising; violence; coalition; statement

(2) enriched; uranium; tension; deadline; correspondent; bureau; Cairo

(3) wonder; eyes; especially; reason; heaven; creation; leaves; breeze; through; mine

Answer the questions

News 1

(1) Iran should seriously consider an international offer of aid in return for limits on Iran's nuclear pangram.

(2) He said so in Shanghai China. He is there to observe a meeting of the Shanghai Cooperation Organization.

News 2

(1) The United States warned the north Korea against launching a long distance missile.

(2) The United States is urging nearby countries to discuss the issue with North Korea.

Part Two

1. Preview Exercises

(1) This is a picture of Shenzhou Ⅶ space shuttle.

How wonderful it is!

That reminds me of a legend of flying to the moon.

I'll never forget the time I watched the launch of Shenzhou Ⅶ.

I was really excited about the first spacewalk of our China.

What impressed me most is the successful landing of Shenzhou Ⅶ.

(2) More ways of expressing something happening in the past:

I used to do ...

In the past I often did ...

Yesterday I met ...

What impressed me most is ...

2. Warming up Exercises

(1) This is a clip showing the first manned spaceship of our China. The taikanout was enjoying the weightless condition. I admire it too much.

(2) Yesterday was one of those awful days for me when everything I did went wrong. First, I didn't hear my alarm clock and arrived late for work. Then, I didn't read my diary properly and forgot to get to an important meeting with my boss. During the coffee break, I dropped my coffee cup and spoilt my new skirt. At lunch time, I left my purse on a bus and lost all the money that was inside. After lunch, my boss was angry because I hadn't gone to the meeting. Then I didn't notice a sign on a door that said "Wet Paint" and so I spoilt my jacket too. When I got home I couldn't get into my flat because I had left my key in my office. So I broke a window to get in and cut my hand.

(3) The ways of expressing the past, describing experience.

① What impressed me most is ...

② I remembered that ...

③ What you said reminds me of the ...

④ This film makes me recall ...

3. Listening Material Review

Task 1

China has successfully launched its manned spacecraft Shenzhou Ⅶ into right orbit on schedule.

Task 2

(1) The Jiuquan launch center.

(2) President Hu Jintao delivered an important speech.

(3) Extra vehicular activity or spacewalk.

Task 3

(1) President Hu Jintao sent his deepest gratitude and respect to all those who had participated in this Shenzhou VII launching mission and congratulations.

(2) After the launching of China's manned spacecraft Shenzhou VII, the signals from a control station in Qingdao, show that everything is going well so far.

Chinese President Hu Jintao has been watching the whole launch process together with other senior Chinese leaders in the Jiuquan Launch Center.

A Chinese officer declared Shenzhou VII had successfully entered its orbit and then he announced the launch was totally successful.

President Hu Jintao delivered a very important speech, sending his gratitude and respect to all the participants in this Shenzhou VII launching mission and congratulations. Then he and other Chinese leaders went to walk about and shake hands with the participants of the launching mission.

Over the next three days, Shenzhou VII will be orbiting the earth and the three astronauts on board will be performing the first extra vehicular activity or spacewalk by Chinese astronauts. All Chinese people are waiting for even more exciting movements in the next three days.

Task 4

(1) Well, now we are looking at the image of Shenzhou VII.

(2) Now Shenzhou VII has been declared into the right orbit on schedule.

(3) Now please welcome President Hu Jintao to deliver a very important speech.

(4) This time, Chinese astronauts will participate in a spacewalk for the first time ever.

4. Video-aural Material Review

Task 1

Shenzhou VII's safe return to the earth.

Task 2

(1) In Shenzhou Ⅶ reentry module.

(2) The distribution of blood in the body.

(3) The ground crew.

Task 3

(1) a. The main parachute was released. Then the Shenzhou Ⅶ reentry module landed on the earth safely.

    b. When the reentry capsule opened, astronauts were having some conversations with the ground crew and went through medical checkups.

    c. When accommodation was over, the astronauts get out of the capsule with the help of the ground crew.

    d. Astronauts received flowers sent by the ground crew and posed for some phote off.

    e. Finally the three astronauts said a few words in turn to the TV viewers to express their thanks.

(2) The first astronaut said that they had successfully accomplishded this Shenzhou Ⅶ man's space flight mission, and that they had just come back to Earth. The day before, Chinese astronauts had done China's first ever EVA. The whole mission had been full of challenges, but it had successfully been completed, He felt proud of his country.

Task 4

(1) We have seen the main parachute has been released.

(2) What we just saw should be taken by the camera on the helicopter.

(3) So after three days being in weightless environment, can the astronauts get back on their feet?

(4) They are making way for the astronauts to get out of the capsule.

5. Additional Video-aural Material

Task 1

China's third man's space flight is now in its final stage of preparation.

Task 2

(1) A succession of fine days.

(2) The Shenzhou Ⅶ rocket, the manned spacecraft, the escape tower and Long March pro-

pelling rocket.

(3) Vibrations. If the frequency of vehicle matches that of the rocket, it can damage parts of the spacecraft.

Task 3

(1) The Shenzhou Ⅶ rocket was being transported in an upright position bound together with the manned spacecraft, the escape tower and Long March propelling rocket.

(2) If wind lasts exceeded 10 meters per second, the state of the equipment will change.

Task 4

(1) This means China's third man's space flight is now in its final stage of preparation.

(2) They were careful to make two stops just to check the state of the equipment.

(3) The whole process took just over an hour.

(4) One of them is scheduled to take a walk in outer space.

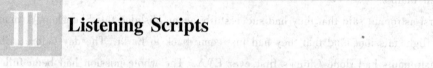

Listening Scripts

Part One

1. Preview Exercises

A primary school in Shanghai had suggested that all schools reduce or even postpone homework assignments to guarantee students enough time to watch the launch of China's Shenzhou Ⅶ space mission live on television.

An article in the Beijing News says that watching the live broadcast of the spacecraft's lift-off is meaningful homework.

The article points out that perceptual knowledge of Shenzhou Ⅶ can broaden and arouse students' interest in science and encourage them to be serious about their studies.

A teacher was quoted as saying that the manned space mission is a vivid science lesson for students to make up for the holes in China's exam-oriented educational system.

The Beijing News says encouraging students to watch such a momentous event is a good example of integrating practice into teaching.

2. Listening Material

From the conversation coming out of Command Center all is going well so far. From a control station located in the east China's Shandong province from the city of Qingdao the signals there show that everything is going fine as well.

People are taking pictures and applauding celebrating the success of the launch.

We are now looking at the image of Shenzhou Ⅶ. Is that real-time image or simulated image? (the left side is the real time, and the right side is the simulated, is on the computer)

And Chinese President Hu Jintao has been watching the whole launch process together with other senior Chinese leaders in the Jiuquan launch center.

Now Shenzhou Ⅶ has been declared into the right orbit on schedule.

"Respected President Hu Jintao , dear senior leaders, distinguished guests, comrades, according to the reports by the Beijing Air Space Command and Control Center, the man spacecraft Shenzhou Ⅶ has successfully entered its orbit and now I hereby announce the launch was totally successful. "

Now please welcome President Hu Jintao to deliver a very important speech.

"Comrades, Shenzhou Ⅶ spacecraft has successfully been launched. This symbolizes the man space flight mission has achieved its initial success. On behalf of the CPC Central Committee, the State Council , the Central Military Commission, I wish to send my deepest gratitude and respect to all those who have participated in this mission and congratulations. Implementing this man space flight mission is a representative mission for our country at state level this year, in the science and technology field. It is another milestone in Chinese people's march towards as the science, and mission in space. This time, Chinese astronauts, will participate in a spacewalk for the first time ever. And this means that the challenge and technological difficulties have been raised to higher level. This has put greater pressure and request on the organization and total planning of this mission. After this spacecraft has actually entered into orbit, I hope that everyone here would be very serious and have a careful attitude towards all the post-launch activities to ensure its complete success. "

We are still looking at live pictures coming out of the Jiuquan satellite launch center in Gansu Province in northwestern China where Chinese President Hu Jintao just gave us a speech congratulating all the scientists and science staff have contributed to the success so far of the launch of Shenzhou Ⅶ into orbit. He, after the speech, went to walk about and shake hands with the people who have been working very hard to ensure the success of the launch vehicle. Once again at this historic moment, for Chinese space exploration program, China's third manned space flight has just been lifted into space in Shenzhou Ⅶ. Now the spacecraft is officially in its scheduled orbit. More Chinese leaders are congratulating scientists who have been working very hard over the past three years for the success of the Shenzhou Ⅶ mission. And we have just seen the success of the first phase which is the launch of Shenzhou Ⅶ spacecraft into its scheduled orbit. Over the next three days, Shenzhen Ⅶ will be orbiting the earth and the three astronauts on board will be performing the first extra vehicular activity or spacewalk by Chinese astronauts. So, more exciting moments are still awaiting us ahead in the next three days.

3. Additional Listening Material

The hatch is about to open. The EVA is about to begin. First it is unlocked and the handle must be turned to 60 degree angle and the pressure inside and outside the module are equal. The hatch can be fully opened. So I believe Zhai Zhigang is about to turn the handle and measure the inside and outside pressure before he finally opens up the hatch.

OK, the hatch has opened. We see a piece of thing is flying out from the capsule into the outer space. That means the hatch has been opened.

We see the helmet. We can see the helmet of Zhai Zhigang with the background of the earth. He is speaking in his helmet.

He said, " I have been out of the hatch. I am feeling good. To all the people in my country, in the world, my greetings, my country, please have faith in me. And I will, my team will finish this mission. "

Helped by the handle bars installed on the outer body of this spacecraft, he is now moving. The flag of PRC is on float by one astronaut, with the background of the earth. We can see the flag. He is waving the flag, the flag of PRC for the first time, being on float by an astronaut.

In outer space the other astronaut is right there in helmet. Yeah.

Ok, Zhai Zhigang is about to reenter the opened module. After he has successfully finished his first EVA, he is collecting all the tie lace and hooks so that he will let free of the body of the spaceship and be able to get back into the orbit module. And you can see the backpack is quite bulgy. And he has to be very careful because the hatch is not very big opening. And this time it is for his feet first entering the hatch. Does he need the support of the other taikonaut? (Guidance perhaps). Some guidance to make sure that he doesn't ... But they are all...they are both in the vacuum environment. EVA activity and back into the orbit module ...

Well, all the activities outside this spacecraft have been finished at this stage. And now they are about to get back to the module, actually they have already return to the module, and the process is exactly opposite to getting out of the module, the astronauts entered the module first with the feet and this process involved closing the module's door...

Because this is first time Chinese have tested this air lock module. This hasn't been done before.

4. Video-aural Material

We have seen the main parachute has been released. That means Shenzhou Ⅶ has safely returned to the atmosphere. Now it is the question of whether the Shenzhou Ⅶ reentry module will land safely.

What we just saw should be taken by the camera on the helicopter. So it means the helicopter is approaching this spacecraft. And very soon we'll see the ground crew taking care of this spacecraft. We can not tell who he is. Obviously he is in good shape. He can move his limps freely and having some conversations with the ground staff. They also have many to follow. It should be their job to ensure that everything is just carrying on the schedule. So after three days being in weightless environment, can the astronauts get back on their feet? No problem. (I will say no problem. The biggest physiological difficulty at the moment may simply be the distribution of blood in their body. When they stand up, their body has to remember how to adjust blood pressure into the brain. So they will stand up slowly. It doesn't mean that there's anything wrong with their muscles.) Because the blood system has been working in the weightless environment for quite some time. I can't tell who this is, but it looks like Liu Guomin . He is about to step out of the reentry module. He is in a medical step. Shielding the hatch, the astronauts come out. They are making way for the astronauts to get out of the capsule. They are putting their hands to help. The accommodation is over. They are about to step out of the capsule. With the mission accomplished, —job well done, and they are receiving flowers sent by the ground crew. Now they are posing for some photo off. This is the moment that they will remember for the rest of their life.

"The three of us has successfully accomplished this Shenzhou Ⅶ man's space flight mission. And we have just come back to earth. Yesterday Chinese astronauts did China's first ever EVA. The whole mission was full of challenges, but it was successfully completed. I feel proud of my country. "

"After we've returned to Earth, we've gone through some experiments and testing and medical checkups. And now I am feeling very good. Chinese astronauts are the best. Thank you. Thank you , my country. "

"After flying for 68 hours, the whole country's attention was on you. What do you want to say to your country? "

"During the past three days in the vast universe. We felt the concern and support of our country. Thank you, my motherland. Thank you, all the people of China. "

"How do you feel during the spacewalk?"

"It felt amazing. Thank you, my country. "

5. Listening Skills

Comprehensive listening practice(2)

Dictation

The President of Iran said his country will carefully consider an international offer of aid in return for limits on Iran's nuclear pangram. President Mohamed Afar Dinajudge Spoke in Shanghai China. He is there to observe a meeting of the Shanghai Cooperation Organization. In Washington Secretary of State said the international community needs an answer to the offer soon. The five permanent members of the United nations security council and Germany developed the plan that have offered Iran aid if it will stop its uranium enrichment work and return to nuclear talks. The United States and other countries believe Iran is trying to make a nuclear weapon. Iran denies this.

Fill in the blanks

(1) A bomb attack in the CI religious center in Baghdad on Friday killed 10 people; more than 20 other were injured. The leader of the religious center blamed the group in Iraq for the attack. But an American army general supervising security in Baghdad says the level of violence has decreased since new security measures began earlier this week. In the separate incident the United States military said one coalition soldier was killed in an attack on the security stop southwest of... A statement said the officials are searching for two other solders who are reportedly missing after the attack.

(2) The President of Iran says the country has successfully enriched the uranium for the first time...The announcement is likely to increase tension of Iran's nuclear program as U. N deadline approaches for Iran to end the nuclear fueling enrichment. VOA correspondent Charles Mick Dona has more from Middle East bureau and Cairo.

(3) Such a feeling is coming over me, there is wonder in most everything I see. Not a cloud in the sky got the sun in my eyes, and I won't be surprised if it's a dream. Everything I want the world to be is now coming true especially for me. And the reason is clear, it is because you are here. You are the nearest thing to heaven that I have seen. I am on the top of the world, down on creation and the only explanation I can find is the love that I've found, ever since you have been around, your love put me at the top of the world. Something in the wind had learned my name, and it is telling me that things are not the same in the leaves on the trees and the touch of the breeze, there is a pleasincense of happiness for me. There is only one wish on my mind, when this day is through I hope that I will find that tomorrow will be just same for you and me, all I need will be mine if you are here.

Answer the questions

News 1

(1) Iran should seriously consider an international offer of aid in return for limits on Iran's nuclear pangram.

(2) He said so in Shanghai China. He is there to observe a meeting of the Shanghai Cooperation Organization.

News 2

(1) The United States warned the north Korea against launching a long distance missile.

(2) The United States is urging nearby countries to discuss the issue with North Korea.

Part two

Additional Video-aural Material

Let's begin with the Shenzhou Ⅶ Spaceship which has been transported to the Jiuquan launching-pad in northwest China's Gansu Province. This means China's third man's space flight is now in its final stage of preparation. Engineers say if the fine weather continues, Shenzhou Ⅶ can expect to blast off late next week. Wang Xiqing has the story.

The Shenzhou Ⅶ rocket was transported in an upright position bound together with the manned spacecraft, the escape tower and Long March propelling rocket. This combined-structure moved along in 1500-meter long rail at a precise speed of 28 meters per minute. Accompanying engineers also kept a close eye on wind speed just in case wind will last exceeded 10 meters per second. They were careful to make two stops just to check the state of the equipment.

Transportation causes vibrations. And if the frequency of vehicle vibration matches that of the rocket, this can damage parts of the spacecraft. We must make sure that doesn't happen. The whole process took just over an hour. Now firmly-positioned in its launching-pad, Shenzhou Ⅶ is all set to take off with three astronauts on board next week. One of them is scheduled to take a walk in outer space. Wang Xiqing, CCTV.

Translation of the Listening Materials

Part One

1. Preview Exercises

（略）

2. Listening Material

从指挥中心传来的消息，到目前为止一切工作正常。来自位于华东山东省青岛市一测控站的信号显示一切工作正常。

人们正在拍照，鼓掌祝贺发射成功。

我们现在看到的是神舟七号飞船的图像。这是实时图像还是模拟图像？（左边的是实时画面，右边的是计算机模拟的画面。）

中国国家主席胡锦涛一直在酒泉发射中心同中国的其他的高级领导人一起观看了发射的全过程。

现在宣布神舟七号已如期准确入轨。

"尊敬的胡主席、各位领导、各位来宾、同志们：根据北京航天指挥控制中心报告，神舟七号载人飞船已进入预定轨道。现在我宣布，神舟七号载人飞船发射圆满成功。"

现在请胡主席发表重要讲话。

"同志们，神舟七号飞船发射成功，标志着这次载人航天飞行任务首战告捷。我代表党中央、国务院、中央军委向参加这次任务的全体科技工作者、干部职工和部队官兵表示热烈的祝贺。实施神舟七号载人航天飞行任务是今年我国最具代表性、最具影响力的国家级重大科研实践活动，中国人民攀登世界科技高峰的又一伟大壮举。这次飞行中，我国航天员将首次实施空间出舱活动。任务技术难度更大，可靠性要求更高，状态变化较多。其任务的组织实施提出了更高的标准。在神舟七号飞船顺利升空、准确入轨之后，希望同志们毫不松懈，再接再厉，聚精会神地做好各项工作，夺取神舟七号任务的全面胜利。"

我们现在仍在观看的是从中国西北的甘肃省酒泉卫星发射中心传来的现场画面。刚才胡锦涛主席在该中心发表了贺词，向为神舟七号成功入轨做出贡献的科学家和科学工作者表示祝贺。胡锦涛主席发表贺辞后走到各处与为确保飞船发射成功一直都在辛勤工作的工作人员握手。中国的第三艘载人飞船神舟七号刚刚发射升空，这是中国空间探测计划的又一历史时刻。现在非常已正式进入预定轨道。中国的其他领导人正在向三年多来为完成神舟七号发射任务而辛勤工作的科学家表示祝贺。我们刚刚看到的是神舟七号发射升空进入预定轨道,完成了第一阶段的任务。在未来的三天里,神舟七号飞船将在轨绕地飞行,飞船上的三名航天员将首次进行出舱活动或由中国航天员进行太空行走。因此,未来的三天里将有更激动人心的时候在前面等着我们。

3. Additional Listening Material

舱盖就要打开了。空间出舱活动就要开始。首先是开舱盖。舱盖的把手必须旋转60度,舱内外的气压要想等。舱盖可以完全打开。因此,我认为翟志刚只有测量完舱内外的气压、转动舱盖的把手后才能打开舱盖。

好的,舱盖打开了。我们看到有一个小东西从太空舱飞向外层空间。这标志着舱盖已经打开。

我们看见了防护罩。我们看到了翟志刚的防护罩,身后背景是地球。他戴着防护罩在说话。

他说:"我已出舱,感觉良好。神舟七号向全国人民问好,向全世界人民问好。请祖国放心。我们坚决完成任务。"

他正在飞船外安装的把杆的帮助下作太空行走。一名航天员正以地球作背景挥舞着中华人民共和国国旗。我们可以看到那面旗子。他正挥舞着旗子。一名中国航天员正挥舞着中华人民共和国国旗。

外层空间还有另一名航天员也戴着防护罩。是的。

好了,翟志刚正要返回开着的飞船船舱。现在他已成功地完成了首次出舱活动,正在收起所有的系带和挂钩以便离开舱外返回到轨道舱内。你可以看到他的宇航背包很鼓胀。他必须小心翼翼,因为舱盖口不是很大。这次他的脚先进舱盖口。他需要其他的中国航天员帮助吗?(也许是指导。)需要一些指导。确认没要帮助……但他们俩都处在真空环境中。完成了出舱活动,返回了轨道舱……

好了,进行到这一步,出舱活动已经完成,并就要回到舱内,实际上他们已经回到了舱内,其程序正好与出舱相反:航天员脚先进舱,该程序还包括关舱门……

这是中国人第一次试用密封舱,因为此前还没有用过。

4. Video-aural Material

我们已经看到主降落伞已经弹出,这意味着神舟七号飞船已安全地返回了大气层。现在的问题是神舟七号飞船的返回舱是否会安全着陆。

我们刚才看到的画面应该是由直升机上的摄像机拍摄的。这表明直升机正在接近飞船。不一会,我们就会看到地勤人员看护飞船。我们分辨不出他是谁,但看得出他的身体状态不错。他可以自如地移动双腿并和地勤人员进行一些对话。他们还要遵守很多程序。确保一切按部就班地进行是他们的工作。那么,经历了三天的失重环境后,这几位航天员还能再站起来吗?没有问题。(我要说没有问题。目前最大的生理问题可能只是血液的分布问题。他们站立起来时,身体必须记住如何调节大脑的血压。因此,他们将慢慢地站起来。这并不意味着他们的肌肉有什么问题。)因为血液系统在失重状态下工作了相当长的一段时间。我分辨不清这是谁,但看起来像是刘国民。他正要走出返回舱。他正在做一项健康检查。航天员们避开舱盖的碰撞后出舱了。他们正在为航天员出舱让路。他们伸出手去搀扶航天员们。调整步骤结束。他们就要出舱了。他们完成了任务,完成得非常出色,正在接受地勤人员献的花。现在他们正在摆姿势拍照。这是他们以后的人生中要铭记的时刻。

"我们三人成功地完成了这次神舟七号的载人航天飞行的任务,刚刚返回地面。昨天我们中国航天员进行了中国人的首次出舱活动。整个任务充满了挑战,但成功地完成了任务。我为祖国感到骄傲。"

"返回地面后,我们经过了一些实验、检测和体检。我现在感觉很好。中国航天员是最棒的。感谢祖国。"

"飞行了 68 小时,全国人民一直都关注着你们。你想对你的祖国人民说点什么?"

"在茫茫太空中所度过的三天里,我感到了祖国的关怀和支持。感谢祖国! 感谢祖国人民!"

"太空行走的感觉如何?"

"太奇妙了。感谢祖国!"

Part two

Additional Video-aural Material

我们首先报道神舟七号飞船的消息。神舟七号飞船系统现已运抵位于中国西北的甘肃省酒泉发射台。这表明中国的第三次载人航天飞行现已进入最后的准备阶段。工程师们说,如果天气持续晴好,神舟七号飞船有望在下周的晚些时候发射。下面是王喜平发回的报道。

神舟七号飞船的火箭部分连同捆绑在一起的载人飞船、逃逸塔和长征推进火箭以竖立的姿势向前运输。这个组合的装置沿着 1500 米长的轨道以 28 米/分的精确速度向前移动。随行的工程师们还在密切注视着风速,以防持续风速超过 10 米/秒。他们小心翼翼地停过两次以检查装置的状态。

　　运输过程中会引起振动。如果运输车辆的振动频率与火箭摆动的频率一致,就会毁坏飞船系统的部件。我们必须确认没有此类情况发生。整个过程仅用一个多小时。现在,神舟七号飞船系统已牢牢地矗立在发射台上,准备下周携带三名航天员升空。按计划,其中将有一名航天员要进行太空行走。中央电视台王喜平报道。